MY CHANCE

MEN OF NEW YORK BOOK FOUR

SAMANTHA SKYE

ISBN 978-0-6452730-7-6 (ebook)

ISBN 978-0-6452730-8-3 (Paperback)

Cover Design: Angela Haddon

www.angelahaddon.com

Editor: Nice Girl Naughty Edits

www.nicegirlnaughtyedits.com

❀ Created with Vellum

CONTENT INFORMATION

This book contains spicy scenes and descriptions of violence. It also alludes to family violence and contains kidnapping.

It is an opposites attract, surprised pregnancy mafia romance that will have you hot under the collar and on the edge of your seat.

Enjoy.

1

NICO MOLENTI

Minutes tick past, the clock on the wall tapping to the beat. Each second grates on my nerves, making me angrier than I already am.

"I have nothing left to give you. You have everything," the sad excuse for a man says as he sits tied to a chair in front of Sebastian and I.

"Stop lying!" Sebastian growls, face twisted from frustration. And I don't blame him. This man tried to take everything from us. He thought that with all his millions, he could simply walk in, change the way business is done in New York, and push us out in the process. The family I have come to know and love would have all perished if this man was successful. But he is hiding something, and unfortunately for him, both Sebastian and I can feel it.

Brian Cole was one of the wealthiest men in New York. But he was greedy. He still wanted more. He wanted to run the streets, run the ports, and run the politics. That is our foothold. I may be the youngest brother of the New

York Mafia, but my blood runs for them, just as theirs runs for me.

"But I have nothing. NOTHING!" he shouts, showing a sudden change in demeanor. He must know he is near the end because his voice pleads to us the longer this goes on, dripping with desperation, still hopeful his heart will beat after today. That we will let him go.

"You have taken my money, my businesses, my property..."

"Your son," I add, dropping the words like lead into the silent room, filling in the gaps of his memory as I stand in front of him. Staring down at the pathetic excuse for a man that he is, I feel nothing. It is true. We did, in fact, kill his son Daniel. His pride and joy. Well, Carter did. Carter was more than ready to end that fucker's life after everything he did to Doc, so he had to die. That was personal for him. But this. Right here, right now. This is something I know very well.

This is business.

"So now it's your time. Your debt is still not paid in full. You planned to end us, so we will offer you the same courtesy," Sebastian says simply, and I grin. Sebastian is like an older brother to me. All the boys are, but he is the one who has really taken me under his wing, and I would do anything for him. Anything for this group of men who are now my family, including hurting someone to get the information we need. Potentially killing him. I will take blood and bleed for my family; it is what I am committed to do.

Sweat beads along Brian's forehead, trailing down his fat face as he looks up at us. His emotions remain skittish, going from outraged to despondent, because at this point, he knows he has to die. Only, we want everything from him first. Once he has nothing else to give us, nothing else of value, we will take his life.

We stand before him in a small cement block room, hidden deep in the basement of our compound. *Our cell.* We don't use it much, but for the past few weeks, this has been his home. In the cold, dark and damp recess of the New York Mob headquarters. He will never see sunlight again. His son is long gone, his businesses sold or burnt to the ground. Brian Cole is no longer a man about town, flaunting his wealth. He is a man who has lost absolutely everything.

Of course, we set up the media landscape, providing them with information of his fraudulent activities and his undesirable business contacts. So far, our hands are clean, and no one has picked up that we even know who he is. Just the way we like it. We have been through his paperwork, and most of his digital files, but we are still missing something, and we need to get to the bottom of what that is.

"Times up, Brian," I say as I step toward him, rolling up my sleeves, ready to get dirty to get revenge for our family. My hands clench and unclench, eager to feel his skin break underneath my fists. The need to hurt him runs through my blood. I'm ready to end his miserable life as I cock my fist back to knock him out.

"WAIT!" he screams, his eyes wide, and I pause. I haven't even touched him, and he is already in a hurry to give us what we want.

"I have something else. I have something you can

have. But then we are even." It's laughable how this man still doesn't seem to understand the situation. We will *never* be even.

"What?" Sebastian steps up next to me and eyes him suspiciously.

"My daughter. You can have my daughter." He smiles, like he thinks he has just saved himself. I feel Sebastian bristle beside me because we don't deal with human trafficking. We love women, cherish them, and treat them well.

"We don't steal women, asshole. Your sick dealings are of no interest to us," I say through gritted teeth. I knew he had a daughter. Sebastian has checked her out and, apparently, she is not part of Brian's activities. She doesn't seem to have much of a relationship with him at all, which makes me wonder why he is ratting her out to the mob.

"Not for pleasure, not to sell, but for business," he clarifies, and my brows pinch together.

Now he has my attention.

"Spit it out. You are talking in riddles." I grab him by the collar, growing increasingly impatient.

"She's a lawyer, a good one. She can work with you, for you." I give nothing away before I punch him across the cheek and finally knock him out cold.

We need time to think.

2

EMILIA COLE

My heels click on the pavement as I run down the street to the office. Late as usual.

I had a meeting that went for hours yesterday afternoon, and by the time I got home and finished the paperwork, it was past one in the morning. It would have been a lot quicker had my potential new client not had a serious case of *I can't stop looking at your chest to actually explain my legal situation to you.* I get more of them now, the type I'd rather not be working with. Ever since my poor excuse for a father went down in flames, something I have been trying to distance myself from for the past few weeks since it all came to light.

Today, however, I made sure my corporate attire is exactly that. Black pencil skirt, pink blouse, and a large black trench coat, which is doing nothing to combat the chill in the air today. The wind whirls through the street, the sun blocked by the tall buildings as I stay in the dark shadows of the early morning, hurrying to get to my office to start my day.

As I see the entrance to the side, I take a breath. I am thankful it's Friday because exhaustion is nipping at my heels and the weekend can't get here quick enough. Working day and night in order to keep my business afloat has been brutal.

I push open the large double glass doors and head to the elevators, giving Antonio, our security guard, a quick smile and a small wave. He is a quiet man, and more of a concierge than security. I almost put money on the fact that he couldn't fight me, let alone anyone else of significant height or build. Antonio is Italian, I think. In his late sixties, at a guess, and he always smiles brightly whenever I come into view. But today, he is not meeting my eye for some reason, which is odd. I have little time to worry about that, though, as I slip into the elevator to head up to my floor.

My floor. It has been five years since I became a practicing lawyer and now I own my own small boutique firm. Obviously, the years of me secretly listening in on my father's business deals served me well because, up until recently, I was one of New York's most up-and-coming, sought-after lawyers. My name was really starting to climb, business was fruitful, and for someone married to their job like me, I finally felt like things were coming together.

Until my father ruined it. Fraud. That is my specialty. White-collar crime. Ironic, really. Even though I have been estranged from my family for years, his name still haunts me and continues to ruin my reputation. Since his fall from grace, I've lost clients left and right, to the point I am now wondering how I can even dig myself out of the small pile of invoices that sit on my desk, begging to be paid. My heart rate increases when I think about them. I'm not sure how I will meet next month's lease payment, and I'm even more concerned I will need to let go of Cindy, my assistant.

The only new clients coming my way now are dirty, and I *don't* do dirty. I am as clean as a whistle, straight as an arrow, and play firmly on the right side of the law. I didn't spend years at law school, dreaming of this career, building my reputation, in order to throw it away like my father did. It's is all I have.

My mom passed away when I was just a baby and growing up, my brother and father treated me like I was nothing. It was a very lonely upbringing that led to me planning for a way out. I buried my head in books, got a full scholarship, and moved to the other side of the country for college. I didn't want him involved in my life, and I especially didn't want his money.

I worked two jobs through college just so I never had to ask my father for anything. To this day, I'm not sure he even realized I left. Once I returned to New York, I built my practice, ignoring both him and my brother completely. I hadn't seen him until my brother's funeral, and I wasn't planning to. I figured that New York is big enough for the both of us, that I could pretend he doesn't exist. Yet that is becoming more and more difficult as the weeks go on.

The elevator opens, and I am not surprised to see the reception desk empty. In desperate need of a coffee, I look at my watch, deciding to wait another thirty minutes until Cindy arrives. Cindy was a barista before she became my assistant. When I saw her working at Bobby's Diner, I knew her sparkling personality was exactly what I needed and offered her a job on the spot. And it's just a bonus that she makes the best cup of coffee I've ever had. In comparison, I still haven't worked out how to use the new fancy coffee machine. It's something I splurged on before shit hit the fan and my professional life started to crumble around me. Probably should have saved that money considering where I'm at now.

I slip off my trench coat as I strut to my office, eager to start on the pile of files I need to work through before I can end the week. As I push through my office door, I make it exactly two steps in before I stop short.

"Who the hell are you, and why are you in my office?" I nearly shriek in both surprise and fear, as I see the back of a man standing near my office window. He is tall, broad, still looking out on the cityscape below, not at all startled by my arrival.

"Hello, Miss Cole." The man's deep, much too calm Italian accent vibrates through me, and I try to steady myself. I watch him as he sips on a takeaway coffee, then turns around slowly, piercing me with his eyes as they immediately lock onto mine. Deep chocolate brown against his olive complexion and dark hair. My eyes search his face for his intentions, but all I notice is how devilishly handsome he is. If I wasn't so startled, I might actually swoon.

"Who are you?" I ask again, my tone firm as I throw my coat and bag on my armchair and put my hands on my hips. In my years of working in law, it was a steep learning curve for me to understand the different intimidation tactics men try to use. I have built a thick layer of protective armor around my body. I now know that in order to succeed in getting what I want, I need to match their energy and demeanor. However, this man has caught me before my morning coffee, so I already feel sorry for him. I feel my wrath building, patience at a zero.

I see his stubble covered jaw tick, and I wait a few beats for him to respond, but he doesn't. He remains silent, just looking at me. His stance is casual, with one hand tucked in his very expensive-looking suit's pocket, as he takes another sip of his coffee. But looks can be deceiving.

"Who are you and what do you want? You are in *my* office, so answer me when I ask you something," I demand this time, breathing slowly and trying to keep them from chattering too much as I watch his eyes narrow ever so slightly. My nervous system is now entirely out of control, from his good looks or fear or his extreme arrogance, I am not yet sure.

"I am acquainted with your father," he states as he begins to walk toward me, like he is approaching a wild animal.

I huff, my teeth now grinding. "How is my father?" I ask sarcastically, because I really don't care.

"A handful. But he speaks highly of you and your career to date. In fact, he recommends you." A smirk quirks his lips, and I feel my stomach churn. I try to remain unaffected and raise my eyebrow a little, my fingers gripping into my sides to prevent my hands from shaking.

"My father is an entitled piece of shit who thinks only

of status and money. I want nothing to do with him or you." I say, making it extremely clear that I am not going to be working for any of my father's men. Despite my career going down the toilet, working for my father or any of his associates is where I draw the line.

"He hasn't been doing too well financially..." the man says as he comes to a stop right in front of me. Mere inches separate the two of us, but I am not budging. He is trying to intimidate me, and I will not show weakness.

"He owes me and my family a lot of money." And the penny drops.

"Well, I am not a bank, so you will have to find it elsewhere. You are not getting a cent from me."

The man's face has softened a little, almost like he finds me humorous, but I am most certainly not joking. Whatever mess my father has landed in is his alone. I am not digging him out. I couldn't even if I wanted to, and that's all because of him.

As my confidence increases and my nerves dissipate, I meet the man in his stare off. He has an air of power to him, along with a healthy dose of cockiness. He is very measured with his words, not really answering me entirely, yet is watching me like he is waiting for me to tell him something. What that is, I still don't know.

"I don't need your money, Miss Cole..." he says, his voice grittier, almost husky. I clench my fists at my sides. The way his voice skirts over my skin is enough to have my heart racing.

"I have no idea what he does or doesn't do. I haven't seen my father in a very long time," I lie.

"You were at your brother's funeral, were you not?"

He cocks an eyebrow, obviously pleased he caught me out. I squint at him, frustration now taking over any nerves. His hand rubs his jaw, eyes melting into my face as he waits for a response.

"Yes, I was at the funeral, and that was the first time I have seen my father since I was seventeen. I have no plans to see him ever again. I don't even know where he is." Whatever it is my father's done has absolutely nothing to do with me.

"He thinks you are an excellent lawyer." I tilt my head at that; my father doesn't give a shit about me. He only cared for Daniel. The pride at having a son to help him rule the world was the only thing that ever mattered to him. He was more than happy to let me leave and move to the other side of the country, no longer wanting me to be an annoying little girl who demanded daddy's attention. The older I got, the more clearly I could see that I was not his precious daughter, but a mere disruption in whatever plan he had at the time.

"He said you are one of the best lawyers he knows. Probably going to be the best lawyer in all of the country soon..." I blanch as he continues. My father *never* took this much of an interest in what I did.

"Well... I don't—" I can't even get myself to form a coherent thought before he cuts me off.

"He also mentioned that you possess a keen eye for white-collar activities..." I feel the world spin on its axis and I shake my head in confusion. "And we want your skill, Miss Cole, in solving a riddle..." he adds, his voice trailing off. As it does, I don't miss his eyes as they flick down to my mouth, and my tongue skims over my bottom lip involuntarily. I watch his pupils dilate, and my chest works overtime to get oxygen into my lungs. He is standing too close to me, probably seeing my nerves written all over my face, where I didn't want them to be, yet I can't move back.

He's a Black Widow, and I am caught in his web, hypnotized by his mere proximity.

"A riddle?" I ask him, my voice coming out clear and steady as I regain my composure. Raising my eyebrow, I'm now even more intrigued as his words sink in. I do love a challenge. My natural fascination with riddles is something that started as a kid. The need to figure things out was my main driving force in becoming a lawyer. But I am not yet sure if this man is playing games with me, looking for representation, or just here to ruin my day.

"I have no intention of working for any of my father's friends or being involved in any of my father's activities, so I think it is time you leave my office and find another solution to your problem. If you ever feel the need to sneak into my office in the early hours of the morning again, at least bring a coffee with cream, because it is way too early for this bullshit." I sigh out a breath, as if completely uninterested, swallowing down any lingering nerves, and move to my office door, holding it open for him to leave.

"I know your client list is getting smaller by the day..." he says to me, his voice thickening with his accent, watching me intently as I lean against the door. His mouth turns up again into a sly smirk, one I really want to slap off his arrogant face.

"I will give you a week. Think about it. I can promise

you will be well paid and will have interesting work to keep you busy." His eyes glisten with amusement. He is enjoying this standoff.

"My answer will be the same next week as it is today." My hands find my hips again, ready to knee this asshole in the balls.

"We will see. A lot can happen in seven days," he says simply, and the air leaves my body as a cold chill encases my spine.

My heart pounds as I try to reconcile what he just said. I hate my father, and if I ever see him again, I will absolutely kill him for putting me in this position. I remain silent as I clench my jaw, and my intruder smiles like a Cheshire Cat, seemingly pleased that he succeeded in whatever he came here to do.

"I will be in touch, Miss Cole." I nod to him as I fold my arms across my chest, now wanting to shield myself. My early morning visitor turns on his heel and leaves, closing my office door behind him. The click of the door sends shock waves through my tense body as I slump into my armchair, exhaling like I've been holding my breath this whole time.

What the hell is going on?

3

NICO

The need to get away from her before I suffocate in her scent is the only thing making me put one foot in front of the other. Rose aroma travels up my nostrils and plants firmly into my chest, reminding me of my upbringing in Lake Como in the springtime. I take one last look at her, glad I shocked the sass right out of her, and walk out of her small city office before another word can be spoken. Stalking away from it like it is on fire.

I don't like to intimidate women, but I sure do want to spank her ass. She is feisty, and already proving to be too stubborn for her own good.

After some investigation on her over the past few days, I soon realized that having her on our team would be an extremely successful move on our behalf. She is an excellent lawyer, top grades in college, and no doubt wants to save the world if her pro bono work is any indication. Now after meeting her, I can see why. She has no fear and says what's on her mind. I wonder how long it will take for her to acclimatize to working for the other side of the law.

I take a deep breath in, clearing my mind and my senses of the woman who also happens to be a complete bombshell. Her blonde tresses would look perfect splayed out across my bed, and I imagine how her incredible, voluptuous figure would feel underneath me as I trace her curves with my tongue and make her mine over and over again. Only, she'd have to leave that attitude behind. Her mouth is already proving to rile me up, and the most frustrating part of that is my body didn't hate it as much as my mind did. I shake my head, trying to pull myself together. It's clear she is going to be a handful, yet another thing I need to manage.

Sebastian has given me the role of business manager of our family, helping to arrange the finances and business deals to get things done. That is why I am now the babysitter of Miss Cole, and it is now my job to ensure she becomes part of our team. That she can work on our things quickly, quietly, and discreetly. I still use my fists and weapons, but Dante and Carter are better at that. It is their forte. Me, I proved myself in Sicily with Sebastian by killing Enzo years ago and have been his constant shadow ever since.

Whatever he needs, whatever he asks, I do it, no question. It is what I have trained for most of my adult life. It is the reason I, an unknown young man from a small town in Italy, was able to support my family back home, by becoming a brother in *the* head crime family of New York.

The elevator opens, and before I can step in, a

woman steps out. Short and stout, with blue eyeshadow and deep red lipstick, her hair perfectly quaffed. I guess her to be in her fifties, the eighties the key decade for her if her style is anything to go by. She looks me up and down, intrigue in her eyes, but I simply smile and nod as I move around her into the lift. I watch her as she heads to the reception desk and dumps her handbag and coat on the chair as the elevator door closes.

Making my way to ground level, I rub my eyes. I need another coffee. It was an early morning for me, but I wanted to catch her by surprise. In fact, I have a few more surprises for Miss Cole. Within the week, I know she will be putty in my hands.

Stepping out into the foyer, I weave through the city workers, making my way over to Antonio.

"Is everything all right, Nico?" he asks me as I approach, worry etched in his features.

"Fine, Antonio," I say, slipping him another $100 discreetly.

"Miss Emilia is a nice girl. She is always kind and respectful. I'm sure whatever trouble she is in—" he starts, but I cut him off.

"She is not in any trouble. How is your lovely wife?" I ask, steering the conversation to safer territory. Antonio and his wife, Pia, have been known to me since I first moved to New York. The fact that he is the doorman at this building was pure coincidence. I couldn't have planned it better because Antonio owes me a few favors. We helped him and his wife on many occasions with rough thugs in their neighborhood, so he was more than willing to let me up to her floor without question this morning.

"Pia is well. Thank you for helping us with the recent burglaries. I appreciate everything you and Sebastian do for us," he says with a nod.

"Anytime, Antonio, you know that. I need to go. Ciao." I shake his hand and strut out of the foyer and into the street. Stepping out in the cool morning air, I get into my car and nod to Tony, my driver, just as my cell phone rings.

"How did it go?" Sebastian questions before I have even had a chance to greet him formally.

"Fine. She won't be an issue. I give her a week before she is onboard and will do anything we need her to." I am greeted with a sigh. He is stressed and, no doubt, relieved I have this handled. We really needed to get someone like her on our team to sort through her father's paperwork, because although we have no proof, we know there is something we are missing. My gut tells me that she will find it, because I have a feeling she is like a dog with a bone and won't give up until she uncovers what we need her to.

I have followed the paper trail her father gave us five times over and I always find blocks. We are not sure who is helping finance his various activities, but we know someone is and that someone is powerful. While not a direct threat to us anymore, whoever he is working with could become a threat again in the future, and our preference is to neutralize them before they become a problem.

"Come back to the compound. I want to run the monthly numbers today and work through the family spreadsheets," Sebastian says, and I hear his wife, Goldie, growling at him in the background—something about him being too bossy—and I smirk.

"Wipe that smirk off your face, Nico. My wife is the boss of this household, you know that," he says in jest, knowing me so well.

"That's right, Nico. You will learn that one day when you find yourself a wife!" Goldie screams out to me, and I laugh. We all love to push Sebastian's buttons, but Goldie dances very close to the flame, getting away with a lot, constantly pushing her husband to the brink.

"See you back here soon. Good job." Then he's cutting off the call, and I rest my head on the back of the seat.

Watching the world pass me by out the window, I can't help but think of my family back home in Italy. I miss them. Especially my sister, Sofia. Younger than me by a few years, we were always close, even more so as we became adults and she got sick. It was heartbreaking watching my parents struggle financially to support her medical bills. They worked tirelessly day and night, while I looked after her at home. We nearly didn't survive it all, but then I met Sebastian.

Well known in Italy, Sebastian and Dante were looking for new soldiers, and I volunteered. He met my family, saw the heartbreaking situation we were in, and paid for Sofia to get the medical attention she needed. In return, he got me. I moved away from my family to New York and now work for him. I owe Sebastian my life, my sister's life, and I will work for him until eternity to repay him for giving her back to me.

I sit in remembrance for a moment, spinning my cell phone in my hand, before I type out a quick text to her.

Me: *Miss you, Sorella.*

Sofia: *You need to come home soon, Fratello. I have found the perfect woman for you!*

At her quick reply, I bristle. She has a fascination with setting me up with nice Italian women and trying to get me to come home more. Arranged marriages are common in the mob, less so in Italy in general. My sister, however, has taken her role of matchmaker for me extremely seriously, and I entertain her for the most part to keep her smiling. I know it is early afternoon in Italy right now, and no doubt, she is busy writing at home. An aspiring author, I already know whatever she publishes will be pure gold.

Taking a silly selfie, I send it to her, my eyes crossed, my tongue poking out, and within moments, she sends one back.

Sofia: *Seriously, when are you coming home? Do you have another visit planned soon?*

Me: *Things are busy here at the moment.*

Me: *Let me see what I can arrange. I miss the sunshine and gelato. Talk later?*

I feel better after checking in with her. The two of us talk almost daily. We're close and have been our entire lives. As Tony pulls into the compound, the shared secure neighborhood where we all live and work, I know I need to get my head in the game. Sebastian wants numbers crunched and deals reviewed, and I still need another espresso.

Sofia: *Deal.*

I pocket my phone and step out of the car, seeing Goldie getting into her car across the garage, obviously heading to work at the gallery.

"Good luck, he is in a mood today!" she hollers to me.

"I heard that!" Sebastian barks out from behind me, hands in his pockets, not amused at his wife's banter.

"I meant for you to!" she says with a smile, and I need to hide my smirk as Sebastian and I stand there, watching Goldie drive out of the lot.

"God, she drives me crazy, that woman," he murmurs, before slapping me on the shoulder and leaving no room for questions. "Come, let's get to work."

4

EMILIA

I smash my hand into my cell phone on the bedside table, cursing myself for not turning off my alarm on a Saturday.

It took me forever to get out of the office yesterday. Paperwork is building up as I try to meet my remaining clients' expectations faster than usual, given that they could leave me at any moment. But I also couldn't concentrate on anything after my early morning visitor. Then, even after all that, sleep still eluded me for most of the night as I tried to reconcile what my father has done and what this all means for me now. The few hours of sleep I did get were full of dreams of chocolate brown eyes and a domineering Italian man.

The buzzing continues as I squeeze my eyes shut, trying to deny the morning's arrival. I thrust my hand out of the covers, slamming the surface on my side table again, wondering why the beeping noise won't stop. Frustrated, I sit up, flinging the covers back, and grab my phone, ready to throw it at the wall. But as I click on it, I realize my phone isn't making any noise. Confused for a moment, I sit quietly and listen as it continues. Rubbing my eyes, I get my bearings and stand, stifling a yawn as I pad out to my kitchen, where I see the coffee machine beeping as it fills to the top.

But that is not what is concerning. The man standing in my kitchen with a smug ass smile on his face is what is concerning. Shocked, my breath hitches, my heart beats out of my chest, and my voice gets stuck in my throat. *What the hell is he doing here?*

"Ah, here she is," he says, looking fresh as a daisy in his pristine black suit, hair slicked like James Bond. Meanwhile, my hair is a bird's nest of activity, my body barely hidden by my slouchy college sweatshirt, with only my underwear on underneath. I am pretty sure I have both dried mascara under my eyes and the remnants of saliva on my chin too.

"Here. For you." He grabs the fresh brew that is now poured into one of my coffee cups and slides it across my kitchen bench.

"With cream, as you requested." I stand there, stunned, watching him from my bedroom doorway. I haven't moved. My body stiff as he moves around my home like it is his own. The smell of fresh coffee finally snaps me out of it.

"What the hell are you doing in my apartment?" I screech at him, my raspy morning voice making me cringe.

"You have great beans," he says as he ignores my question and sips his coffee.

"*What?*" I ask, now even more perplexed.

"Are they Italian?" he asks, taking another small sip of his small espresso.

"Is *what* Italian?" My eyes narrow, growing even more confused.

"The beans?" he repeats, as his tall body leans against my kitchen wall, looking like he belongs in a luxury appliance commercial.

"What the hell are you talking about?"

"Your coffee beans. What did you think I was talking about?"

"I don't even know what is happening right now!"

"We are talking about beans, Miss Cole."

I can only stand and gawk at him. Five minutes ago, I was lost in my slumber, and now I am talking about coffee beans with a strange man who broke into my apartment.

Who knows how long he has been here already, probably casing the place while I slept. Not that he would find anything here; I am not someone who is sentimental. I have no photos or knickknacks, so my apartment is modern and stark just like my life. Anything of value is in my safe deposit box.

But still... should be calling the police? Should I be trying to run? Why am I just standing here?!

I don't miss his eyes as they flick up and down my body, and while I should be embarrassed that this dapper man has now seen me at my worst, I can't part with the anger swelling in my chest at having someone uninvited in my home.

"Who the hell are you?" Although this is the second time he has been in my space, I realize I still don't even know his name. He ignores my question and walks over to my dining table, taking a seat and relaxing back.

"Please, just make yourself at home," I say sarcastically as I wave my hands around my space.

He smirks at me again, and I ignore his eyes as I look at the steaming coffee he made me sitting on the kitchen bench. My mouth waters, so I decide to pretend like I am actually playing this game of doing what he wants. I keep my eyes on him as I walk forward and grab the coffee, trying to wrack my brain for a plan. It is one thing to be in my workplace, but it is something else entirely to be standing here, in my home. My apartment is the only place just for me. Now it has been invaded, by whoever this jerk is.

Sipping the hot brew, my eyes close as the coffee hits my tongue and slides down my throat. This is a damn good coffee. Walking toward him, I put my cup down on the dining table as he looks me up and down once more. His trademark smirk stays plastered on his face, one any other woman would find panty dropping, but I find infuriating. Mostly.

"Seriously, this coffee is really good," he says, still ignoring my question as he finishes his espresso and crosses one leg over the top of his knee.

"Okay, enough of this game. What is your name? You want something from me, but I have no idea who you are." Standing tall, I cross my arms over my chest. I'm not sure if I actually want to know, but knowledge is power, and I need all the power I can get at the moment.

"Nico," he finally answers, quickly and sternly, folding his arms across his chest, matching my stance. I guess he isn't too happy to play this game of *get to know your intruder.*

"Nico who?" I fire back and watch his nostrils flair. It's clear he doesn't like me asking questions, but I am not continuing any conversation without knowing exactly who I am dealing with.

"Nico Molenti. I work for the mob," he states, deadpan, and I laugh. I laugh so hard, tears form in my eyes, and I start to ugly snort, not able to control myself. He looks at me as though I am crazy and have lost my mind. Maybe I have.

"Sure, and I am a direct descendant of the Queen of England," I say in a mock English accent as I give him a royal wave. "Seriously." I wipe my eyes, not missing the dark smudge of the mascara I obviously missed in the shower last night. "Who are you? Do you need support with one of the top five banks, or are you just some jerk who likes to break into young women's apartments and scare them on a Saturday morning?"

"I am Nico Molenti, and I work for the mob." Something about his tone this time has my smile wiped from my face, and my body stills. Understanding washes over me that he is, in fact, not joking. The anger I felt now starts to dissipate, the nerves from earlier rearing back into gear. I couldn't have heard him right...

"Excuse me?" I barely whisper, my eyes staring into his, all humor gone.. "As in, Sebastian Romano Mob, or.." My voice wavers. Everyone knows Sebastian Romano.

"Sebastian is my brother," he says like he is asking for creamer in his coffee and not like he just dropped a bomb on my life.

Once again, I'm unmoving, eyes bulging and mouth agape. I want to say something, but nothing comes out. The shock of what he just told me renders me speechless for a moment, my fight-or-flight instincts battling each other.

"You know, looking at me with your mouth wide open like that makes me think of some ways we can pass the time... unless you have something else to say? Hmm?" Lifting a brow, he takes another sip of his coffee.

My lips find each other instantly, pressing down firmly as I growl under my breath. My fight senses taking over. I roll my shoulders back, feigning confidence I usually have but which seems to elude me every time I am around this man.

"You need to leave," I say sternly, taking a few steps away from him. I want no part of being in any way associated with the mob.

He makes no move to leave.

"I am a lawyer, for Christ's sake! I work to put people like you behind bars! I can lose my license just from being in your presence!" My voice gets higher in pitch and more panicked the more I talk. "I can't believe you are here in my apartment! Oh my God. Have you spiked my coffee? Are you going to kidnap me? I'm too heavy to kidnap. You won't be able to carry me. Me as a dead weight would be even worse... You could totally put your back out, maybe really hurt yourself. Yeah, you would most certainly need backup. Shit, do you have backup? Are there more men waiting outside?" I can barely catch my breath as I pace back and forth before him.

This is what happens to me when I am pushed too far

or caught off guard, I ramble. It is a good quality to have in the court of law, I can pull many things out of my hat of awkwardness and it is often worked in my advantage. But right here, right now, I have a case of verbal diarrhea and no idea how to stop it. He stands at seeing my obvious distress, pushing in the chair he was sitting on, leaving no trace of him being here. I suppose my nerves worked in my favor this time. Annoy the man until he leaves me alone.

"You have until Friday, Miss Cole. Think about it. You are losing clients each day, and I know your assistant, Cindy, is saving her money for her wedding anniversary trip to Europe. Her heart will break if she loses her job because you can't afford to keep her."

Nico has obviously done his homework and knows exactly where to hit to make it hurt. He heads toward my door, strolling like he has all the time in the world.

"Why?" I ask to his back, and he stops and turns to face me. "Why me?"

"Because you're the best," he says before giving me a smile walking out my door.

What the hell just happened?

I rub my face with my hands, trying to wake myself up, hoping it is all a bad dream, but as my vision returns, I'm still standing in the middle of my apartment, wearing my sweatshirt that barely covers my ass, staring at a cup of coffee I didn't make myself.

"Emi, Emi, Emi..." I quietly scold myself, not liking how out of sorts this man makes me feel. I rub my face again, because... this can't be happening.

I walk back to my bedroom, and as I do, I catch myself

in my standing mirror and gasp. I look like I have put my finger in the electrical outlet. My hair is everywhere, looking much worse than I thought. Stepping closer, I see lines along my cheek where I obviously laid on my crumpled sheets for too long, and mascara under my eyes as I suspected.

What am I going to do? He isn't wrong, my business is going down the toilet. Rapidly. And I don't want to lose Cindy or impact the once-in-a-lifetime holiday she has been planning for close to a year. But he is a freaking mobster! I can't work with him. I can't even be seen with him. If I am, then I can kiss my career goodbye for good. Literally the only thing I have in my life. The only thing I have focused on for years.

Without it, I don't even know who I am.

I stand in her office, admiring the view. It's not bad; you can see most of the streetscape below, and the windows let in a lot of light as the sun rises over the dark New York skyline. My eyes flick to her desk. It is neat, with nothing out of place. Pristine. Much like her apartment.

As I move around, I notice her filing drawers are locked—*smart girl*—her computer is not here at all, and there are no photos or keepsakes anywhere to give me any further insight into the woman who now has to be the center of my attention.

I bite my lips as I try not to laugh at the memory of her walking out of her bedroom early Saturday morning, still half asleep. The vision of her messy hair and fire in her eyes, her long, smooth, tan legs, with her soft pink painted toes now firmly ingrained in my mind. She has great fucking legs. The kind I know would look amazing wrapped around my waist. She looks like a bambolina; short, blonde, with pouty pink lips and a sharp mouth, the complete opposite to any of the Italian women my sister tries to set me up with.

Hearing a familiar chime, I know it is her arriving to work. The elevator giving her away. Her coffee with cream already waits on her desk, still hot as the steam rises from the cup. It matches the steam coming from her ears as she stops abruptly as she spots me in her office again.

"Again?! What are you doing here on Monday morning? You said I had until Friday!" she screeches out, and I smirk.

"I am eager to start our arrangement." It is not entirely untrue, because if she can start on the work I have for her sooner, that would be even better. But I only came here today to get another chance to see her, push her a bit more. I enjoy teasing her. It's very entertaining.

"I have not changed my mind, Nico." She sighs like I am annoying her.

"Ahh, but you will." I walk around her office, taking in the books in the bookshelves and her certificates, which all shine behind the glass frames on the wall.

"Oh, really? And what makes you think I will?" she asks with a bite, watching me as I saunter around her space, not really afraid of me, yet not trusting me either.

"Because you will have no choice, and I always get what I want. You will come and work for me, Emilia. You know it, and I know it. We might as well start today, but I'll be generous and not go back on my word. You'll get the week to *think* about it." As soon as I emphasize the word "think," her eyes light up with rage. My cock twitches at the sight.

"Oh my God! You are so arrogant. Such an asshole! Is this how you do business? Continually harass people until you get your own way?" When her huffed insults and questioning garner no reaction from me, she roughly sets her bag and coat down. Straightening, she crosses her arms over her ample chest, just as she spots the coffee. Then her eyes are back on mine.

"You only have five days now, Emilia. Tick Tock..." I say mockingly, leaving the light threat sitting between us. I respect her confidence in standing her ground, but she will take this deal. She doesn't have a choice.

"I don't think so, Nico. I am sure you can find someone else for your illegal activities," she says, waving her hand around. I rub my mouth with my hand, covering the smirk that is forming. She speaks with her hands a lot, especially when her feathers are ruffled, which I'm taking too much joy in. I wonder where she picked it up. It is a very European mannerism, one that reminds me of my family.

Striding forward, she snatches up the coffee and takes a sip. Her body relaxes visibly, eyes closing just for a moment and a little *"mmm"* sounding from her throat before she catches herself. "Maybe you can work for me instead. I could get used to this little luxury of you bringing me coffee.." She speaks with a tight smile, one that says *"fuck you"* as she leans against her desk, giving me a perfect view of her curves in her black suit and sky high heels. "Where did you learn to make coffee so well?" she asks, taking another sip immediately. And for some reason, I find myself answering.

"My father was a coffee merchant in Italy, selling the

best beans in the north. I think I had coffee before milk when I was a baby." She observes me, trying to decide if I'm being genuine. When her face softens ever so slightly, I know she believes me.

"Speaking of fathers... since mine is why you're here." She crosses her legs at the ankle, taking a breath, her gaze dropping to the ground. "I don't think you understand my need to stay away from him and everything he's involved in. His decisions have created a tsunami of problems I now have to deal with, and it's been hell. You want to work with me, but don't you realize I won't be a working lawyer anymore if that's discovered. My reputation has already been dragged down, and that will be the nail in the coffin." With a rough swallow, her eyes meet mine again, and whatever she sees there hardens her on the spot. "But I am sure you know all about that already, don't you, Nico?" she says, eyeing me with an accusing glare.

"I know a lot of things Emilia," I say, letting my voice drift off, not really answering her question, which I know she doesn't like. Her shoulders stiffen when I remain silent. I imagine in a court of law, she would push her subjects further, drill a proper answer from them, but she leaves mine lingering in the air.

As I approach her, I watch her big blue eyes, which are like a beacon showing me the way. Stopping mere inches from her body, I don't miss the way her breasts move up and down as her breathing increases in pace.

"Five. Days. And then you will be all mine." My statement is said in a way that ensures she understands, my tone one made to intimidate. But it does just the opposite. I see a flash of defiance in her eyes, feel the flames of anger welling inside her that she is trying very hard not to let out. We stand close, staring at each other, neither of us wanting to be the first one to move in this standoff. I can feel her warm breath skirting across my skin, and my fingers twitch to touch her.

My cell vibrates in my pocket, startling me from my thoughts, and I smile as I look at the screen and see my sister's name. Emilia not so subtly looks at the screen as well, and I smirk.

"Five days, Emilia. Make the right *choice*." I step away before I do something stupid, like put my lips on hers. Being that close to her is something I should be avoiding. My eyes trail over her form, drinking her in, and I see fire in her gaze as they land back on her face. Walking out the door, closing it behind me, I grab my phone.

"Ciao, bella!" I say as I answer the phone, a smile immediately coming to my face when hearing my sister on the other end. She starts talking in Italian a million miles a minute about Mama and Papa and the happen-ings of her day. I let her talk, as my mind is still back in the office, still picturing my frustrated bambolina.

"So, Fratello, there is a girl. Her name is Jasmina," she starts, and even though I have no interest, I decide to entertain her as I step into the elevator.

"And, tell me about her." I play along, wondering if I'll ever end up marrying one of these girls she tells me about. I pretend to listen, giving Antonio a wave as I walk out of the building and step into the morning light. My sister's strong desire to set me up and get me married is her one and only frustrating attribute.

"She is from Milan. Tall, beautiful, a model..." she

says the last part tentatively, already knowing it will be a no from me. The last model she set me up with was purely after my money and connections. We are well known in Italy and that means a lot of women want to date men like me. The problem is finding the right one, something that has not yet happened.

It is one thing to be in an arranged marriage for Sebastian. That is business and I will do what I need to if that was ever presented. He has never asked, but it is not entirely impossible. But if my sister plans to set me up with one of her friends, then it needs to be the real deal. I want the kind of love my parents have, the everlasting kind. I grew up in a household full of it and I want the same for my children, no question.

"Ahhh, no model, Sorella, not for me." I can hear her sigh, so I change the topic of conversation.

"Tell me, Sorella, how is your health. Everything going okay? You haven't given me any updates lately." My sister had breast cancer years ago. It has not reappeared yet, but I know it is something that can come back, and with Dante so precautious with Annie's health, it constantly plays on my mind.

"I am fine, Fratello. Now, back to your love life! You need to come home and find a beautiful Italian woman, get married, and make babies!" she says excitedly.

"What if I find a nice American girl instead?" I ask as I jump into my car, thinking of the beautiful curvy blonde I just left. Though, the way my mind went right to her has me pausing for a moment.

"What? No! You must marry a nice Italian girl, Fratello. That way, you can come home more. You don't want anything or anyone else to keep you over there. You need to be home with us!" I let the conversation flow, not pushing her anymore. I don't have the heart to tell her I think New York is my home now. Italy will always be a special place, somewhere I go and visit all the time, but my life is here. I pledged my allegiance to Sebastian, and that is the kind of deal you take for a lifetime. And I wouldn't change it.

"Sorella, you need to stop playing matchmaker. I don't need a woman just yet."

"I know, Fratello. It's just... you gave so much up for me. You joined Sebastian's family for me. I want to see you happy," she says solemnly, and I am glad she is being honest. Now I understand why she's so focused on this.

"You don't owe me anything, Sorella. I am happy. Sebastian is fantastic, and I would do it all again in a heartbeat," I say, trying to reassure her.

"Just promise me you will be safe, Fratello."

"Always, Sorella. Tell me about your love life? Is there anyone I have to kill for touching my little sister?" I joke, successful in annoying her.

"Fratello! This is why I don't date. The last boy I was interested in ran for the hills the moment you turned up and scowled at him," she says, laughing, knowing the last boy I scowled at was her teenage crush who lived across the street. Since then, she has been sick and focused on herself, love not something that has come across her mind. I talk with her for a few more minutes, then end the call as we get to the compound.

I have work to do. I need to have things in order before our lawyer officially starts on Friday.

6

EMILIA

As I sip my morning coffee, I see a note next to it with the words '*24 hours*' scribbled on it. His handwriting is scrawly, but legible. I don't even have to think about who wrote it because it looks the same as the one that was left on my desk yesterday and the day before that. Every morning this week, as I have stepped into my office, a steaming cup of delicious coffee has been waiting for me on my desk, along with a note reminding me of the timeline I am on.

He is extremely sure of himself, and as much as that grinds my gears, I am getting used to the nice hot coffee each morning. I wonder what he will say on Friday when I reject him for the third time. I have a feeling Nico is not a man who is told no very often.

My body sinks into my office chair, feeling deflated because I lost another three clients this week. And I already know my remaining two are hanging on by a thread. I have been trying to drum up new business, calling all my contacts, reaching out to new prospects, but no one wants to come near me. It's like I am tarnished or have an infectious disease. I even had one guy hang up on me the moment I said my name.

The other few businessmen I have chatted with have been nice enough, telling me that in any other circumstance, they would hire me in an instant. But the fact remains I am a Cole, and my father is currently wanted for one of the biggest cases of fraud the country has ever seen.

It is most certainly not good for business to be associated with me at this time.

My eyes travel to the pile of invoices sitting on my desk, the ones I have been ignoring. I am not usually someone who doesn't pay accounts when they are due. My affairs are, for the most part, up to date and papers filed neatly away. But this batch is marked with 'OVER-DUE' in red ink, making it obvious I am not as in control of my life as I once was. As a woman who has had to do things on her own her entire life, being in this position leaves me feeling sick.

My bank account is nearly empty and the office lease is paid up for another week. I have put the coffee machine up for sale online, and I have already canceled the cleaners and my business insurance. With what I have remaining, I plan to pay out what Cindy is owed.

I sip the coffee, and it is perfect as usual, even if the man who makes it is an arrogant thorn in my side.

"Good morning," Cindy greets me quietly as she walks in with her notepad, a coffee, and a tray of freshly baked brownies—my favorite.

"Oh, you didn't have to!" I say to her, standing to help

her with the tray as she takes a seat opposite me, ready for our usual morning catch-up.

"Well, we lost Symons, Catcher, and Sycamore yesterday, so I thought we needed chocolate." She gives me a sad smile.

I sigh, offering her a sad smile in return. I don't have the energy to fake it anymore. "Thanks, Cindy."

"And I saw this at the newspaper stand this morning..." The look on her face is one of remorse, and I glance down at the newspaper she is handing over to me.

The front page has a large photo of my father, one which I think was taken a while ago. He is in his business suit, fat and happy, with a young blonde on his arm, who is wearing a tight red dress that would work better as a t-shirt, and they both are stepping into a limo. The headline is in big black bold letters.

Disgraced Business Man Gone Underground: Where are you, Brian Cole?

My eyes quickly read through the article. It doesn't mention anything new, just that he is a fraud, owes various people millions, and hasn't been seen since my brother's funeral, all of which I know, as I have been interviewed by the FBI multiple times now about his whereabouts. My eyes stall on the paragraph at the end of his article.

Brian Cole's sole surviving daughter, Emilia Cole, was one of New York's most up-and-coming corporate lawyers until her father's criminal activities came to light. However, her father's activities have tarnished her reputation, with our sources saying she is now needing to find a new career, her lifestyle no longer feasible in the current climate.

"Oh my God..." I whisper out as my body falls back into my seat. Sure, the newspaper has written about me before, but it has all been how estranged I have been from my father, showcasing the distance I have kept from him. This article today has sealed my fate. No one is going to want to work with me ever again.

"Oh, Emi, I know. It's tough, but you are one of the best young lawyers in the city, if not the country. Surely people will see that?" While her loyalty is heartwarming, her expectations of other people are way off.

"I have called everyone I know. I am just not sure what else to do," I say to her, my eyes showing her how sorry I am for letting her down.

"I know this is not the best time to ask, but do I need to be looking for a new job, Emi?" Cindy asks, and the bite of brownie I just took feels like sludge as it travels down to my stomach. Cindy was my first and only hire. Everyone else I have paid on retainer, and I let go of them a few weeks ago, but Cindy was all mine from the start. I feel terrible she is going to be out of a job.

"Cindy, I am so sorry..." I watch her grab a brownie, taking a big bite as well. Decades ago, before Cindy had kids and her job at the diner, she was a law clerk. She has a great eye for detail. Her skills came through within weeks of me hiring her, so I know law is where she really wants to be.

"It's okay, I think I can cancel Europe and get most of my money back," she says glumly.

"Are you sure there is nothing we can do?" she asks me, her eyebrows high in question. My gaze flicks to the note sitting next to my coffee, then back to Cindy.

"There is one opportunity, but I haven't made up my mind on whether to take it or not," I say to her honestly, still trying to weigh up the short-term gain for the long-term pain.

"Does it have anything to do with the dashing young man who brings you coffee each morning?"

"You've seen him?" My eyebrows rise in shock. Clearly his visits haven't been as inconspicuous as I was hoping.

"Yes. I usually see him each morning on his way out. He seems nice enough, always polite, and he is pretty easy on the eyes too," she says with a hopeful smile, and she perks up a bit. Seeing her happy again gives me warm fuzzies. Having not had a mother figure in my life, Cindy does a really good job of filling some of that void.

"He also dresses impeccably well, and I see him talking to Antonio downstairs a lot too, so he is obviously friendly." I don't have the heart to tell her he is actually more like a snake, slithering along the perimeter of my life, waiting to strike.

"Yes, well, he does appreciate good coffee," I grumble, acknowledging his only rewarding attribute.

"Maybe you should take his job? What other choice do you have?" she presses, her tone hopeful.

"There is a bit more to it than that, unfortunately." I'm not sure how much detail to tell her. "He operates on the other side of the law to what we usually work with."

"Ooohh..." she says with a nod, tight-lipped as she takes in my dilemma, sipping her coffee quietly.

"I think he knows my father," I add, and she nods again. I can see her digesting this information.

"Whatever you decide, just know that I am with you one hundred percent."

"Cindy, if this is something I do, I don't want you to —" I start to say, already shaking my head.

"Nonsense, I am a law clerk. I file, I type, I answer calls. Half the businesses we help are probably a little bit shady anyway. Besides, just because he might operate on the other side of the law doesn't mean the work he will have you do leans that way as well. Have you asked him exactly what he needs?" I can only look at her in slight shock and awe as I try to untangle the fact she has literally not only given me permission to tread outside of the lines to save myself, but also offered herself up to do the same.

"No. We haven't discussed it in detail. I suspect he will want me to agree to it before I know exactly what it is," I tell her with a sigh, taking the last sip of coffee.

"Well, think about it. Options at this point aren't plentiful," she says, just as my office phone rings. Leaning over Cindy grabs it from my desk.

"Emilia Cole's office," She greets, sounding upbeat as ever, but then her eyes look at me, and sadness sweeps through them. "One moment, please." She puts the phone on hold.

"It is Mr. Jefferson for you." Mr. Jefferson is one of my last two clients. We both know why he is calling. One of my last lifelines is about to be taken away.

"Okay, thanks." I grab the phone and Cindy stands, taking the remaining brownies and walking out of my office, closing the door softly behind her.

I take a big breath in and try to put my armor on, but

it is cracking. For the first time since this whole debacle started, my armor feels too heavy. Before I think too hard about that, I answer the call, knowing that unless I can pull off an absolute miracle, this is going to be the last time I speak with Mr. Jefferson.

7

NICO

Stepping into her office, carrying her coffee and a box of papers, it is me that is surprised for once. The whole office is quiet, dark, no Cindy at reception and no other people around. That has been the usual case for me this week when I come to deliver her coffee and her note. But this morning is different. Sitting in her large leather chair behind her desk is the bambolina herself, looking at me as though she is going to end me and take great pleasure in doing so.

"Ahhh, she is up early today," I say to her, putting the box on her desk and then handing her coffee over to her.

"Might as well get this over with. Give me that goddamn coffee," she says with a groan, reaching for the cup.

I smile at her, which irritates her more.

"You're especially delightful this morning. Are you finally ready to come to the dark side?" I ask her, as I take a seat on the small sofa in her office. I watch her as she sips the hot brew, noticing her long delicate throat as she swallows. Dressed casually today in jeans, a white t-shirt, and black blazer, I don't miss the hint of black lace peeking out of the top of her V-neck, giving me a small glimpse of what she is hiding underneath. Crossing my leg over my knee and leaning back, I wait for her to talk.

"Tell me your terms," she grits out, and I know this is killing her. I feel bad for her... a little. Her father really did a number on her and none of this is her fault, yet here we are.

"You work for me. I have a project I need you to investigate. Lots of paperwork to review and catalog. I am trying to find a needle in a haystack." The two of us staring at each other from across the room, her with narrowed eyes and me with a straight face.

"What about Cindy?" she asks, and I realize if she does this, she is probably doing it to look after her staff more so than for herself. It is admirable and also incredibly stupid.

"I will continue to pay her a salary and offer her a silencing bonus for her to keep all this confidential. She can't be involved in the project, but she will be looked after, and may need to provide some administrative support at some point. Until then, she can stay here with you, answer calls, and do your company admin, as required and as you need her. She can even keep her holiday plans too." I see the tension leave her shoulders as she relaxes a little.

"So you will pay her to do nothing?" she asks, sounding astounded.

"I am not totally unreasonable. It is not her fault she is losing her job, and I am sure she has a hint of what is going on anyway, so we need to keep her quiet. Money is one of the best ways of doing that, wouldn't you say?" I say, a small threat leaking out, and Emilia nods in understanding. Though, she looks like she's biting her tongue to stop from biting back at me.

"Likewise, we will pay you too. Your standard hourly rate, plus a little extra. While I know there is lawyer-client privilege, I am sure I don't need to tell you whatever you see, hear, or do is not to be repeated to anyone. At any time. Under any circumstances."

"Will there be anything illegal required?" she asks, and I tilt my head.

"What do you think?" I lift a brow, smirking at the dread taking over her gorgeous face.

"Jesus," I hear her mumble as she runs her hand through her hair, and I have a sudden urge to grip it and pull her head back, just so I can see more of her.

"Can I work from here?" she asks, bringing my attention back to the matter at hand.

"Maybe. The paperwork I have is sensitive. I have an office set up for you at a secure location. But I can bring you boxes here. If needed, I can place some protection on you as well."

"Are you saying working with you will put a target on my head?" she counters. Her quick questioning shows how good of a lawyer she is. She makes sure I answer all of her questions clearly, leaving no room for conjecture.

"Yes. It's possible. I'm not going to lie, we have a lot of enemies." I offer her nothing but the truth. She needs to understand what she is getting herself into.

She is silent for a moment, and I wait for her, giving her time to process.

"What is the project?" she asks. "I would like to know about the project before I agree to anything."

I nod my head in approval, because she is exactly what I need. She is thorough, thinks everything through, and will ensure every *t* is crossed and every *i* is dotted.

"Your father," I say, then watch her and wait. It doesn't take long.

"No," She barks, her arms waving a big X in front of her.

"I need you to look over his entire business portfolio," I continue, though now, she's about to freak out. That much is obvious.

"No. Absolutely not," she says, jumping up from her chair, and beginning to pace the length of her office.

"He is hiding something, and I want to know what it is." I slowly stand, her nervous energy near palpable as I move closer.

"I don't know him. I don't know anything about him. I can't even believe that we share blood. My blood is tainted because of him. I am too scared to even donate blood to the blood bank because of how tainted it is; I don't want to infect anyone else. Could you imagine if there were more people like my father out in the world? It would turn into the white-collar crime version of the zombie apocalypse. I can't be responsible for that. I can't do it, Nico. I don't want to. I just... I can't."

I don't even think she took a breath. Her father has done some damage, and she's victim number one.

Walking up to her, I stand in front of her, cutting off

her walking path and causing her to stop pacing. As she looks up at me, I watch her swallow, her throat the prettiest damn throat I have ever seen draped in a fine gold chain that highlights her bone structure. So fucking feminine and dainty, I want to run my tongue along it. Her hair is flowing down her back, and I clench my fists by my side so I don't fulfill my newest fantasy and wrap it around my wrist to keep her eyes on mine.

"You are the best fucking lawyer in the city. You have more insight into your father than any of us. You are fucking perfect for this, and you *will* do this for me," I say to her, my tone is demanding, but I want to shock her from her fluster. She remains quiet, her breathing still rapid, so I continue.

"You have so many issues with who he is, what he's done, this is your chance to take him down. While what you uncover will never have him land in a court of law, it will provide consequences to his actions. And make no mistake, my bambolina," I say as my hand unconsciously comes up and pushes her hair back from her face. "I will make him pay. For everything." I feel her soft locks in between my fingers as I grit out my declaration. Her lips part just a little, and if I wasn't so focused on doing my job, I would probably fuck her against her desk right now.

She is looking at me, wide-eyed, the various blue hues sparkling in her office lights, but her breathing slowly calms. I can see the wheels in her head turning as she thinks about all I have told her.

She clears her throat, and I let her hair fall from my

fingers as she straightens her spine, her breasts pushing out toward me. If only she could read my mind.

"What are you looking for in the boxes?" she asks me, her hands now on her hips. Her defiance fucking turns me on. I want to devour her whole.

"I'm not sure."

"You're not sure? So how do I know what to look for?" she presses, her eyebrow raising in a challenge.

"Believe me, you will know when you see it."

Her eyes flick to the table, and she glances at the box before looking back at me.

"Fine. You have a deal. But I need more coffee," she huffs, waving her hand in the air as she steps around me and strides into her small bathroom. I smile.

I knew she would come around.

8

EMILIA

I look at myself in the mirror of my office bathroom, wondering what the hell I just agreed to. As I repeat the conversation over and over in my mind, I know it doesn't really matter because I can't go back on it now. I just made a deal with the devil, and there is no way out.

I turn on the taps and run cold water onto the inside of my wrists, trying to cool down. The tension between Nico and I was all-encompassing, and I walked straight to the bathroom to collect myself while he got to work on fresh coffees. But even I know there is not enough caffeine in this world to get me through what I know will be one of the toughest cases of my entire life. One that will never end up in a court of law.

I take a deep breath and straighten my spine, meeting my eyes in my reflection.

"C'mon, Emi. Put on your big girl panties and show these men what you can do," I say to myself by way of a pep talk, because I know now I need to bring my A-game.

The mob are paying me to find information and they will expect results. This will be unlike any other project I have worked on before. I don't want to know what would happen if I don't deliver.

Sucking in one last deep breath, I throw open the door and stalk back to my office.

"Right, where do we…" My voice gets stuck in my throat as I see him sitting at the small conference table, laptop open in front of him, and an open box full of papers nearby.

"I need you to open your father's files," he says, spinning the laptop to face me. I hold back my groan of frustration. He really wastes no time, does he? Well, he'll just have to wait.

"Right now? I haven't even had my coffee!" Walking over to my desk, I pick up the steamy cup, taking a small sip. My eyes flick to Nico, who is watching me swallow, and I see his eyes trailing the movement of my throat. Putting the cup back down, I move around my desk and grab my handbag, pulling out a lip gloss and coating my pout until it shimmers before I take another sip, leaving a stain of color on the cup.

"Are you finished?" Nico says, looking exasperated as he sits, waiting for me. I see his jaw tick slightly, and I am glad that I frustrate him as much as he frustrates me.

"You know, I don't think I am," I throw back at him, taking my time to tidy up the non-existing mess on my desk.

"Are you always this infuriating?" He leans back, legs spread a little as his hand rubs his chin like he is assessing what to do with me. He takes up nearly all the room at my table, his presence almost overpowering.

"What makes you think I know how to access his files? I haven't seen my father for years. Have you not researched our past, or do you just not believe it? You have recently found out that he is an evil bastard, but I have known that fact for most of my life."

"Try." One word, and it was an order. I look at the screen, and I see the blinking cursor in front of me. The webpage open is to my father's private business account, one where he stores a range of things, I'm sure.

I sigh out in defeat as I walk over to where he is sitting and pull the laptop toward me. Just for fun, I type in the word *'asshole'* into the password section and hit enter. The words *'Please Enter the Correct Password'* flash across the screen in red text and the man next to me raises his eyebrow, clearly knowing what I typed and running out of patience. I give him a smartass smirk of my own in return.

Leaning against the table, I drill my fingernails in succession, creating a beat as I think, wanting to annoy him but also trying to get my mind into gear. I am already frazzled by the events of this morning. I didn't miss the way he looked at me, the way his fingers felt against my cheek, and although he drives me absolutely crazy, when he pushed my hair out of my face just moments ago, I nearly whimpered. With Nico now sitting so close to me, I can feel the soft material of his shirt grazing my arm, and it's enough to distract me.

With his woodsy cologne invading my senses, my

thoughts remain jumbled, so I stand up and begin to pace the floor again to get away from him.

"What have you tried?" I ask. Surely the mob has tried to crack the system already. Surely they haven't just left it all to me.

"We have tried thousands of different combinations; birthdays, holidays, names, addresses, recurring trips..." Nico replies as he leans back in his chair, watching me as I continue to pace back and forth, wearing a line in my carpet.

"Well, that's your first mistake." I see him grit his teeth, his jaw clenching.

"He doesn't think like a normal person. He has no empathy, no love for anything or anyone. The last thing it would be is someone's name or birth date," I state with an eye roll. These mob men can't be that smart if they haven't figured out that small fact.

"So what do you think it is, then?" His body is more open now, his body language more accepting. Less demanding and more collaborative, an approach I prefer, even if he is still an asshole.

"What deals made him money? Lots of money? What properties has he bought, what person did he fuck over...?" I feel myself get into work mode. The buzz of the riddle already starting to spark in my belly as I try to recall anything I know about the man whose blood I share, but coming up empty.

I look at Nico, and his eyes are already on me. I don't think they've left for a second. "What?" I bark out to him as I pause my steps.

"You really have no idea who your father is, do you?" he says slowly, almost somewhat fascinated.

"If you are referring to what deals he has done, where his investments are, or what he has for breakfast each morning, no. I have absolutely no idea," I state honestly, and it appears Nico is only just starting to understand exactly how estranged my father and I are.

"And before you say anything else, I think I prefer not to know. Let's just go through the paperwork and see if that gives us any clues," I murmur as I take the seat next to him at the table again, now in full concentration mode as I delve into the files Nico has brought with him.

We sit close together in silence, each of us looking over the paperwork, but I don't miss the heat radiating from his body or the way I see his eyes flick over me from time to time in my peripheral vision. I feel unsettled, but not scared. If anything, my body lights up under his attention. Which should concern me more than it does, frankly.

It has been a very long time since a man invaded my space like this. Sure, I have male clients all the time, but not ones that show up to my apartment, bring me coffee every day, and whose one simple touch has me itching for them to do it again. I'm not sure why I let him touch me in the first place. If it was anyone else, I would have slapped his hand away. Maybe I should have, maybe that would have set up some boundaries. Formal working expectations. Although I already know that nothing about this arrangement is going to be as expected.

Men have never been a priority for me. I constantly had my head stuck in my school books at college, rarely coming up for air. I did have a few short-term boyfriends here and there, but no one of significance. The term *career focused* was invented just for me, as I have done nothing but work day and night, seven days a week, for the past few years to build my career.

Yet here I am, sitting next to a man from the mob, looking through piles and piles of corporate jargon belonging to the man who's responsible for my life crumbling around me, still not sure exactly what I am looking for, but praying it isn't something so bad the mob decides to end me for it.

I swallow at that thought, and I look over at Nico. He is gruff, arrogant, and obviously deadly, but would he kill me? That is such a stupid question, of course he would.

There are so many statements, bank letters, company contracts, and every kind of document in between to go through, so thankfully that keeps me occupied from my spiraling thoughts. My eyes scan for anything and everything, hoping some clue jumps out and slaps me in the face so this whole ordeal can be over with already.

After an hour of slowly processing letters, statements, file notes, and even his personal diary (which was extremely eye opening), I sit on my office floor with paperwork scattered around me, ready for a mental breakdown.

"More coffee?" Nico asks as he stands up from the table, obviously sensing my need for a refresher.

"Sure," I reply, rubbing my eyes and stretching my arms out. I'll be lucky if I don't get a migraine from staring at the papers for so long.

I watch him walk out of my office, leaving the door

open as he goes to the small kitchenette behind Cindy's desk to make us two cups of coffee. He opens the fridge for the cream, which is just for me, him being a straight black coffee man himself.

As I watch his tall frame approach me, reaching down to hand me my cup, it dawns on me that no man has ever made me a coffee before. At least not like this. I actually need to stretch my memory to think if any male work colleges in the past have done such a thing, but I come up blank.

Nico might be the first.

Grabbing the coffee from him, I take a quick sip, looking at him over the rim of my cup as he takes a seat on the sofa behind me. With me now sitting on the floor at his feet, the power dynamics are evident. I don't like it one bit.

"What do you think?" he asks, waving his hands across the pile of papers surrounding me on the floor as his body sinks into the white pillowy softness of my sofa, a place I am already wishing to relax into. To anyone else, the papers look a mess, but to me, it is organized exactly how I've processed it.

"Too early to say... but..." I trail off and take another sip of the coffee. He really does make it good, I will give him that.

"But what?" he barks out sharply, and I turn slowly to face him, my eyes searing. Patience is not his strong point.

"You know, if you want me to work *with* you, I think you could start with being a little *nicer* to me. I could just sit here and shuffle papers and put random names into the laptop and you would have no idea if I was being helpful or not." I shrug, giving him a big cheesy sarcastic smile, and batting my eyelashes in an overt attempt to grate on his nerves. His total lack of gratitude is frustrating.

"I like when you get fiery..." he says, smirking, taking a sip of his coffee. Of course he likes it. Dammit. Doesn't he get it that he needs me, not the other way around. This man is so maddening.

"Tell me what you are thinking, bambolina." I have no idea if he is being genuine or taunting me, but regardless, calling me a nickname gives me butterflies. Only, these butterflies seem to have a death wish.

"What does bambolina mean?" I ask with a huff, assuming it is something crass, and straightening my back, ready to think of a smart response.

"Little doll," he replies without hesitation, his eyes skimming my hair and my body, filling me with warmth, before settling back on to my face. I remain quiet, but my heart skips a beat, and I raise an eyebrow in question, but he doesn't elaborate.

Rolling my lips, I take a deep breath and release it slowly before putting down my cup on the coffee table and sitting on my knees. I decide to get back to business. Best to ignore the way that just made me feel the exact opposite of how I was expecting. "So, we have bank statements, insurance policies, company files..." I start to explain, flipping through the papers to find something, then looking up at him. "What is this?" I ask, handing a letter to Nico.

"A letter from the Swiss bank where your father had millions. But we have already looked here, already scanned every account we could find," he says, handing it back to me.

"So what about this one?" I ask again, pushing another paper into his face.

"From the Seychelles, his hidden bank account," Nico says, eyeing me suspiciously. "Go on." He leans forward, now clearly interested in what I have to say.

"Well, there are no investment notices, no medical documents, no trust fund information..." He moves even closer, and I swallow past the growing lump in my throat. I should really tell him to never wear that delicious cologne again.

"Hmmm, and?" His dark eyes shine with anticipation as he looks into mine, waiting for what I am going to say next.

"There is also no passport," I state, clearing my throat as I wait for him to put the pieces together. Only, his face remains blank as he watches me.

"Nico, all of this paperwork is international documentation, but we don't have his passport or travel details, plane log book, hours for his jet, or anything like that," I say, looking up at him again to see if he understands what I am getting at.

"What are you saying?" he asks me, his eyes penetrating mine, his forehead crinkled in thought.

"There has to be another box. There has to be more... there is so much that is missing. And..." I stop as I watch him process, seeing his jaw tighten.

"And?" he prods.

"And, I think whatever you are looking for is in international borders..." I say in merely a whisper because I am afraid to say anything out loud, not sure of his reaction, suddenly feeling like I am swimming in dangerous territory. I hope he doesn't think I know more than I really do. Being on the wrong side of the mob is not my preferred position.

He moves a little in his seat, and I immediately stiffen and move away from him slightly, not wanting to meet his eye. Tilting his head, he pauses, looking at me questioningly.

"Are you afraid of me, Emilia?" his eyes crease a little as he asks the question. My first instinct is to lie, because screw him, but why even bother at this point.

"You are the mob, Nico. Everyone is afraid of you."

"But are you? Or are you just afraid because you think you should be?" Nico searches my face as I try to understand his question.

His hand comes out and grabs my chin, the action making me gasp as he tilts my face up toward his, which is now mere inches away.

His grip is warm and firm, and I don't want to move away. My body craves to move closer, while my mind is telling me to run. The warring feelings slam into me, making me second guess everything.

"I won't ever hurt you, Emilia. You are not in danger from me. I promise you." I momentarily forget to breathe as his breath ghosts across my face, making my body hum. A wave of his protectiveness seems to flow over me, putting me slightly at ease. I nod a little, not even realizing I am at first, as his fingers run down my jawline, skimming my face, his eyes looking at me intensely.

I am not sure what is happening other than my heart

is pounding out of my chest and those butterflies dancing in my stomach have multiplied. Whether it is from stress or an entirely new feeling, I have no idea, but I have never had a man say something like that to me before. Feeling safe is foreign to me, and I will admit, it's a slight turn on.

"You have passed the test, bambolina. There is another box, many in fact. It's time to take you to the compound," he whispers to me, and for the first time since I first met him, he smiles.

A small, but genuine smile.

9

NICO

I sit in the car, with her positioning herself as far away from me as possible, looking everywhere but at me. She wasn't keen to come with me. In fact, she bolted up from the floor so fast, her coffee nearly spilt all over her carpet. But with the rest of her father's boxes locked away at the compound, it was a hell of a lot easier to take her to them instead of bringing them to her.

I only took one box over with me this morning, along with the laptop as a test to see what she is made of, and she didn't disappoint. I have thought about who would be supporting her father internationally, but who he knows remains a mystery, having not found any evidence linking him to anyone. He has covered his tracks extremely well. Given it took her less than a day to come to the same conclusion, it reinforces that I made the right choice in getting her to help us.

If only I could stop touching her. This is business, and I need to focus. The fact her blonde tresses and shimmering blue eyes continue to float around in my subconscious is not helping. Not to mention, her rose scent that wraps around me the instant I'm in her presence.

I glance over at her again to see her face firmly planted at the window, watching the world blur past as Tony drives us from her office to the compound. Her arms are crossed across her chest, but it's not in the willful way I've become familiar with. It's like she's protecting herself; she is cautious of me, and I am not sure how I feel about that.

We don't hurt women ever, and I tried to make it clear to her that she was not in danger. I love women, especially having grown up close to both my mother and sister, so hurting a woman in any way is something I could never do. While I am okay with people being afraid of me, like all us mafia men encourage, I don't want Emilia to be. My gut churned when she flinched away from me back in her office.

I don't want her to feel fear around me. Ever.

The car gets dark as we enter our basement car park, piquing her interest.

"Where are we?" Emilia demands, and I try not to chuckle because she has yet to learn that no one demands anything from me. My eyes flick down to her hands that have now moved and are white knuckled on the leather seats, her head whipping around to see out the other windows, trying to decipher our surroundings. She is a strong woman, but I can see the doubt in her face about what she's gotten herself into. Without thinking, I extend my hand and wrap it over hers on the seat in between us. I don't hold anyone's hand, but around her, my body seems to do things all on its own.

I hear her gasp, and she looks at me. Our gazes lock, but she doesn't move her hand away and neither do I. For a brief moment, I wonder what the fuck I am doing, but her hand curls around and she grips mine tight, I don't hesitate. I squeeze hers in return to help settle her nerves, telling myself it is because I need her focused and settled in order for her to do good work. But my actions have caught me off guard, and I don't entirely know if that is true.

"My home. My office. We call it the compound. All your father's files are here," I state, clearing my throat as the car comes to a stop, then removing my hand from hers. Opening the car door, I step out into the garage and lean in to offer her my hand—only because my mother raised a gentleman. I watch her face as she hesitates for a moment before she steps out and takes mine in a death grip. I can't help but smirk and, if I am honest, I don't actually mind having her hand in mine. The two couldn't look any more different; mine large, tanned, and scared, with tattoos, and many stories to tell, hers small, delicate, and soft. So fucking soft.

"Oh my God, I'm in your web," I hear her say quietly, seemingly in awe as she eyes the men working down here and the various cars and trucks that are parked throughout the garage.

"I'm sorry?" I question, wanting to ensure I heard her correctly.

"Oh... nothing." She flashes me a fake smile, and I growl. I need her to be honest with me if this business relationship is going to work. We'll have to work on that.

She stands beside me, near the car, but I don't let go

of her hand, choosing to keep her close as I see her eyes flick around the space. I notice her blonde hair again, as it dazzles under the overhead lights, but I grit my teeth, realizing we have lots to hide down here.

"Let's go," I say sharply, her head whipping around as her eyes now meet mine. I pull her along, getting to the side of the garage and in through the door and out of sight of anyone else. We make our way through the maze of corridors inside, with me quickening our pace.

I now know this place like the back of my hand, due to the fact I was forced to run around these hallways in pitch black as part of my training when I first moved to New York. I can find any room with my eyes closed, including those on the other levels. But I am aware Emilia would get lost easily, would become very disoriented, with the way the hallways are decorated, making it look like we are heading in circles and offering no clear pattern or directive of where we might be. Her grip on my hand remains tense, as her steps struggle to keep up with me from behind. But I keep moving forward without pause; she doesn't need to see any more than is necessary, no need for her to see anything at all, really. Not yet. Once she completes this project, then who knows, maybe I will keep her on permanently after that. I mean, she is not going to have her business much longer, so she will need another job soon enough anyway.

I stop in front of a glossy black door, putting my handprint to the screen on the wall to the side. The new, fail-safe security system is something we put in after Annie and Little Leo were attacked over a year ago. I hear her breath hitch at the action and see her eyes widen as she looks at the screen. My palm lights up green, and as soon as the door opens, I push her inside before closing the door behind me.

She turns to face me immediately.

"I don't belong here," she states breathily, sounding nervous. But nevertheless, her hands find her hips, feigning confidence as she straightens her back and inhales deeply. I brush a hand over my mouth to hide the chuckle that threatens to break through.

"Come, bambolina. Let's just look at the files and see what we can find." I walk past her and into the apartment, expecting her to follow me. But she does not. What a surprise.

I get to the living room before I turn around, finding her arms now crossed across her chest, pushing her perfect breasts up higher. I admire the view for a second or two, as does my dick.

"I suggest you get your pretty little ass in here. You work for me now, and we have work to do." I watch her internal debate, like she has a choice. I've observed her this past week, seen how she operates, and what makes her perform best is always when I push her. She gets fiery, competitive almost, needing to prove something, and I can't say I mind frustrating her. It is fast becoming one of my favorite pastimes.

"I need to leave, Nico. I really don't belong here," she states more firmly this time, still not budging. Her shoulders are stiff, and I can practically see her second thoughts swirling around in her mind.

"If you want to leave, then you'll need to put yourself to work before you do. Let's go." There's an edge to my tone, but I stay where I am, crooking my finger to motion her closer.

"No." That's it. One word, and instead of moving forward, she takes one step back. And I just know it's meant to piss me off.

"Why are you so infuriating?" I say on a groan, taking slow, threatening steps in her direction until I'm an arm's reach away. "We made a deal, and now you belong to me. Don't you forget that bambolina."

"Stop calling me that," she fires back at me, her fists clenching, and I smile. I love her fighting spirit, even if it is redundant. I see her swallow roughly, my eyes trailing the movement of her throat, the action making a tingle run down my spine and right to my balls. I am a sucker for a delicate neck, and hers is making me mindless. Looking down at her, my eyes travel up to her perfect bow-shaped lips, to her cute button nose, then finally reach her big blue eyes framed by long lashes. She doesn't blink as she meets my stare, still waiting for my response.

"What? Bambolina? You don't like the name I gave you?" I tease her. She licks her lips, the movement briefly catching my eyes before I flick them back to hers. Quiet for a beat, she then sighs, the noise bringing me back to the present.

"Asshole." Dropping her hands from her chest, she struts into the room. I smirk as I follow her, watching her voluptuous round ass as I do.

"This is one of our private residences," I tell her, looking around the room with her, trying to take it in from her perspective. It is deluxe, as all of our apartments

are. This one is situated farther away from the other residences, and is here purely for business. It is where our
visitors usually stay, but at the moment, it is full to the
brim with boxes. I brought all the paperwork here
because I can sift through it until I fall asleep, and then
just crash in the bedroom upstairs. I keep the kitchen
stocked, and for the last few weeks, I haven't really left
this place, my head buried so deep in her father's business affairs, I have barely had time for anything else.

Her face remains stoic, but having already seen where
she currently lives, I know she is impressed. While we
may hate her father, I want her to feel somewhat
welcome. She is our employee now after all. We will treat
her with respect as long as she does the same to us.

"So where are the boxes? Might as well get this over
with." I like her sassy optimism, even if it comes with an
eye roll.

"This way." I head down the hall to the large room
that now contains storage boxes, most of which were
packed in a hurry when our team raided his many
homes. "In here," I say as I open two large timber doors,
pushing them inwards to a large living space. The furni-
ture is minimal, only containing a large sofa and a small
table with some chairs, but they're not here for comfort,
just here for me to take a breather while reviewing files.

"Oh my God," she says, as she looks around, eyes
wide and face bewildered. "How many boxes are there
here?"

I smirk. "Hundreds."

"You're kidding." Her eyes scrunch as she looks at me

like I am crazy. "You want me to go through all these boxes?" she confirms in disbelief.

"Yes. We have been through them, but I figure you will see something we haven't." I state honestly, because we have been through every single one of them. Both Sebastian and I have. Carter has spent some time reviewing things too, and as have Dante and a few other men in our team. Many things we followed up on, and have been successful, but there is something we are missing. I know it is big, and I need to find it.

"This is going to take forever! There is no way I can get through all those boxes today, or even this entire weekend. It will take me weeks!"

"It takes as long as it takes. You work for me now, remember?" I can basically see the smoke coming from her ears as her anger rises.

"I have a business, and I have... a client," she states, once again being too damn stubborn. The urge I have for her to submit to me is becoming all-encompassing.

"*A* client?" I ask as I step towards her. I look right down at her, displaying my dominance, reveling in the momentary shift in her expression. Strong-willed to questioning and back again, all in a matter of seconds. "Did I not make myself clear, bambolina? You work for *me*. No other clients. Just me." I clench my jaw, watching her trying not to say what she really wants to.

"I have a business, Nico. I cannot designate all my time to you and you alone," she says simply, her posture firm.

"I'm your business, your only business," I say just as

casually, keeping my hands in my pockets and looking at her inquisitively, curious as to what she'll say next.

"I still have one client I need to manage outside of this... arrangement." I see the defiance in her eyes as she holds firm. She's unrelenting. "And I still need to try to get new clients too..." I remain silent, my gaze on her unwavering.

"Nico! I still need to focus on getting my business back! This is not my only priority!" Her pitch rises with her frustration. It isn't yet a beg, but fuck I want it to be.

"You work for me, when and where I need you to. What you do in between is up to you, but you drop everything when I call, and right now, we have hundreds of boxes to make a start on. I suggest you get to it," I say as she looks back across at all the boxes, and then I turn to leave.

"Where are you going?" she asks me in a rush, sounding shocked.

"I have a meeting with Sebastian." The color drains from her face.

"I will be back to check on you later." Then I'm walking out the door, but not before I hear her murmur, "*asshole.*" And I grin, because now, I really want to spank her.

10

EMILIA

I watch his smug ass leave as I continue to stew in frustration at the man who appears to be one step ahead of me all the time. I have never experienced that before, being top of my class every year, and smart enough to know things others didn't. But Nico is becoming insufferable, especially when he smirks at me like he does, and even more so when he touches me and makes my mind turn to mush.

I look across at the boxes again. It is already early afternoon, and I know it is going to be a long night. *Exactly how I want to spend my Friday night*, I think to myself sarcastically, even though I didn't have plans. I never have plans. I am married to my job. Even more so now it appears.

When you work as hard as I do, there is little time for men or even friends. I left all my college friends back on the West Coast, many of them California natives. Although we keep in touch, our time together is usually limited to a large group vacation every year.

The last man I took an interest in was Adam. He's a young, successful, drop dead gorgeous man who works in finance. We met briefly at a business event a few weeks ago and even swapped numbers. But due to us both being so busy with work, we haven't been able to catch up since. And who knows if we ever will with my life imploding before my very eyes.

As I slowly walk toward the wall of boxes, I feel like a prisoner in this place. With no way out and no one to talk to. Being here in this room, with all that's left of my father's possessions, I already know I am not going to like what I uncover. I feel like whatever my father has done is now transferring onto me, and I don't like it one bit.

I grab a box and sit on the floor, my most relaxing and comfortable place to be, made even better by the soft, luxurious carpet adorning this amazing apartment. Whether it is Nico's or not, I have no idea, but it certainly looks lived in.

Opening the lid, I pull out some papers and start shuffling through them. As my eyes scan over one document to the next, my thoughts continue going back to Nico. I was quiet during the car ride because I really didn't want to go anywhere with him. A week ago, I never knew he existed, and now where do I find myself?

Right in his lair.

The last place an upstanding lawyer like me needs to be. The fact I am even here is enough to absolutely ruin my reputation, although my father has already done more than enough in that department. I thought this job for Nico would take the weekend, a week tops. Then I could go on my way, trying to obtain new clients and building my business back up, this small indiscretion never to be thought of again. But now as I stare at the giant wall of boxes, I feel like I am digging myself into a deeper hole, one that is going to be very difficult to get out of, and I am not sure what that is going to mean for me and my career.

I wonder about Nico and what his story is. Clearly Italian, his English is fantastic, but his accent is thick. I am not ashamed to admit that I tried to listen to the fast-paced Italian conversation he had walking from my office yesterday, and I didn't miss the female's name that flashed on his cell phone screen. As I pull out the next piece of paper, I huff out in frustration. Sometimes I feel like I am the only single person left on the planet. Although, he doesn't wear a ring on his finger, so maybe it was his girlfriend? If that is the case, he shouldn't be touching me the way he has been. Either way, she needs a gold medal for dealing with him and his arrogance on a regular basis.

I shake my head, trying to refocus. I start to sort the paperwork into piles, constructing a system I know will make sense only to me, but this is how I work.

Moving to the second box, I find much of the same. All of these papers were thrown into these boxes without a care, and no doubt have already been looked over by Nico and whoever else. Nothing's organized or set aside; this is like starting from ground zero.

As the hours tick by, I dig into the third and then the fourth box. My paper piles are now almost as tall as me as I sit beside them, my sorting skills being pushed to the limit. It isn't until I am halfway through the fourth box that I find something interesting.

It is a small envelope. It looks old, and it's stuck in between the pages of an old ledger book. By the looks of it, it hasn't been opened in a while, making me think this is something Nico hasn't seen.

I sink into the carpeted floor and lean my back against the sofa, keeping the ledger book open on my knees. There is nothing but a blank page staring at me, though, giving me no indication of what this envelope may contain. It's clean except for the words *'My Darling'* on the front in a feminine, black cursive script.

Opening the envelope, I take out a small handwritten note that is nicely folded on white parchment paper. The paper is thin and feels like it is about to crumble under my touch. Unfolding the note gently, I begin to read the cursive.

My Darling

I miss you. Your laugh, your voice, the way you make me feel like the only woman in the world, the most important person in the room. I wait breathlessly for your letters each month, hoping that we can be together soon. The desperation I have to be with you overwhelming.

Emilia and I are well. She is such a delight, and I can't wait for you to see her again.

All my love

Your angel always, Jacqueline

Jacqueline is my mother's name, so I look at the top of the note and read the date. It is dated just over a year after I was born and a week before she died in a car accident. I never thought my father would be a love note type of man, as he certainly didn't show any love when I was growing up, but I guess I never really knew him when my mother was alive. I was too young to remember her and have limited knowledge of her appearance since my father didn't have any photos of her in the house. I remember asking my father about her, but he always shouted at me to stop, and eventually, I did. Her name was blasphemy in our house, and as such, I have not much memory of her at all. Not even a photograph. Maybe he was just heartbroken. Maybe her death was what sent him down this dark path of life.

I read it again, then let my fingers trace the words, trying to feel connected to the woman who gave me life, but who I know nothing about. I try to imagine what she was feeling when writing this. She sounds so infatuated with my father, and so in love. There is a small sketch of some wings at the bottom next to her name, but it is faded. Maybe it's a butterfly or an angel, I am not sure.

I fold the note again and put it back into the envelope, securing it inside the ledger and away from prying eyes. I make a mental note of the box number and place it inside, hidden among years' old bank statements and other seemingly unimportant documents.

As I start to pull across a fresh box, I am still so deep in thought about the letter, I don't hear footsteps approaching.

"Any luck?" Nico asks, and I practically jump out of my skin.

I scream and my body jolts in surprise, and he looks at me like I have lost my mind.

"Don't just creep up on a person like that!" I yell at

him, my hand planted firmly on my chest, willing my heart to calm down. He looks at me from where he stands near the doorway with what looks like yet another cup of coffee.

"Do you bleed brown?" I ask him with a bit of sass, as I calm down and look up at him. His brows furrow in confusion.

"Coffee. I have never known anyone to drink so much coffee."

"I'm Italian," he replies with a shrug while flashing me his trademark smirk, and I purse my lips. That smirk is going to be the death of me. "What have you found?"

"Nothing yet, much of the same," I say as my eyes go back to the paperwork piles on the floor.

"You will know when you do. We think it is something pretty significant." He takes another sip of his strong black, his gaze roving over the piles around me.

"What do you think it is? Do you have any thoughts?" It would be good if he gave me some idea of what to look for.

"He has a lot of money, your father. Not all of it is clean. I think he is working with someone, perhaps washing it, perhaps he stole it, but who, how, or where, I don't know."

I think about what he says. It is, of course, possible. My father, through his quest of wanting more, could have made some deals with people he shouldn't have. Considering I am now in the mob's compound in New York City is evident of that fact at least. I sigh and rub my eyes, feeling weary and emotional, yet trying to display an air of confidence I know I need around this man. I'm also on high alert, since I don't know what he, or anyone else in this building, is capable of.

"Come and eat. You have a long few hours ahead of you still," he says before turning on his heel and walking back out the door. I watch him leave, surprised by the offer. But I guess prisoners get meal time in jail and I suppose this is no different.

I get up to follow him, my stomach rumbling because I haven't eaten all day. Walking slowly out of the room, I take in my surroundings and commit everything to memory. As I step down the small hallway into the open-plan kitchen and living room I walked past earlier, I stand, mesmerized for a moment, as the late afternoon sun shines brightly now. The high ceilings, with the large glass windows, let in some beautiful light, making the whole room shine. Looking around, I spot two bowls of pasta and some water at the dining table, with Nico already sitting down and waiting for me.

Wordlessly, he pulls out a chair for me, waving me in. I take a seat, and he passes me some bread, the whole thing entirely domesticated, like he's a perfect host. This is odd. Or at least it should be. Me sitting at a dining table, having a meal with a mob soldier. My eyes continue to flick around the room, like I am waiting for someone to jump out and spook me, but keeping a straight back and relaxed expression to hide my wariness. But that seems to be wasted on him.

"Will you relax and eat your pasta? You are not in danger. Besides, even if I wanted to kill you, I still need you. You are too valuable for me to harm yet," he says with a wink that should have me shaking in my boots, but has the complete opposite effect of warming me from the inside out.

What the hell is wrong with me?

I pick up my fork and begin to eat the most amazing meal I have ever had in my life. There is something to be said for Italians and their cooking, and if something happens and this deal I have with Nico takes a bad turn, then I might order this dish as my last meal. I look at Nico then, and his smirk returns, looking at me like he knows exactly what I am thinking as I continue to shove the pasta in my mouth.

Asshole.

11

NICO

We have been in this room, going through boxes, for the past hour. I have been pulling them down and moving them around as Emilia sits on the floor, sorting and reviewing each piece of paper from top to bottom. She has piles of paper around her, all systematically sorted in a way that makes absolutely no sense to me.

Having been through each of these boxes over the past few weeks, I can't imagine she will find anything, but she may see something we haven't. Having no other leads, I need to try everything.

As she rummages through the latest box, I notice her pause, her hands holding something I can't yet see. Intrigued, I step closer.

"What is it?" I ask her, but she doesn't answer me, her eyes not moving from the box, from whatever is in her hands.

"Emilia?" I ask again, taking another few steps in her direction. She is holding a photo. I vaguely remember

78

SAMANTHA SKYE

seeing it, but paid little attention to the family paraphernalia at the time, preferring to look at the paperwork, trying to find a trail.

"Is that you?" I squat next to her, looking more closely at the old photo in her hand. It is crumbled in the corners, but the little girl, with big blue sparkling eyes is front and center. She is sitting near a cake, a small chocolate one. I notice her hands are crossed against her chest and she has a grumpy look on her face. It's adorable to know she has always been a handful.

"Yes. I think this was my birthday..." she says quietly, lost in thought. I watch her for a beat, caught up in her memories, before my body automatically moves and I sit on the floor next to her. Intrigued by the photo, I lean over to get a better look before she hands the photo over to me. "I remember it because it was the only birthday cake I ever had." My head whips around to look at her.

"Really?" I ask, gobsmacked. As a child, I had birthday cakes and parties every year. Hell, if I am in Italy on my birthday, even now, my parents put on a celebration. It strikes me then at how different our upbringings were. Me in a house with both parents and a sibling, full of love, laughter, and quality time. Hers, by contrast, seemingly alone, with no mother to guide her, a father who didn't care, and a brother who should have protected her but didn't.

Now I am working for a criminal family, and she is the one on the right side of the law. Yet we both sit here in the apartment, looking over the same information, working together.

"The housekeeper found out it was my birthday and

made me a small cake. It was delicious. But then my father heard what she did, and she was fired that night. The next day, I woke up to a new housekeeper, one who wasn't allowed to speak to me and who ignored me every day." I can see her eyes filling with tears, though her voice doesn't waver. I wonder how a father can treat his own child like that, his daughter, no less. What were his motives?

She looks back at the box and pulls out something else. Following her gaze, I see an old newspaper clipping in her hand. I can't read the story, but the headline says *'New York Socialite Laid to Rest After Car accident on Local Freeway.'*

I watch her as she reads it, noticing her breaths coming quicker than before, the clipping shaking in her hands. My chest aches for her.

"Emilia?" I'm not sure what it is about this woman that makes me so soft, my voice no longer the demanding mafia soldier, but the young gentleman from Italy.

"This is about my mother..." she says, her words sounding broken. I know her mother died years ago, but paid little attention to the cause. "I didn't know her. She died when I was just a year old." Pausing, she swallows roughly. "It says here she was buried in the Woodlawn Cemetery."

"You didn't know?" I ask, already coming to the conclusion she didn't. She looks at me then and shakes her head slowly, as a lone tear trails down her cheek.

I move quickly, my hand reaching for it before she can. Her glassy eyes look at me questioningly as I brush the tear away with my thumb, but don't pull away. We stare at each other for a beat, my hand slowly cupping her jaw, and she leans into it a little. It's the first sign she has given me that lets me know she feels at ease in my presence. And that show of trust...

"Nico," Dante barks as he walks into the room, effectively snapping us both out of the moment. I swing my gaze to him, feeling her body jolt beside me. Instinctively, I put my hand down and rest it on her thigh, letting her know she's okay. I give her a reassuring squeeze, a move Dante notices, and even though he has a scowl on his face, his eyebrows raise in question.

"We've got to go. Something has come up," Dante says to me, then walks back out the door. I jump up, knowing something important must be going down.

"I'll be back. I need to go and take care of some things," I tell her. I don't need to provide her any type of reason, but I can't stop myself from trying to ease her mind.

"Wait!" she says quickly, just as I reach the doorway.

I stop and turn, looking at her, her eyes flicking between me and the door.

"How long will I be here? I've been here for hours, and it's almost eight. I'm not sleeping here, am I?" I can see her exhaustion, the long day taking more out of her than I thought it would.

"I'll take you home when I get back." I answer her the only way I know how, and she nods in understanding.

"Okay," she says, relief in her tone, and her shoulders relax. I don't wait a second longer before I am out of the room and walking with pace to catch up to the boys.

"WHY DID you bring her here so soon, Nico? Are you sure she can be trusted?" Sebastian asks me the minute I step into the meeting room. Dante and Carter are sitting with him around the table, everyone's attention on me.

"She needs to go through the boxes. It is going to take weeks, and we need to get started," I state nonchalantly as I take a seat at the table, not looking him in the eye.

"Bullshit," Carter says, covering it like a cough, and I throw my pen at him.

"We'll talk about it later," Sebastian says, looking at me pointedly. "Right now, we have a bigger issue at play."

"What's going on?" I ask, feeling like I've missed something if he's this concerned.

"We picked up a guy loitering around the compound. He has been here walking the perimeter since early this afternoon. When our boys questioned him, he just grinned at them like some psychopath and didn't answer any of their questions. They tried to push him on, but he continued his circuit around the block, so they brought him in," Dante answers, leaning back in his seat.

Having people walk around our compound is nothing new. People do it all the time.

"What's different about him?"

"We're not sure, but something's off," Carter says, and we all know what we need to do.

Five minutes later, the four of us stand in the basement of our compound in one of our holding cells. A white male covered in tattoos, in his mid-thirties, at a guess, is sitting on a chair, tied by his hands and feet in the center of the room. He is not yelling, screaming, pulling or tugging on the ropes. He is not panicked, doesn't even look the slightest bit scared. In fact, just the opposite. He looks like the cat who got the canary, and it doesn't sit well with me.

Dante and Carter start firing questions at him while Sebastian and I stand back and watch. He answers none of them. The boys grow increasingly threatening, asking him again why he is here, what he is doing, and he simply smiles at them. He is certainly not a lost tourist, and from what we can see, he's fully coherent. Carter was right; something is off.

As Dante and Carter continue with the man, Sebastian turns to me.

"So why is the girl here again?" Sebastian questions. I am about to answer when the man in the chair whips his head to the side and looks right at me.

"What?" I jolt up straight, observing him for a moment. I look over his features, and as I do, something just doesn't sit right with me. What is he hiding?

When he says nothing, I move toward him slowly, not taking my eyes off him. "What was that look for?" I ask him, and he gives me a sadistic smile.

"Nico?" Sebastian asks, stepping up beside me.

"Are you here for the girl?" I ask the man, but his eyes are now focused forward, staring at the blank wall in front of him, giving me no indication of his reasons for being here. I am suddenly feeling like we are dancing around a bee's nest, about to get swarmed.

I look sharply at Dante and Carter while I roll up my sleeves. They nod and take a step back.

"What is your name?" I bark at him, and when he doesn't reply, I hit him right across his jaw. He head jerks back, and I see him swallow, but his eyes remain on the wall, not looking at any of us.

"Who do you work for?" I bark at him again, and he remains silent. I send a punch into his nose this time, which breaks on impact, and blood flies from his face onto me. He growls then, the pain searing, so his mental toughness is admirable.

I hit him a few more times, my anger rising, because I know I didn't imagine it. I have a feeling it has to do with Emilia or her father, and I don't like it one bit.

After another hour of unanswered questions and a tremendous amount of pain, the man slumps in the chair. He has remained quiet as a mouse for the entire afternoon, and now he is barely conscious, but even so, he looks right at me. As his swollen eyes connect with mine, a bloody red grin spreads across his bloody mouth. He parts his lips, looking like he's about to speak, but then his eyes glaze over, and I watch the life leave his body.

"This is a problem. He was here for a reason. Nobody sits through a beating like that and stays silent unless they're loyal to someone else's cause," I say, looking at the boys, all who have the same concerned look on their faces.

"Agree. But this is enough for tonight. Get someone in here to clean up this mess and let's regroup tomorrow. I will see each of you in the conference room in the morning. We need to work this out and we need to do it quickly," Sebastian orders before turning on his heel and walking out of the room. I follow as Dante and Carter organize the cleaning crew and finish up down here.

Swiftly, I head to my private house here in the compound and go straight into the shower, feeling on edge. I step beneath the warm water, the heat hitting my back and washing away the sins of today as I think about the man in our cell and what he could be doing here. We have absolutely nothing to go on, but in my gut, I know something isn't right.

All is quiet and dark as I walk into the apartment where I left Emilia and look at my watch. "Shit," I whisper to myself, seeing it's already past 11 pm. I had hoped I would be back sooner to take her home. As I step around the corner into the office, I see her curled up on her side, fast asleep on the floor. Standing in the doorway, I look at her, watching her for a moment as small puffs of air leave her lips, her face completely relaxed, her top riding up just a little giving me a glimpse of her curved, soft stomach and her flawless skin. In her hands, I see she's hugging a photograph. Stepping closer, I pluck it from her loose grip to inspect it further, realizing it's a picture of her mother holding her as a baby, the pink jumpsuit and the handwritten date on the back giving it away.

I rub my face, sighing deeply. It has been a long fucking day, and I feel a little bad for keeping her here so long. And now seeing this photo, I feel even worse. What I told Sebastian was correct; I need her to make a start on these boxes because it will take her weeks, but I would be lying if I said I didn't want to make her feel slightly uncomfortable. On edge. Push her a little to see what she can uncover. What I didn't consider is how going through her father's belongings would bring up parts of her past she's probably left behind, or truths she's always wanted to know about her mother. Not only could that deter her from finding what *we* need, but after seeing her cry earlier, I know I won't be able to witness that again without getting too close. Closer than I should be with her, as someone who's working for me and my family.

After putting the photo back into the box, I step out of the room to call Tony to get the car ready downstairs. Walking back in, I lean over and pick her up, folding her against my chest. She wakes a little, startling in my arms.

"Nico?" she murmurs, her eyes sleepy, but they lock on mine. I continue down the hall with her in my arms, and even though she is still half asleep, I can see her wanting to resist.

"Have you been crying again, bambolina?" I murmur to her, noticing her eyes and nose are both a little red.

"No." It's an obvious lie, one she doesn't try to make convincing. "You can let me down. I am way too heavy to carry," she says at the same time as she yawns, her hands hanging around my neck, and my grip on her tightens.

"Sleep. I will take you home." I don't know if she understands or if she is purely exhausted from the events of the day, but she rests her head in the crook of my neck and snuggles into my chest, making my heart pump.

"I can walk... I don't want *my boss* thinking he can just pick me up and take me anywhere he wants," she sasses. Although, there is less of a punch in her tone as she barely whispers the words against my skin, where her head is resting, telling me she is already close to half asleep again.

"I don't need to be your boss to do anything I want to do with you, bambolina. I just will," I growl to her quietly, to which she only *"mhmms."*

"You better have a strong coffee waiting for me tomorrow... and remember the cream." Her breaths are warm on my chest as she murmurs, and I find myself holding her impossibly closer.

"Fuck," I mutter to myself as I approach the garage, all the while watching her face now that her eyes are closed, committing her soft lips and long lashes to my memory.

I keep her on my lap for the duration of the car ride, holding her tight and brushing the hair off her face that had fallen across her cheek.

I don't know her well, but I would put money on the fact she has never had anyone look after her before, and has lived a pretty lonely life for the most part. Now, even as an adult, she doesn't have anyone in her life to count on. Our research on her didn't unearth even one close friend or long-term boyfriend, only her career to keep her company.

As the lights of New York night filter through the car window, I think back to the man we picked up today. What he wanted, who he was, and if there are any more men coming for us.

But I already know the answer. Whoever it is, they are coming.

12

EMILIA

I wake to the sun streaming on my face from the window in my bedroom, cursing that I forgot to close the blinds. As I rub my hands across my face and stretch out my body, I wonder why I am still fully dressed, and then I sit with a start.

Eyes now wide, my chest thumping, I look around my bedroom wildly and see nothing amiss.

Nico brought me home.

I try to recall my memory of last night. I remember getting lost in the history of photographs and newspaper clippings and then resting my head. I must have fallen asleep because I can vaguely remember Nico picking me up, but then I don't remember much more. The vision I have of being carried flashes into my mind, something no man has ever done. Clearly, the events of the week have made me even more exhausted than usual.

I fling back the blankets and slip from bed, opening my bedroom door tentatively. Looking around, my apartment is empty. No Nico. I am not sure why, but I am disappointed.

My eyes catch on the cup sitting on the kitchen bench, and I walk over. A steamy hot cup of coffee, freshly brewed, so he must have just left as I woke. I smile as I take a sip. He remembered. He has made it perfectly every time.

My thoughts drift back to how good it felt to be swept up in his strong, protective arms. How he said something when I was half asleep that I'm just now remembering... how he will do whatever he wants with me, or something to that effect.

The words should scare me to death, but the way he said them, as he pulled me tight, it brought nothing but comfort to my soul, and a little longing.

Taking another sip, I snap myself out of thinking like that. I can't go there.

Relieved to have a nice quiet house, with no mob soldier ordering me around, I take a seat on my comfy sofa, and think instead about my mother.

Once I got over the fact that the work Nico requires will take much longer than the weekend, unpacking the boxes gave me the ability to discover parts of my history I never thought I'd have the chance to. I didn't bring home any of the things I found, but I will ask Nico if I can take the photos and the newspaper clippings that have to do with her.

My eyes flick to my door, half expecting him to walk in, and that thought isn't as annoying as it was yesterday. I wonder when I'll see him again. Looking to the window, I pause as I take in the blue sunny sky, before I look at the wall clock. It is early, and I want to see her. Having never known where she was laid to rest before, now the impulse I have to grab a taxi and haul myself across town to the cemetery is festering with renewed enthusiasm.

Instead of waiting around for the mobster to call, I sit up, throw back the rest of my coffee, and jump in the shower.

I am going to see my mother today.

THE TAXI RIDE was reasonably quick and now as I stand in the cemetery, clenching a small posy of yellow roses I picked up from the corner florist—who obviously does a roaring trade simply due to proximity. A calming sense of peace washes over me. I walk slowly in the direction where the office receptionist at the front of the cemetery pointed me. This place is huge, and I am glad I wore comfy sneakers.

I see different memorials as I step along the pathway; some are so beautiful, large and opulent. Many of them are old, with no flowers, no color, no sign that anyone visits. I look in the direction of where I am going and see a small headstone. It is nothing too big or unusual, but it catches my eye because there is a large bouquet of bright red roses resting in front of it. The color is striking in the sea of gray cement and grass. I'm pulled closer by my interest to see who is held in memory so beautifully by someone all these years later.

I pause as I look down and read before my breath gets caught in my chest.

Jacqueline Grace Cole

My mother. Startled by my sudden find, I take a small step back and read over the rest of the text on the headstone; the date of her birth, followed by the date of her death. She was only in her mid-thirties. The prime of her life. I squat and lay my posy of yellow at the base and look at the large bouquet of red roses as I do. They are fresh, like they have only been placed in the last day or two. There is a small card with them, and although I feel like I am snooping, I flick it open to read.

mon ange toujours

That's all it says, and I wish I had stuck to my French lessons in high school, because I have no idea what it means. I flip the card over and see the florist sticker on the back. *Le Rose Fleurs* is stamped on the back, so it appears the florist is even French.

"Mon ange toujours," I say out loud to myself, feeling how it sounds on my tongue and committing the saying to memory. I lean back and sit on the grass in front of my mother, wondering who is placing flowers at her grave with mysterious French messages.

As I look around, I see no one and feel shy all of a sudden. I am quiet for a few beats before I take a deep breath and talk to her. I stumble at first, as it feels weird, but I have so much to say. So much to ask her. Within moments, it is like I have forgotten where I am as I start telling her everything. Everything about me, my life and what has happened. It feels so good to get it out. Get it off my chest. Tell her how Dad never treated me with love, only contempt. Tell her the best thing to ever happen to me was when I got a full college scholarship and moved to the other side of the country to get away from him, and how I often wonder why I ever came back.

I apologize to her for not coming sooner, explaining how I didn't know where she was or what had happened until last night after reading it in the old newspaper clipping.

Then I tell her about Nico, about his demands, but also the odd sense of comfort I feel around him, the coffee he makes me, the way he instinctively put his hand on my thigh last night when he knew I was scared of his friend. He was protecting me. I have never had that before. I have always looked after myself, never wanting to get too close to people, not wanting to feel the pain of rejection. If my own father didn't want me, then it became apparent to me very early on that no one else would either, and that has been fine with me.

But Nico is different. A virtual stranger, yet he seems to care for some reason. And I'm not sure how I feel about that... or if it's more about being sure of how much I like him, but knowing I shouldn't.

The sun is high in the sky by the time I finish, my voice hoarse, and my throat now dry. The tears that have slowly crept out and over my cheeks now finished. My heart beats in a steady rhythm, and a little weight has been lifted from my shoulders. A small breeze flutters past me, and when I look up, I immediately spot a man standing in the distance who looks like he is watching me. I squint a little, trying to see if it is someone I know, but he simply nods his head to me and turns and walks away. But as he does, I notice a large winged tattoo on his neck... it looks familiar, but I can't place it. My eyes remain on his back until his body is a mere dot in the distance.

Looking back at the grave, I lean forward and touch the cold stone with my fingers.

"I will come again soon, Mom. I promise," I say to her, knowing I will make an effort to come regularly from now on, now I know she is here.

Standing, I take one last look at the red and yellow roses, happy she still has at least one other visitor, and I turn and walk away. I grab my cell from my handbag and type the French words into the search before I forget them.

Mon ange toujours it confirms is French, which is what I thought, so my French can't be too rusty. I hit translate. The words '*My Angel Always*' pop up on the screen and my feet halt as I come to a stop. That was what she had scripted in the letter I read last night. Looking back at my phone, I read on. A term of endearment for love. *What the hell*? I already know this isn't the work of my father. He couldn't give a damn about my mother now. There is no way he would be placing flowers on her grave decades after her death, given how much he despises her.

So if it isn't her husband delivering flowers to her grave, then who is it?

13

NICO

"What's going on?" Sebastian's voice is rough as we sit together in the conference room, waiting for the others. He takes a sip of his morning coffee, and I take a sip of mine. It's my third for the morning already, having had one when I was at Emilia's apartment earlier, then another when I arrived back home not long after. I tell myself it is because she has a good coffee machine and great Italian beans, because there is no other reason to be stalking my new employee so early in the morning.

"She got through about five boxes yesterday," I tell him, my eyes flicking to him and watching for his response.

Sebastian nods. "Not bad, but she will need to work faster," he says, eyeing me suspiciously.

"I don't want to push her. It's a lot for her." I think back to her tears at seeing her family photos, and then seeing her asleep on the floor. She is an employee, I know this. I shouldn't care. Sebastian would tell me to have her working even more, and that is my job to get her to do so.

"So I ask you again. What is going on?" Sebastian presses. He puts the cup on the table in front of him, placing his hands face down beside it.

"Nothing," I say simply. "What do you mean?" I wish he'd just get to the point.

"Are you fucking her?" Sebastian asks, and I rear my head back.

"No," I answer smoothly and immediately, though I'm surprised by the question. I run my hands through my hair, frustrated that Sebastian has made such an observation. We have known each other merely a week, but he can already see the writing on the wall. I need to do a much better job of schooling my features, because he picks up on everything.

He sighs.

"Nico. We need her to find whatever it is we are looking for. She is the only one who is remotely capable of figuring out her father's mess of paperwork. Not only because she is his daughter, but because she is fucking excellent at her job," he says this like I don't already know, his eyes not leaving mine. "Regardless of how fucking beautiful she is." He watches me, and my eyes narrow, not liking him looking at her in that way. The blood starts pumping around my body, and I feel the light flames of possessiveness flicking at my skin. I scratch my neck, frustrated by my reaction.

"Hmmm, just as I thought. You haven't fucked her, but you want to," he states, picking his coffee back up and taking another sip. I suddenly want to rip it out of his grasp so I can tell him to stop talking about Emilia like that.

"Be careful, Nico. Business first. Pleasure later. I need you both focused on the work, not each other."

"Is that what you did with Goldie?" I ask, knowing full well it wasn't and that I am treading on very thin ice. No one questions Sebastian, especially about Goldie.

Sebastian grunts. "That woman had me by the balls the minute we met," he says honestly, and I smile. But then he continues. "We need to sort out this shit and we need to sort it out fast. She is the daughter of our enemy, Nico. I think you need to sort out where her loyalties lie before you start making her yours." And of course he's right. Business before pleasure, always.

"She is not on his side. She isn't on anyone's side. But it's more than that. She is more than that." The words leave me before I think about what I am saying.

"What do you mean?" Sebastian looks at me with concern.

What I want to say is that she isn't just a quick, meaningless, lust-driven fuck. She's vibrant, and beautiful, and she challenges me. Her pushing me is like an aphrodisiac. Emilia is the kind of woman who will make me work for every inch, every comment, every thought of hers. And what had me sleeping like shit last night was the fact that I want her so badly and not just for sex. I've never been so consumed by thoughts of a woman before.

But instead, I say nothing, letting my silence speak for itself. He's too damn perceptive and knows where my head is at anyway; there's no point in dragging Emilia into this any more than she already is.

"As I said, business first, Nico. I need you focused," he says after a moment of silence, eyeing me warily.

I grind my teeth together in thought as the others walk into the room. Sebastian giving me his permission, albeit under his requirement to keep our project as the priority, unlocks a barrier I didn't even realize existed. Something clicks into place, making that possessive need to make her mine the center of my thoughts. Yet I don't even know if she feels the same. I can only assume she doesn't, considering the circumstances I've put her under.

She has turned me inside out. I need to get my shit together.

"Boys," Dante says, taking a seat next to Sebastian, as Carter merely grunts before punching me in the shoulder and taking a seat next to me.

"What's up with you?" Carter asks me, grinning.

"I'm trying to decide if I liked you better before you met Doc or after," I snark, finishing my coffee, because he is always so damn happy now. He's always smiling, and laughter a daily occurrence. The love he has for his new family radiates from him. Before he met Doc, he was a grumpy violent asshole.

"Right," Sebastian says, pulling us all to attention. "Let's sort out what we know about this guy, and why he was so comfortable to die in our basement last night. We're starting from scratch."

I CRACK my neck to try to relieve the tension building. We have been here all day reviewing footage, looking through facial recognition databases, searching for any possible motive, and my body is tired. I wanted to check in on Emilia today, maybe even bring her back here to work together on some more boxes, but that didn't happen.

As we all get up to leave, my cell rings, and I see it is my sister Sofia. For our daily chat, no doubt.

"Go, Nico, we've got it," Sebastian says, waving me off. I nod as I leave the conference room and pick up the call, making my way through the corridors to my apartment.

"Hey, Sorella," I say, trying to sound upbeat even though I could fall asleep standing.

"Fratello!" she yells into the phone, and I hear music thumping in the background.

"Where are you?" I ask, refusing to believe she is an adult who can now make her own decisions, being out so late at night.

"I'm out in Milan with Jasmina!" she squeals with a laugh. Who the hell is Jasmina?

"If you are having so much fun, Sorella, why are you calling me?" I push into my apartment and walk quickly down the hall to my bedroom.

"She really is the prettiest woman, Fratello..." Sofia's voice skims across the phone line, and I huff out in frustration.

"Sorella," I say in warning, really not in the mood for drunk women to be calling me from parties, not being a party man myself.

"Fratello, put it on FaceTime so you can meet!" she screams in excitement, and I want to hang up. But it is Sofia, so I will give her my time.

I pull the phone from my ear and hit the video call button before I see my sister, looking all made up and glitzy. Wearing too much makeup and not enough clothes.

"Nico, this is Jasmina!" Sofia says as she turns the camera to the side a little, and a woman's face comes into view. She is stunning, with sun-tanned skin and dark hair, very Mediterranean, clearly from a long line of Italians. But she does nothing for me. I can admire her beauty, of course, but as she smiles and her eyes sparkle at me, I feel nothing.

"Hello, Nico. Pleasure," she purrs out like she is in a porn movie, sitting back with what looks like a pout on her lips that shows me she is trying too hard to be sexy. When in reality, all it takes is a woman to walk out of bed, with her hair messy, mascara smudges on her face, and sassing me endlessly to make me weak at the knees.

"Ladies, it looks like you are having a great time there. Why don't you go and enjoy, I have had a big day." I rub my face, wishing this call would just end already.

"Hmmm... okay, Nico, love you!" Sofia sing-songs.

"Be safe, Sofia."

I end the call and look at my phone, pondering. I think of Emilia, and before I can think twice, I dial her number.

"Hello?" Her voice comes across unsure, and I smile at hearing it.

"Emilia." I lie back on my bed, waiting for her to question me.

"Nico. Bit late for a work call, isn't it?" she says, and I grin, glad she's feeling better than she was yesterday and also amused she thinks that working for me is a nine-to-five job.

"I'm checking in," I say, already feeling my body relaxing at talking to her. "How are you today? I know you must have been tired."

"Do you call all the people who work for you on a Saturday night, or just me?" she asks, and my smile widens.

"All of them. I need to ensure our work gets done," I say just to ruffle her feathers.

"I need to know what days or hours you expect from me, Nico. I have other things I need to organize."

"You clearly didn't understand our previous discussions around this, because I should be your only focus, Emilia. Your only priority."

"Oh, I understood just fine, but I need a schedule. I can't make the work I do for you center to my entire life." I imagine her standing, jutting out her hips.

"I need you to always be available." I give her the answer she is not wanting to hear.

"What can I say, I'm not really the beck-and-call kind of girl." The way her voice wraps around the words, it almost sounds like she's flirting. But I know better.

"Don't I know it."

"I am a businesswoman, Nico. I need structure and schedules. I can't just focus on you and your needs."

"Too bad, that was the deal you made." I grit out. She infuriates me, yet I'm getting harder by the second at her constantly pushing me.

"What do you want from me? Do you want me to call your *sir*? Do you want me to cater to you, just like all other men seem to want these days? Shall I forget that I actually have my own business to run and just run around looking after you instead? Stroking your ego, telling you how fabulous you are, then run around behind your back, fixing all your mistakes and making things right, like I should've just done the first time?"

"Ahhh, there she is, my feisty bambolina. I will always make sure you are looked after; I won't work you into the ground. Besides, I will always ensure I have good coffee," I say smoothly, heat building unexpectedly throughout my body, my dick pushing painfully against my zipper.

She sighs, and it sound like giving in. "Thanks for the coffee this morning. Can't say I'm thrilled about having you break in again, however the hell you did that, but your barist*o* talents make up for it, I suppose." A dark chuckle escapes my throat before I get to business.

"I need you back here tomorrow." I should just bring her here and lock her in the room. Sebastian will get what he wants, and so will I.

"Sure. Fine. I can focus on getting other clients during the week from my office then," she says, and I bristle. She *still* doesn't seem to understand our arrangement, yet a strange feeling of respect spreads across my chest at her strong work ethic.

"Like I said, I am your only client, Emilia. Don't forget that," I say in warning, and she groans, the sound going straight to my cock.

"Nico, you are not my only client. No matter how many time you say it, it doesn't make it true." I wait for something more, but she is quiet. Eerily so.

"What? That's it? No more arguing with me? You know I like it," I ask her in jest.

"I'm sure you do, but I'm quite tired, and if you have nothing else to say, I'd rather be sleeping." Her change in tone is confusing, making me push for a reason.

"Why are you so tired, bambolina? You said yourself it's the weekend. No days off with you, are there?" I hear an intake of breath over the line, then she starts to speak, only to stop again. Finally, she answers me, and it's not what I was expecting.

"I went to see my mother today," she whispers, and now it makes sense. I know it would have been a big deal, especially after only finding out last night where she was buried.

"And?" I ask her, wanting to see how she feels.

"And... it was nice," she says on another sigh.

"Good." My voice softens as I match hers. I wish I was there with her to catch any of her tears that might be falling, to see her so vulnerable. Knowing she doesn't show that side of herself often, but she did with me, just like she is now, I want to be the only one.

"Thank you, Nico. I wouldn't have found her if it wasn't for you and those boxes." I swallow, not expecting her gratitude and surprised that after all that she is doing, she can still see a silver lining.

"You better rest up. There are still many boxes for us to get through," I say, steering the conversation into safer territory. More so for me than for her.

"Yes, boss," she says, back to her usual tone.

"Goodnight, Emilia."

"Goodnight, Nico," she replies softly, and I end the call.

Throwing my phone on the bedside table, I stand, needing a shower to wash the day away. I make my way to the bathroom, stripping my clothes as I go, and my body relaxes as soon as the hot spray of water hits my skin. I grab the soap as I think about Emilia. I think about her soft skin, her bright blue eyes, and her lips. Her fucking lips are what my dreams are made of.

My hand travels down to my cock. I am hard, so fucking hard, just thinking about her. I begin to move my hand up and down my length as I remember her bare legs and her pink-painted toes, her soft stomach, full breasts, and the curve of her ample hips. Her sharp, sassy mouth, and all the things I want to do with it. I grit my teeth, imagining my hand is her lips, taking me into her throat, the warm water her mouth, sucking me, swallowing all of me, before I come undone at the mental image, losing control and emptying myself in my shower.

Losing control to her.

14

EMILIA

As the car drives down into the darkened basement, I can't help but get chills. Without him in the car next to me, I feel cold and uneasy. I wring my hands together, the knot in my stomach only relaxing when the car pulls up in the cleanest basement I have ever seen and I see Nico standing and waiting for me.

"Morning, bambolina," he says, opening my door. The nickname he has given me now warms me like a soft blanket as I step out of the door toward him. He is one of the most powerful men in this country, he could kill someone with the flick of his wrist, yet his soft tone with me makes me feel like we're on equal footing. Like he cares truly about me.

We are both tough, yet soft when we need to be, it seems. It's something I haven't experienced before from someone else, yet I crave it. When I told him about visiting my mother, he didn't say much at all, but his tone was kind. Even throughout the whole conversation, he was pressing my buttons, only I was enjoying it. It felt like something shifted in me. I've opened up to him more last night than I have with any other man, and I wonder why it seems to be so easy to do with him.

"Morning," I say, as my eyes hone in on him, He looks devilishly handsome as always in his black slacks and black shirt. His hand grips mine as he helps me out of the car, and with his sleeves rolled up, I can see his forearms, covered in tattoos, with thick veins that run from his wrists to his elbows.

I, on the other hand, kept it casual today. Wearing my jeans, and basic white t-shirt, I dressed for comfort, considering I will be sprawled out on the floor again, no doubt surrounded by paperwork. The only saving grace for me is the soft carpet that already beckons me.

"Let's go," he says, not letting go of my hand, and together we walk through the basement to the door.

"You don't need to hold my hand. I won't run away, you know," I say with a smirk.

"I know," he replies, giving me a wicked grin and a wink as he grips my hand firmer, and my heart beats even harder. There he goes again. Hand holding, the coffee, carrying me to the car. The small everyday things, that cost nothing but mean everything, they mean so much to me. Even though I should be fully professional and keep my guard up, bit by bit, the man belonging to the mob cracks away at my wall of independence. I expected him to be so different from who he is, and now, instead of my heart beating out of fear of him, it beats for an entirely different reason.

We are walking slower today, so I take the time to

look around. While there are still many men down here, there are less than before. Perhaps they actually get a day of rest unlike me. They are all dressed impeccably, in dark clothes similar to Nico's, and I see a tall man over to the side who I recognize. He looks up at me, giving me a brief nod with a small smile, which I return.

Nico squeezes my hand again as we walk through the side door and down the corridors and hallways to the apartment.

"Here." He pushes a cup in my direction, and as soon as the coffee aroma hits my nostrils, I immediately relax even more.

"Thanks." I hold the coffee in both my hands, feeling the warmth as I bring it to my lips and sip. My eyes flick to his over the top of my mug. He is staring right at me, watching me as I pull the cup down and swallow.

"Why are you looking at me like that?" I question him. The way his eyes are on me, it is like he can look into my soul.

"I like looking at you," he says confidently, giving nothing else away, yet butterflies take flight in my belly and the world is still for a moment. I like him looking at me. I like his eyes wandering my body, like they are undressing me slowly. It has been a long time since any man made me feel like this. Nico is doing a damn fine job at making my knees weak.

I remain quiet, watching him openly admiring me. Heat swarms my body under his gaze.

"I like the look of your neck when you swallow..." he comments, as he takes a small step toward me. I remain still, too shocked to move a muscle. My heart pounds out of my chest.

"I like the way your tongue swipes your lips, tasting every last drop of coffee I make you," he continues, taking another step. My stomach dips.

"There are many things I like to look at..." he pauses, his eyes locked on mine for whatever he's about to say next, "but I am more of a doing man, than a talking man."

I'm silent for a moment, my breath caught in my chest.

"Should we make a start then?" I stutter out, so unlike myself. If he continues to look at me like he currently is, I am certain my underwear will disintegrate right here in his kitchen.

"Let's go," he says, flashing me his smirk as he turns, and I follow him down the hallway to the boxes, coffee in hand, trying my hardest to stop my hand from shaking and spilling it everywhere. God, just his talk gets me all worked up. I need to get a grip. And it doesn't take long, because as we enter the room, I get exactly that, a hard dose of reality slapping me across the face.

"I swear there were less boxes yesterday," I moan as my eyes run across the still piled-high paperwork along the wall. The ones I got through yesterday are in a different spot, looking comically small in comparison.

"Do you think I can do some from my office this week?" I ask. I want to try to still be at my office Monday through Friday.

"Why? You don't like coming here?" His eyebrow cocks in question. Not this again. We've already been through this.

"There is more space, and I think I would work quicker," I say as justification, seeing how flexible he is when I'm not being completely honest. He knows damn well why I want to be in my own office. I have other things to do, a business to rebuild.

"Let's see how we go today," he says, moving a box toward me, encouraging me to start.

"Fine," I sigh, sitting on the floor, opening the lid and starting the process.

Hours later, I roll my head to relax my shoulders, which are now stiff after sitting in the same position for so long. I look over at Nico, who is leaning back a little more relaxed, reading through a log book from my father's private jet, one I would be extremely confident in saying is incomplete or at least missing some vital information. My father's jet was his pride and joy, but he had a few other aircraft as well, so unless we find all of the plane logs, the information Nico gleams may not be overly fruitful.

Opening the next box, I shuffle through. Sorting each document, then reviewing the contents before sorting them into immediate actions or just simply cataloging for a later date. I pause as I see some information from a winery. At first glance, it's just an invoice for cartons of wine, my father constantly filling his cellar with the latest and greatest wine from Bordeaux or something.

But given it is French, I pause to take a closer look.

It is an invoice for a large shipment of wine. A lot for most people, but my father never did anything by halves so it's probably a drop in the ocean for him. There is nothing else of interest on the invoice, but the more I stare at it, the more I feel it's important. Though I can't put my finger on why.

My eyes flick to Nico, and I see him engrossed in some other paperwork, so I don't say anything. It's probably nothing. I put it in the pile to review further and keep digging.

Deeper in the box, I find some older flight logs, mostly for his helicopter, the one he would take to business meetings up and down the East Coast. Mostly to the Hamptons, where he would often go, leaving me at home with the hired help as a young teenager. I flick through the logbook, New York, Washington D.C., Boston, the cities repeated every month or so, for his various board meetings, no doubt.

I notice some numbers scribbled on the inside cover of the logbook in pencil, very light and faint, but they are there. I grab my phone, take a photo, and then put them in the search to see if they represent anything.

"What have you found?" Nico asks, and I glance up at him briefly before looking back at my phone.

"Nothing," I say as my search pulls up a blank. "I was looking to see if these numbers mean anything, but nope, just scribbles." I point to the logbook, and he gives me a nod, going back to his papers.

Nico's phone rings, breaking our silence, and he sighs and rubs his head.

"Hey, Sofia," he says, and I look away to try to focus on my box, not wanting to eavesdrop on his conversation. But I am curious, since Sofia was the name on the screen of his cell when I looked last week. My shoulders tense, in a way they really shouldn't, but I can't help the jealous ball that starts to form in my gut, making me feel a little unwell.

The next box I grab ends up being one full of more family history, as I see photos and newspaper clippings galore. My eyes are glued to the contents, no longer paying any attention to Nico and his conversation as I get on my knees and start digging through. I feel a mix of excitement and anxiety as I begin to look over it all, wondering what I might possibly uncover about myself.

I see a photo of my father, one that looks staged, as he sits behind his desk. From memory, it was taken by a business magazine who put him on the front cover almost a decade ago. He looks strong, broad, and in total control. He is wearing a suit and tie, and looks every inch a billionaire businessman. The only odd thing is the cat in his lap.

"Kitty," I murmur out to myself, remembering the cat we had when I was younger. Turns out, I am allergic, but my father, for some reason, absolutely loved that cat. It went with him nearly everywhere he did. Which meant I had to keep my distance all the time for fear my throat would close up and I'd break out in hives.

I put down the photo and pull out some of the newspaper clippings. A few of them are the same, about my father making some business deals and such, and then I see one of him and another man I remember being one of his closest friends. It is Dr. Wakeford, a heart surgeon and Catherine's father, who died a few months ago around the same time as Daniel, I believe. I saw him a few times around the house. Both he and my father were widows, his wife having died years earlier in a car accident... And that's when I pause. My breathing falters.

A car accident. Both of their wives died in car accidents.

I stare at the image, feeling my breathing starting to get out of control. My hands shake, my heart beating so fast I'm suddenly lightheaded.

My palm rests on my chest, as I try to take in a breath, only my lungs don't feel like they're expanding enough. Nerves take over as I start to sweat, feeling hot all over.

"What is it, bambolina?" I hear Nico ask, standing immediately and walking toward me. I can hear a woman on the other end of the phone yelling, "*Bambolina? Who is Bambolina?*" but I ignore it. As does he when he immediately hangs up on the call, then throws his phone on the sofa and kneels next to me.

"It's okay, Emilia, just breathe," he says, as his hands cup my jaw, and I struggle to take a full breath. I look at him, my eyes wide as fear grips my body. I try to say his name, but nothing comes out. My hand pulls at my collar, feeling like I'm suffocating, my eyes watering and running down my face. I feel helpless, like I can't do anything. I can't stop this feeling. I have no control over my own body.

"Breathe with me, bambolina. You can do it. Come on, we will do it together." His thumbs glide along my jaw, caressing my skin, his soft voice doing wonders to calm me. I watch him take a big breath, and I try to copy him.

"That's it, nice, big breaths. I've got you." He pulls me toward him, his arm coming around my shoulder, his hand rubbing my body softly. His eyes pin mine as we breathe together, his touch relaxing my coiled-tight muscles and my body melting against his. I close my eyes and concentrate on my breathing, my hand resting on his chest so I can feel his deep breaths and heartbeat.

"Nico." I manage to say his name, hating how pathetic I sound, embarrassed that Nico witnessed yet another moment of vulnerability from me.

"Are you feeling better now?" He searches my eyes as I nod subtly. "What happened?" he asks me, and I show him the newspaper clipping of my father and his friend.

"What about it? What upset you?" he asks, removing his hands from my face, and sitting next to me on the floor.

"This is Doctor Wakeford..." I say quietly to him as he watches me intently.

"Yes, I know." He nods, waiting for more.

"His wife died years ago too..." I say, my heart rate is starting to elevate again. "In a car accident... just like my mom..." I barely get the words out past the lump in my throat. Could it be a horrible coincidence? Possibly. Is it likely to be a coincidence? No.

I watch Nico as his jaw clenches, taking in this information.

"Yeah, well, his daughter Catherine is with my brother Carter now. Apparently, her mother didn't die in a car accident, but it was made to look that way."

"So perhaps my mother didn't die in a car accident either, Nico." I don't want the words out in the universe, but I can't help but believe it's the truth.

"Perhaps she didn't." Nico says as he takes the newspaper clipping from my hand, looking at it again before looking back at me and studying my face.

"Come on. Let's go and take a break. I will make you some lunch," he says, standing before grabbing my hands and lifting me up so I am standing next to him on shaky legs. I am lost in thought as I let him take me by the hand and walk me out of the room, and down the hallway into the kitchen. I pause at the bench while Nico gets busy with ingredients. It seems he likes to cook.

"Nico, why would my father kill my mother?" I'm so confused, trying to reconcile everything in my jumbled brain. "Why would he do that?" I ask again, looking at Nico like he has all the answers. I'm not sure why I'm even asking him. How would he know? Why would he even care? But I still feel raw, not like my usual self, and he is the only person in the world I can talk to about this.

He walks back to me then, his hand coming up to my face, the backs of his fingers draping across my cheekbone. My skin prickles with heat under his touch. What is it about this man that makes me feel things I have never felt before? How does he break my barriers and pick me up whenever I feel out of control, yet do so in a way that makes me crave it instead wanting to shield myself or run way?

He looks at me, drinking me in, a sadness in his eyes. "I don't know, bambolina, but I have a feeling you are going to find the answer in those boxes."

15

NICO

I plate our pasta and sit with Emilia, letting her eat quietly with her thoughts. This is the second time she has become a little overwhelmed with the personal belongings she finds, and even though it is understandable, it is not something I considered when I decided she was the right fit for this job.

She was perfect for this job without her connection to Brian Cole. The fact he is her father is an added bonus. But the emotional roller-coaster she is on has taken us both by surprise. While I knew their relationship wasn't a close one, I had no idea how detached they really are from each other. It is like she didn't even have any parents, essentially growing up entirely on her own.

I clench and unclench my hand under the table, still feeling the buzz from when I brushed her cheek. I need to stop fucking touching her. I need to remain professional, not cross the lines of boss and employee for the time being. Sebastian's voice repeats in my head about business first, about staying focused until our job is done.

I always do as he says. I always follow his directions, but there is something about her that gets under my skin to the point where I don't know if I can hold myself back much longer. She is festering in my chest, making my mind and body weak for her.

She moves the spaghetti around on her plate, obviously not hungry, but we still have the whole afternoon ahead of us, so she needs to eat.

"Eat, you need the energy," I say to her. Her eyes flick to mine suddenly, like she has only just become aware I am sitting here.

"Yes. Sure," she says quietly, almost absentmindedly, and I watch her put a few spoonfuls in her mouth.

I don't have it on me, but I know my cell phone is blowing up right now. I didn't hesitate to hang up on my sister, and I am already stressed about the twenty questions she will ask me later.

"My father has a lot to answer for. If I ever find him, I am going to make him tell me everything," she grits out, and I see the flames now in her eyes as her body becomes rigid. The more she eats, it seems her sadness turns to anger.

"I have a feeling there are probably a lot of people looking for your father," I say to her, leaning back in my chair, eyes on her.

"Where do you think he is?"

I pretend to think about it.

"Where do you think he is?" I answer her question with one of my own, not liking the idea of lying to her face.

"Probably Russia or China, or one of the countries we don't have an extradition treaty with," she says with a shake of her head, making complete sense, although I know better.

"If he is overseas, do you think he will ever come back?"

"I don't think so. He only ever thinks of himself, not the trail of destruction he leaves behind." She puts her fork down, giving up on eating for the moment.

"It really is like finding a needle in a haystack. We have been through at least ten boxes. I've found information on my past, but there doesn't seem to be anything that leads us to any money trail." I can see her mind starting to work again, moving past her personal heartbreak and frustrations and back into work mode.

"His plane log book doesn't hold anything of interest. He flew everywhere, all over the world; there is not one country that sticks out more than any other. Did he ever take you anywhere as a kid? Was there any special holiday spot?" There has to be a lead in it all somewhere.

"Huh," she huffs out a laugh. "No. Nowhere. I was barely allowed to leave the house. I left for school, some sports, and things like that, but I never went on a holiday, and most certainly never traveled overseas. He kept me pretty enclosed. That's why I flew across the country to go to college. I needed to get away, have some freedom and explore. I guess since I was pretty much an adult, he no longer needed to care for me, so let me go, never to see me again." Again, I am reminded of how different our upbringings were.

"Did he go overseas a lot when you were a kid?" I ask again, trying to get a glimpse into anything that might give us a lead.

"No. I mean... I don't think so. But to be honest, I never really knew where he was most of the time. He could have traveled anywhere and I wouldn't have known. I guess there were times when he wasn't around for a while, so who knows, he could have been overseas then, but I have no idea. We were not really the *sit around the dinner table and tell me about your day* type of family," she says with a roll of her eyes, and I am glad to hear her getting back to normal.

"What about you?" she asks, sitting back in her chair, looking at me.

"What about me?" I retort, wondering what she wants to know. I feel myself wanting to talk to her about my life, eager for her to know about me.

"Well, did you grow up in a big family?" she asks expectantly.

"Just my parents and my sister, but we are close, always have been." Divulging personal details is easy to do with Emilia. If this were anyone else, I wouldn't even be sitting here.

"Do you see them much?"

"A few times a year. They are in Italy, I am based here now." I have her full attention as she listens to me inquisitively, her chin resting on her palm.

"Where did you learn to cook?"

"My mother. She is one of the best cooks in our town. She taught me from a young age." I catch myself and stop before I tell her the reason I learned to cook was because my sister was so sick, and I needed to help around the house more than a normal kid my age.

"Well, she did a good job. Your food is delicious," she says with a smile I'd like to see more of, and I nod to her, accepting her compliment. Her admiration has me feeling warmer.

"Nico, do you know where my father is?" she asks, adjusting in her seat and turning to face me. I've come to realize that all her questions were just to warm me up for this one. No doubt she was planning to ask me this all along. I rub my hand on my jaw, rolling her question around in my head. Do I tell her he is underneath us in a cell here at the compound, or do I lie and tell her I have no idea. I decide to not admit to either.

"How are you feeling?" I ask, changing the subject. I'm not ready to answer her question, and I don't think she is ready to hear the answer. And we have to get back to work anyway.

"I'm fine," she says with another small smile, only this one doesn't reach her eyes.

"I can take you home, or to your office, if you need a break?"

"No, I'm fine." She waves off the concern.

"We have more boxes to get to. I think we should head back up." I end the conversation as I stand and start to clear the table. She sits for a moment, watching me, and I meet her eyes, not wavering. It is the lawyer in her. She knows that I know where her father is. And I know she knows, yet neither of us push it.

She stands and grabs her dishes, coming to stand beside me at the sink. "Well, if you ever do find him, Nico, I would like the chance to speak to him. I have a lot of questions of my own," she says in an ominous tone, before walking away to start on a fresh box for the afternoon.

16

EMILIA

It is Wednesday afternoon. I sit at my desk, shuffling paperwork, and my eye catches on the now empty morning cup of coffee. It was waiting for me when I arrived, and was delicious.

So far this week, I have come to work and found a steamy hot coffee on my desk every day, next to a new box of my father's paperwork. I know this is all Nico. One box a day is slow going, and with the amount of boxes to go, it will take weeks, but I am grateful I can work from the office and still try to drum up other business while here.

I haven't spoken to Nico since he dropped me home on Sunday night, which although odd at the time, was also strangely comforting. Even though I have been busy trying to keep my one client on board, my mind has been wandering to him constantly. Thinking about what he is doing, where he is, and when I will see him again.

Unfortunately, my daydreaming has been more successful than my business skills because I lost my last client. Which is probably a good thing, all things considered. It is becoming harder for me to focus on anything other than my father's current predicament, and Nico's deep chocolate eyes and the smirk that lives permanently on his face.

"Emi, an Adam Shaw is on line two," Cindy's voice bellows into my office, startling me from my thoughts.

Adam Shaw? I think to myself before realizing who it is.

"Thanks, Cindy!" I say to her and take a calming breath before I pick up the call.

"Adam? Hi!" I say, sounding surprised because I am. It has been six weeks since I met Adam, and I really didn't think he'd call with so much time having passed.

"Hi, Emilia, great to speak to you," he says, sounding equally upbeat. "Listen, I know we haven't spoken for a while, but I am free tonight and, well, I thought if you were free, it may be nice if we could meet for dinner?" I suck in a breath.

Adam is exactly the kind of man I like. Only, my eyes flick to the coffee cup on my desk, and my mind briefly considers Nico before I mentally scold myself. He is in the mob. My boss for the time being. It's ridiculous to even think he could be a possibility.

"Emilia?" Adam says again before I realize I haven't answered him.

"Sorry, yes, I'm free. I would love that!" It might actually be nice to go out for a change.

"Great, I have a late meeting, so can we meet at Mario's at 7?" he asks, and I grit my teeth. I'm old school. I like to be picked up for dates, perhaps given flowers. I like a man who can wine and dine me. However, I am also single, and haven't been on a date in months, so I ignore the doubt creeping into my mind.

"Sure. Great. I will meet you there," I say, plastering a smile on my face.

"I look forward to it." Then I hear the click of the phone, not even saying goodbye before he ends the call.

Does the kind of man I want even exist anymore? The kind that takes your hand when you walk, opens doors, picks you up for a date, and pulls out the chair for you when you sit.

The kind that takes your coat and makes you coffee just how you like it.

My body jolts, and I sit up, not sure where that last thought came from, but I shake my head and push the coffee cup off my desk, replacing it with some paperwork. Might as well start getting to work on finalizing my former client's file before I leave for the day.

Less than six hours later, I step out of the taxi in front of Mario's. It is an amazing Italian place I have only been to once before, but it is popular. I pull my coat around my frame, the little black dress I settled on doing nothing to keep me warm, but it's extremely complimentary to both my chest and my ass. I may be out of practice in the dating game, but even I know a girl has to highlight her assets.

Not sure where this night will take me, I put on a beautiful black lace underwear set to match, something that makes me feel sexy and confident. Although it wasn't Adam's eyes I was dreaming of when I put it on, but the deep brown ones that keep appearing in my dreams.

With my hair shiny and falling down my back, and

my makeup perfectly done, I look surprisingly put together for a woman who has lost her family, is on the track to losing her career, and who also happens to currently be in cahoots with the mob.

Stepping inside the restaurant, mouthwatering aromas of fine Italian cooking immediately hit my nose, along with the quiet chatter of the patrons inside.

The maître d sweeps up to me, and after giving him Adam's name, he takes my coat. All without complaint and with a bright smile and a welcoming tone. I sigh a little, feeling the stresses of my life melt away slightly, committed to enjoying myself tonight since it is the first time I have been out in months. My phone buzzes in my purse, and I pull it out quickly. I see it is Nico, and ignore the call, not needing to think about him or work tonight. Looking around the restaurant, I see Adam already here. Spotting me, he stands as the waiter takes me to the table to join him.

He is just as good looking as I remember. Tall, blonde, fit, his smile so white it is blinding. I smile, because I am glad to see him, but I would be lying if I said I didn't wish he had dark hair and a smirk instead.

"Emilia, you look beautiful!" he says, taking my hand and kissing it in greeting before sitting straight back down, not pulling out my chair or waiting for me to sit. I long for old school chivalry.

"You look great too, Adam." I take a seat and meet the eyes of the waiter, who seems to know exactly what I am thinking, and nods like he is agreeing with me.

I feel my purse vibrate again, but I keep it closed. I don't want to be rude.

"Wine, madame?" the waiter says to me, holding out a bottle of a nice Italian red.

"Sure, thank you," I say with a smile, which he returns.

"So, how have you been? Has work been busy for you?" Adam asks, launching straight into work talk, something I would like to forget.

"Yes, always, you?" I answer, deflecting the conversation back to him, which proves to be a good maneuver since he proceeds to tell me all about his work, the big clients he has, the large deals he has done, taking up the next fifteen minutes without drawing breath. I continue to smile and nod at the right times, but he is clearly elaborating to make himself look good.

"So, yeah, we've been really busy, talking to a few Wall Street guys just today, actually." He continues to name drop, while my purse continues to vibrate.

"So sorry to interrupt, but have you had a chance to look over the menu?" the waiter asks, giving me a knowing look, and I mouth the words thank you to him when Adam isn't paying attention.

"I would love the steak, please," Adam replies first, folding his menu closed and passing it back to the waiter swiftly before taking another gulp of his wine.

I see the menu has pasta, and while I would normally stay away from anything like that on a first date, I already know there won't be a second one. And it doesn't help that I have been dreaming of pasta since Nico's place on Saturday night.

"I will have the spaghetti, please," I say with a smile.

"Good choice," he says with a nod, before retreating again.

"So you like carbs, then?" Adam says as his eyes roam my body.

"Excuse me?" What is he implying...

"Not many women order pasta these days," he says with a laugh while his eyes continue to assess my cleavage.

"Okay?" is all I say in reply, wanting nothing more than to get the pasta to go. Why I even found this man remotely attractive when we met weeks ago, I will never understand.

My purse vibrates again, and I can't hold back my huff.

"Excuse me, I just need the bathroom," I say and he nods, but again, doesn't stand or offer to take my chair as I grab my purse and head for the bathrooms.

As I zig-zag through the restaurant, I pull out my phone on the way and answer it.

"What!" I blurt out more aggressively than I intended to.

"Where are you?" Nico demands, his voice sending a flash of heat through my body, even though my patience is running thin from my disastrous date.

"I'm off the clock, so it is none of your concern!" I duck around a dark corner, closer to the restaurant kitchen, which was a bad move because the chef here sings while he cooks. Not loud enough to hear in the restaurant, of course, but from where I am standing, I can hear him clear as day.

"Are you at Mario's?" Nico asks, and I wonder how he

knows. He always seems to know everything, though, so I shouldn't be surprised. That fact has me even more annoyed.

"Yes, I am on a date, since you're so interested. Is there anything else you want to know?" I hiss. This man is unbelievable.

"Who is he?" Nico asks, and he sounds angry. For the first time in our dance for dominance, I finally feel like I have an edge on him.

"He is none of your business. Just like the rest of my life," I say sassily, my mood already lighter for pissing him off.

"You are my business, Emilia, and therefore, who you are with becomes my business," Nico grits out, sounding harsher than I have ever heard him. I wonder if there is something else going on. I pause for a moment to consider my next words, but come to the conclusion that he doesn't need details.

"Look, I will be happy to tell you all about it tomorrow over a morning coffee, but right now, I need to go. Bye-bye now." I sing-song my sendoff, then hang up before anything else can be said. I just need this night to end, and then I'll refocus on work, because clearly this dating game is just not for me.

I finally make it to the bathroom and take my time, hoping the food will be at the table by the time I get back and then I can eat and run.

As I head back to the table, I notice how full the restaurant is, large groups and couples, the waiters walking swiftly, looking after everyone, and I quickly take my seat.

"Did you know the chef here sings?" I ask Adam as I fix my napkin to try to introduce a conversation that's not work-related into the evening.

"Urgh, I know, it is so annoying." I raise my eyebrows in surprise because I actually thought it was pretty endearing.

"I thought it was nice, very authentic," I say, and Adam huffs in response.

"I can't think of anything worse than listening to an old man sing while making my dinner. That reminds me of this deal I closed today..." Adam progresses with another work conversation, and I tune out, my mind wandering back to the phone call with Nico and wondering what made him so upset.

The waiter comes and places our food down, breaking Adam's conversation. As the basil aroma hits my nose, my mouth waters and my stomach rumbles. I am so busy looking at the plate of deliciousness in front of me, I pay no attention to the form standing next to me, only looking up as a dark shadow looms over the table.

"You're in my seat," Nico says roughly, and my head whips up so fast, I fear it will fall off my neck.

"Nico!" I gasp, wide-eyed, but he isn't looking at me. He is glaring straight at Adam, and if looks could kill, Adam would be a dead man already.

"Excuse me?" Adam says dismissively, and I cringe. He really needs to just shut up.

"Nico, what are you doing here?" I grit out to him quietly as I tug on his sleeve to try to get his attention. All eyes in the restaurant are on us, but Nico's eyes won't leave Adam.

Adam pushes out his chair and stands, expanding his chest as the two are now face to face in what would be a hilarious case of posturing any other time, but humor is not the emotion I am feeling right now. They are the same height, similar build, and although I know Adam works out, he has absolutely no idea who Nico is and what he is capable of.

"You. Are. In. My. Seat." Nico punctuates back to him, making himself very clear. I can see the anger in his eyes, and his jaw working overtime; he is really pissed. His hand clenches by his side, his fingers twitch, and for a beat I hold my breath.

Could he be jealous? Has he caught feelings for me like I have for him?

Adam looks from Nico to me and back again.

"I don't think so, buddy," Adam says with a grin that even I want to slap off his face, and I already know this isn't going to end well. Not unless I step in and do something.

"You know, I'm going to call it a night." I grab my bag and look at the waiter, who scurries to get my coat. The longer I watch this standoff, the more annoyed I get. Nico hasn't even looked at me since he arrived, so what is his point in being here? I wonder if he will follow me out of the restaurant. My breathing shallows as I realize that I secretly hope he does. "Thank you, Adam, but I need to go," I say through gritted teeth, not talking to Nico as both men look at me. Then I walk out of the restaurant, taking my coat from the waiter on the way.

My strides are quick, and before I know it, I am out of the restaurant and not looking back. I strut down the sidewalk, putting on my coat as I go, keeping my steps fast. Adam was not who I thought he was, and as I hear my heels click on the sidewalk, I try to listen for any steps behind me, hoping like hell he leaves me alone. I'm frustrated. Life keeps throwing me curve balls. Perhaps I need to change my name, change my identity, maybe move to a sunny town in Mexico and make jewelry on the beach.

"Where do you think you are going?" Nico growls from behind me, sending a welcome chill down my spine, and swivel on my heel to look at him.

He is murderous. His eyes lock with mine, and I have never seen a man so angry.

"You own me for work, not for pleasure, Nico. I can still go on dates." Maybe if I push him hard enough, he'll actually admit why he showed up tonight.

For a moment, he doesn't respond, just stands there with his darkened gaze on me. With a huff, I go to turn around, ready to leave him in the dust, but he speaks just as I do.

"You are not going on any dates unless they are with me." His words halt me in place as he stalks toward me, stopping right in front of me. The light from the lamppost shines on my face, but he is in darkness as he looms above me. I'm still for a beat... did I hear him correctly? I barely breathe as I look at him, his face so serious. It dawns on me that this is not business related anymore. The heat in gaze is enough to prove that point.

But because I'm me, I give him another verbal shove in the right direction.

"It is a date, Nico. It has nothing to do with work. A

girl has needs, Nico!" I sweep my coat aside, putting my hands on my hips.

"You have needs, bambolina?" he says as he closes the small gap between us, his face now mere inches from mine. My hear thumps in my chest as I feel his warm breath skirt across my lips. I try to stand firm, my fingers gripping into my hips to remain upright as butterflies twirl and flap their wings in places they haven't ventured in a very long time, making my knees weak and my nipples peak.

"We all have needs, Nico... except for you, it appears?" I say in a challenge, raising my eyebrow, meeting him head on. His movement is quick as his hand snaps up and grabs my jaw, holding my gaze on his as he leans his head in closer, his nose touching my cheek where he then trails it over my cheekbone.

"Perhaps I should fuck those needs right out of you, hmm?" he whispers to me so softly, my ears barely hear the words, but my pussy does as it clenches.

"You're such an asshole. Don't say things you have no intention of following through with," I say with a light shove to his chest, and I turn and walk exactly three steps away before he grabs my elbow.

"This way, bambolina. You're coming with me," he growls, as he maneuvers me toward a dark car parked right out the front of the restaurant.

"Oh my god, you are kidnapping me now? If you take me back to that room of boxes, I think I will scream, Nico! I need a break!" I'm hungry, horny, and now he is taking me back to work?! I have no idea how I will manage even one box in the current state I am in.

I huff as I slide into the car, my body sinking into the soft leather seats, as he walks around the vehicle and gets into the back seat with me, before the driver starts the car and we begin to move.

"You know, you said I could do the boxes around my clients and other activities. You never said I needed to have my head in those boxes every waking hour," I continue my rant, turning to face at him, as he remains frustratingly silent next to me.

"Adam is the first date I have been on in months, Nico. Months! Maybe even close to a year. I never go out, I never enjoy a beautiful meal, and now I am starving because you just had to come and ruin my night. I haven't eaten all day, and I am craving stupid Italian-made pasta ever since you cooked for me last weekend!" When he doesn't even look at me, I keep going. He's going to hear everything on my mind if he wants to test me like this.

"You want me to die of starvation, don't you? That, or death by papercut with the amount of paperwork you have me going through. I wonder if anyone has ever died of a paper cut before. Maybe I will be the first? Maybe I will get a paper cut, it will get infected, and my hand will drop off, Nico. Have you ever thought about that!" I say to him like I have just expressed a very valid argument in court, and not at all like I am a raving lunatic in the back seat of his car, going who knows where. But this is what he does to me; he drives me crazy.

"If that will shut you up, then I won't say no," he mutters, his eyes flicking to me, nostrils flaring.

I am about to unload on him again with another nonsensical tirade, but the car pulls up and comes to a stop. He is quick to jump out, slamming his door and walking around the back of the car and coming to open my door before I can even think to. He offers me his hand, and I take it, feeling another dose of word vomit about to come out.

"You know," I say as I shuffle out of the car, gripping his hand, feeling his warmth. "Come to think of it, maybe I will die from starvation. It is entirely possible that due to you turning up to the restaurant, not allowing me to eat, my stomach could start eating me from the inside out." I huff as I stand next to him on the sidewalk. "From the INSIDE, Nico." His face is set, jaw tight. "I could die never having seen the Eiffel Tower, never having swam with dolphins... never having had a man give me an orgasm..." I lift a brow at him in challenge, ready to finish my list.

But before I know what is happening, Nico growls, grabbing my neck. He smashes his lips onto mine, completely muting any thoughts flying through my mind. I am stunned for a moment, before I realize what is happening, and start kissing him back. He groans against my lips, his other hand coming up the inside of my coat and gripping around my waist. Maneuvering his body, so it is flush with mine, his leg pushes against my center, pinning my back to the car and pulling a moan from my chest.

I am throbbing with desire, and I whimper at his manhandling of me. "Nico..." I breathe out his name against his lips, and he takes advantage, sweeping his tongue across my bottom lip before delving it into my mouth. Between his soft yet powerful lips and talented tongue, I think I will melt on the spot. My hands grip onto his lapels of his jacket as my legs wrap onto his. The kiss gets hungrier by the second, both of us fighting for dominance, right here outside on the sidewalk.

Slowly, he pulls away just an inch, and I am panting, shocked into silence.

"Good, that should keep you quiet for at least a few minutes. Let's go," he says, stepping back, grabbing my hand and pulling me along with him. I shake my head, processing if that actually just happened, a small smile gracing my lips for the first time tonight.

"Where are we?" I ask as I try to center myself and take a quick look around, my small steps fast behind him. He slows as we approach a restaurant.

"Piccolo, in Little Italy. They make the most authentic Italian spaghetti in the city." When he opens the doors to a quaint little Italian restaurant, my heart skips a beat.

I look around the small place as an older man comes and greets Nico in a warm embrace, the two of them back slapping and speaking fluent Italian to each other.

"Ahhh, who is this, Nico?" the man asks, looking at me. He has a full head of hair, although it is gray near his ears. He almost looks grandfatherly, and his smile is warm.

"This is Emilia. Emilia, this is Guillermo," Nico introduces me, and I smile and put out my hand to shake, but he shakes his head and grabs me by the upper arms, pulling me in close and kissing me on both cheeks.

"Bella, Emilia. Bella!" I flush a little, not used to the contact.

"Your usual table is ready," he says to Nico, and we

both follow him down the back of the restaurant to a secluded table.

It is quiet and intimate, with the cute little red-and-white checkered tablecloth, and I stand looking at it for a moment.

"Bambolina," Nico says, and I look at him, seeing him waiting to take my jacket. Smirking, he looks extremely happy with himself right now. I shrug it off, still not entirely sure what is going on. *Is Nico taking me on a date? Was he serious?*

"Why are you looking so smug?" I narrow my eyes, watching him pass my coat to the older man before he pulls out my chair for me. I nearly hyperventilate.

"Not smug, just happy," he replies honestly. *What is going on?* My heart stops, and my body stills as I try to take everything in, my lips still throbbing from our kiss. I don't think I have ever been kissed so thoroughly as Nico just kissed me outside.

"Come on, Emilia, we don't have all night." As I sit, I finally take a breath. This is nice. A man taking charge, a man who knows exactly what he wants. Looking at him as he then sits opposite me, I realize that what he wants is me. For the first time ever, somebody wants me. And I want him too.

Then it dawns on me. He is a gentleman. Nico Molenti is a gentleman.

17

NICO

She is infuriating. Stunningly beautiful, smart, genuine, and funny. I have never met a woman so successful and so sexy and so damn aggravating.

She calmed down the minute my lips touched hers. The kiss was fucking electric, unlike any I've experienced. I needed to pull away from her quickly, otherwise I would have fucked her in the car, or against it. My need to have her thrums strong through my veins. Seeing her with that all-American guy back at Mario's restaurant nearly ended in a 911 call, because I was going to kill him. Or her. I was too angry to know which one. I nearly lost my shit. Which is dangerous for a man like me.

I shouldn't touch her. If the boys knew, then my work ethic would be questioned, but if anyone would understand, I think Sebastian would. So I am not hiding it anymore. I want her. That's that. I want her in my arms, in my bed, underneath me, screaming my fucking name so loud everyone knows she is mine.

Guillermo brings out a carafe of red wine and some

bread fresh from the oven, and I see her eyes zone in on it so I pick up the basket and offer her a piece.

"Here. I wouldn't want you to die from starvation from the inside," I say to her mockingly, loving the way she huffs out at me like a sulky teenager, when she is anything but. No, she is *all* woman.

"Oh my God," she groans as she takes a bite of the bread. Her eyes are closed, and it is like the most magnificent thing she has ever eaten. I look around the restaurant to ensure no one else is watching her as intently as I am, because her moans shoot me directly in the balls.

"This is amazing," she says, as she chews the bread, and I swirl my wine, needing something to get my mind back into working order.

"Your usual, Nico?" Guillermo asks as he comes to the table to check on us.

"Due, per favore," I say to him, holding up two fingers, and he nods and walks away.

"What did you order?" Emilia asks me, as she takes a sip of her wine.

"I got us the spaghetti, bambolina. That is what you are craving, no?" I can feel my accent growing thicker now that I am in what feels like a restaurant in my hometown.

"What would your girlfriend think of you kissing another woman and bringing her out to dinner?" she says to me, crossing her arms across her chest, looking a little vulnerable even with her sharpened body language.

"Girlfriend?" My brow quirks as I lean back in my chair, taking another sip of my wine. What the hell she is talking about?

"You know, the Italian woman who calls you." There it is. Someone's almost just as jealous as me.

"Ahhh... my darling Sofia." I sip my wine and nod. "Well, she won't be happy, of course," I say, trying to stifle my grin. "But she is my sister, so she will do anything for me as long as I am happy." I watch her as she comes to the realization that I am, in fact, single.

"So what is this, then? Do you kiss all your employees before feeding them pasta on a Wednesday night?" Grabbing her wineglass, she raises her eyebrows at me in a challenge.

"Kissing you was the only way to shut you up." I shrug, not able to hide my smirk. I'm still not certain she has lost her fear of me, although the way she was yelling at me in the car just now, I feel like she is certainly more comfortable in my presence.

"Are you sure this isn't a date, Nico?" she asks in a teasing tone, before flicking her hair behind her shoulder, giving me a great view of her ample breasts.

I take my time looking at her. I know what she is doing, and my dick really, really likes it.

"I don't date, Bambolina." I relax into my chair and rub my chin, waiting to see what she does next.

"This sure feels like a date..." A small grin comes to her face. "Although what was it that you said outside, that you wanted to fuck me? Yes, I am sure that is what you said. Mhmm." She loves pushing me. My eyes follow her hand as it lifts her wineglass, bringing it to her lips again and swallowing.

I wait until she places it back on the table, and then reach forward, grabbing her chair and pulling it across the timber floor, directly to me. Her legs now in-between my thighs and I lean on her chair, my arms now on either side of her body, caging her in.

"You keep teasing me like you are, and I will make good on my promise sooner rather than later, Emilia," I grit out to her, really wanting to empty out this restaurant and fuck her right here, right now. Her hands rest on my thighs, and the feeling of her fingers as they grip into my muscles is almost enough to send me over the edge.

"I bet you are the kind of man who keeps all his promises, aren't you, Nico?" Her flirtatious tone might as well be casting a spell on me. All it does is make me want to rip her fucking dress off and spread her legs wide on this table and eat her for dinner until I am satisfied.

"You want me to show you, bambolina? Because I am so fucking hard for you right now that all I want to do is put my mouth on your pussy until you come on my tongue." My words are a deep whisper, and her breath catches when my hand moves to caress her arm. Biting her lip, she straightens her back, only effectively putting another inch of space between us.

"I'm just hangry." That brings my thoughts back from the dark side.

"Hangry?" I ask her, brow furrowed, not sure what she is referring to.

"Yeah, I get angry when I don't eat. Hungry plus angry means hangry," she explains, and I look at her, perplexed. Here I am, falling into her trap, telling her exactly what I want to eat, but she is talking about actual food. Goddamn.

And then she smiles, because she knows exactly what she's doing.

"So I need to make sure you are always well fed. Good to know," I say, huffing a laugh, entertained by her quirks and still so fucking turned on.

"What is with that smirk?" she questions with a sigh. I pick up the bread basket, offering it to her again.

"Hangry?" I ask, which makes her laugh. I watch as her whole face lights up, and I wonder how this woman has remained single for so long.

"Ahh... a pretty rose for the pretty lady?" an older man says, walking up to our table with a basket of individually wrapped long-stem red roses. Emilia fixes her seat, sitting back to face the table, and my eyes flick to the man. I see him around here during the nights, selling roses to all the restaurant guests, and I nod to him and he passes one to me. Pulling a $100 from my pocket, I slip it to him, knowing he needs it more than I do.

"Gracias, thank you so much," he says quickly with a big but surprised smile on his face before he turns and leaves us in peace.

"A pretty rose for a pretty lady." I repeat the man's words and give the beautiful rose to Emilia. Only, she looks baffled.

"Nico, you just gave that man $100 dollars for one rose! Are you crazy?"

"It isn't enough to change his life, but it might just make his week a little easier, bambolina. Here, take the rose. It is for you." She takes it, lifting it to her nose, where she takes a sniff of the petals before putting it to the side of the table.

Guillermo takes that moment to return with our spaghetti, before leaving us to enjoy.

"You didn't get them to poison this or anything, did you?" she asks me with humor as she picks up her cutlery.

"Maybe." I shrug and give her a grin, one which she returns before shaking her head and digging in.

"So what made you study law?" I ask, seeing if I can get her to open up to me a little more.

"As a kid, I was left on my own a lot, didn't have any friends or family around, really, so I used to sneak around the house and listen to my father during his business calls and meetings. I was young, so I didn't really understand what anything was about, but I think that sparked an interest in business." She looks at me, then continues. "What about you? Is working for the mob like a lifelong dream?" she asks me, her sassy pants clearly back on.

"Sebastian saved my sister's life, so I owe him mine in return," I answer her honestly.

"What? How so?" she asks, and I stir in my seat. I usually don't like talking about it.

"My sister had cancer, and her prognosis wasn't good. Our family was able to comfort her with love, but we did not have a lot of money. Not enough to heal her. Sebastian heard about our plight and offered the best medical care money could buy. My sister Sofia got better, and I pledged my loyalty to him. We have been brothers ever since." I take a sip of my wine, the history of how I became part of the fold feeling like it was decades ago now.

"Is your sister okay now?" I am surprised by the question. She is a lawyer, obviously always wanting the answers, but instead of prodding more about the mob, she asks about the welfare of my sister.

"She is. She is very healthy and very happy and really annoying," I tell her with a smile, feeling lighter for sharing a piece of myself with someone.

She smiles then too, a big megawatt smile. It looks good on her.

We continue talking throughout the evening, the conversation easy, and the two of us, although total opposites, find some common ground around business. I even open up and tell her more about my family, about Sofia, and a little about my parents and upbringing. Her eyes dazzle in delight at hearing about the strong family connections I still have to them all, even though they are far away in Italy.

We talk a little about her father, the boxes and paperwork, and it isn't until she yawns that I look around and see we are the last ones here, and the streets outside are dark and empty.

"Let me get you home. It's late," I say, noticing it is close to midnight. I stand, before pulling out her seat and grabbing her coat from Guillermo, slipping him a few hundred dollars as I do.

"Not only are you bossy, but you are also full of surprises, Nico." She belts up her coat, looking at me in slight wonder.

"How so?" I take her hand in mine and lead her out of the restaurant. It isn't until we are out in the cool night air that she answers me.

"Who knew that you could be both a gentleman and

want to fuck my needs away in one night? Quite the turn of events, I'd say." She laughs as we get to the car, and I look at her, head shaking, wanting to lift her dress and push her underwear to the side right here in the street. Rolling my shoulders, I push her body back against the car and put my hands on either side of her head.

"Don't push me, bambolina, I will bite," I warn her, just so I can see the fire in her eyes, knowing she loves a challenge.

"Oh no, where has my gentleman gone?" she feigns distress.

I open the back door of the car for her and watch her sultry frame slip inside, relaxing against the soft black leather. Leaning on the door, I stare down at her. How I am meant to work alongside her now and not want to fuck her brains out instead?

She gives me a small smile, and I give her my smirk in return.

"Let me assure you Emilia... I am anything but gentle." Then I step back and close the door to take her home. I will be on my best behavior tonight, dropping her at her door, but this good behavior won't last long.

I wonder if she is ready for it.

18

EMILIA

I have never been more grateful to work near Bobby's diner in my life than I am today. Between working all day on finalizing the paperwork for my former client and then working all night on the boxes Nico keeps bringing me, I haven't had time to go grocery shopping and am living off takeaway most nights and his coffee most days. But today is Friday, and I need a bagel, preferably one freshly toasted with cream cheese, and Bobby's makes them the best.

As I scurry down the street, I think back to the dinner with Nico. He was the perfect gentleman, for the most part. Hard to believe, really, given who he is, but he was. We still pushed each other, our banter something I enjoy. I like challenging him, and I like him challenging me too. It makes me feel alive, and I think he feels the same way. It is a sad realization for me that I've never felt the way I do with him with anyone else before. . To be honest, until my evening with Nico, I thought it was all in the movies, those men who pull out your chair, spoil you with flowers, maybe dance with you in the kitchen.

Unsurprisingly, Adam never called to see if I was okay after I walked out of the restaurant.

I stop on the sidewalk, waiting for the lights to change, and I touch my lips, remembering Nico's scorching kiss. It was incredible. One of those kisses you can get lost in. One that I never thought I would ever experience. One that makes me wonder what it would feel like to have more of him. He is protective, strong-willed, my match in every way. But he is in the mob, and I am a lawyer, and a part of me wonders if I have absolutely lost my mind.

I roll my eyes at myself because whether I like it or not, Nico has infiltrated my life like no other man ever has. The main problem now is keeping my head on straight to get through this job with them. I can worry about the rest later.

I take the opportunity to look around. Usually, I have my head buried in my phone, but the lack of clientele means I am not as attached to it as usual, and with the morning sun streaking through the buildings, I stop and smell the roses for just a moment. Well, the trash, since New York is not really a potted flower scent type of place. But I enjoy looking over the buildings and notice some subtle changes from when I first moved back here and found my office.

As I turn my head to look behind me, my eyes catch on a man some distance away, staring right at me. He glances away the minute he sees me looking at him, and I can't help but feel like he looks familiar. I squint to try to see him better, but the pedestrian lights turn, and I get a push from behind, so I shrug to myself and keep walking, eager to get to Bobby's.

Seeing the diner up ahead, a smile comes to my lips as I step inside, feeling the warmth immediately.

"Welcome to Bobby's. What can I get you?" the lady from behind the counter asks with a smile, one I can't help returning.

While I already know a coffee is probably waiting for me at my office, no doubt getting cold because I slept in this morning, I give her my order and wait patiently off to the side near the front window for the bagel to be prepared, my mouth watering in the process.

I look outside and watch the rushing people, all getting to their nine-to-five, looking like ants as they scurry about. Except for one person. Across the street is the same man I saw before and again he is looking right at me, but this time, his eyes don't waver as they pin me in place, and my heart races. I can't move my eyes as I swallow the fear building in my stomach, and I see a familiar tattoo on the side of his neck. It's the same man who was watching me from the cemetery. I quickly look around and behind me to ensure I am not seeing things, trying to ascertain if there could be anything or anyone else he could be looking at. Seeing nothing and no one, I look back at him, but he is gone.

A cold shiver runs through me as I stand completely still for a moment.

"Bagel for Emi!" the counter lady calls, and I jump out of my skin at the sound of my name.

"Emi! Bagel for Emi!" she yells again, and I shake my

head.

"Yes, sorry, that's me." I step forward and grab my bagel before I walk quickly out the door. Looking around me, I don't pause my steps the remaining five minutes to my office, my pace much faster than it was before.

By the time I hit my building foyer, I am out of breath, holding my bagel to my chest by way of protection. I strut to the elevators, all the while my eyes continue to scour every person I pass.

"Emilia? Are you alright?" Antonio asks, obviously spotting me from the concierge desk. I still, my eyes flicking to his, and I see his expression change, the fright clearly evident in my face.

"Fine. I'm fine," I say, and force a smile before heading right into the open elevator and taking it up to my floor.

I just need to get to my office, close the door, and take a breath.

The elevator opens on my floor, and I see Cindy at the desk.

"Good morning, Emi!" she says cheerily.

"Hi, Cindy. Do I have any appointments today?" I ask, hoping nothing has been scheduled for me since I saw my calendar yesterday. Purposefully leaving today clear so I can go through another box thoroughly. That need is stronger than ever now.

"No, all clear, just as you asked."

"Great. Please hold all calls too." I don't miss her look of question as I step past her and straight into my office, closing the door right behind me.

I throw my bag on the floor and take off my coat, as I

look at the coffee and box sitting on my desk.

Could it be Nico? I haven't seen him since Wednesday night, and he hasn't mentioned having anyone follow me, *but it could be him*. I begin to calm a little because I feel like if it was him, that would be more for my protection than for any harm.

But that tattoo. The shape, the angle, the wings. Scampering to my desk, I boot up my computer before opening a search engine.

My mind flicks through the image, and I try to search for butterfly tattoos, but nothing similar comes up in the image search. I drill my nails into the desk, the strumming rhythm helping me to think.

I think about how I saw him at the cemetery. *The flower note. Le Rose Fleurs.*

Why didn't I look that up before?

I type in Le Rose Fleurs and hit enter, my bagel now all but forgotten.

Within seconds, I can see the florist is a boutique French flower store on the Upper East Side. I grab my phone and look at their social media pages. Their arrangements are amazing, and prices sky high; it's pure luxury.

I see bunches of perfect roses, red, white, pink. Long-stemmed, tight petals, the kind that look like they belong on the counter at a Tiffany's store, not on the grave of a woman who has been dead for twenty-five years. My body wants to grab a taxi and run to the florist, but I already know they won't tell me any customer details.

So even though my heart is pumping, I look at Nico's boxes and know I need to get to work. The sooner I can get through these boxes, the sooner I can try to investigate who is leaving the flowers and if they are the same person who is following me. And why.

I grab my bagel and take a bite, then push it back to the side of my desk. I have lost my appetite.

Hours later, I have paperwork sprawled across the floor of my office, have kicked off my heels, my pen is lost in my hair, and I am in dire need of another coffee. Just as I am about to shout out to Cindy, my door opens, and Nico walks right through. No knock, no announcement, but he stops short at seeing me sitting cross-legged on the floor, surrounded by piles of paperwork.

His eyebrows shoot up, and his trademark smirk comes to his face.

"You look... busy?" he says, his smirk turning into a bright smile, one that makes my heart flip and my breath get temporarily stuck in my chest. *God, when did he start looking this handsome?*

I clear my throat to try to pull myself together, because I am a professional goddamnit, and technically, he is my boss.

"I just wanted to get these boxes done. How many more do we have?" I ask quickly, looking up at him, and he stares down at me inquisitively.

"Why? What's going on?" he asks me, as he walks in farther, closing the door behind him before standing right next to me.

"Nothing other than drowning in a sea of paperwork that I can't make heads or tails of," I say sarcastically, glancing around at the piles. He follows my gaze, assessing the mess, and spots my half eaten bagel.

"Not hungry today, bambolina?" Slight concern etches his tone as he looks down at me, his hands firmly in his pockets. I debate whether to say anything. I don't want to make a big deal out of it, but I want to find out if they are his men.

"Nico, is anyone on your team following me?" I peer up at him, waiting to see if I can spot the answer on his face. If they are his men, it makes sense. He is watching me for his business reasons, and I kind of get it. But if they are not his men, then... who are they?

"What?" His shoulders stiffen, and my heart starts to race, his body language telling me everything I wanted to know. I scurry to stand before I ask him again, needing to hear it from his lips.

"Do you have men following me?" I ask again, very clearly, my eyes watching his every move.

I see his nostrils flare, his jaw clench. "Is someone following you, Emilia?" he grits out, and I nod quickly.

"I noticed a man when I visited my mother at the cemetery over the weekend... and then I noticed him again this morning," I say before I swallow, waiting for his reaction.

"And you're just telling me now?" His voice gets louder, and I jump a little.

"Don't yell at me! I don't need to tell you my every waking move!" I bite back, folding my arms across my chest in defiance.

When he looks at me then, I get lost in his eyes for a moment. His hands cup my jaw, and I stand unmoving, my toes curling into my office carpet as he leans his head in and presses his forehead to mine.

"Are you okay?" he asks, and the seriousness of the situation makes my spine shiver, but I nod my head in his hands. Reaching out, I grab onto his jacket to support myself before I collapse into a frightened heap on the floor.

"You need to move into the compound," he says, his face still only an inch from mine, and my eyes widen at his request.

"I don't think that is necessary." I am an independent woman; I can take care of myself.

"It isn't a question." Rearing my head back, I look up into his eyes. My frustrations at being told what to do begin to mix with fear at his sudden push to keep me secure.

"Nico, I can look after myself." I take a step back, away from his tall frame, trying to pull myself together. I'm tougher than this. I can handle myself. Always have, always will.

"It wasn't a question," he grits out, his hands leaving my face, his eyes like a hawk watching me.

"What if I say no?" I put my hands on my hips and lift my head, making myself feel taller, even if he still beats me by a few inches.

"As I said, bambolina, I wasn't asking. I know you enjoy making me repeat myself, and I'll do it all day, but you're going to be safe while doing it." He steps back to me, not letting me out of his proximity. Grabbing my hips, he lowers his face slowly, and his lips brush against mine, light as a feather. Any arguments I had been trying to think up leave my head at the feel of him against me.

"You're coming with me."

19

NICO

I have come to realize that the way for me to get Emilia exactly where I want her is to touch her, and I am not complaining. I have been itching to have my hands on her since the day we first met. Our demanding kiss the other night was the first sign of my fraying armor when it comes to her, and now that I've had a taste, my appetite is growing.

I have jerked off more times in the past few days than I have in my entire life. But this is business, and I need to remain professional. I don't need distractions; especially not sexy ones like her.

Yet here I am, walking into her office, and brushing my lips with hers, needing her like the air I breathe.

Should I have kissed her? No. We still have a mountain of boxes to get through and her father is still in my basement, a fact I am sure she won't like, even if she despises him. But now, even though my blood is boiling from this new information, as soon as my hand is on her body, my lips automatically follow and the slightest touch has us both on edge.

"You should have told me you saw someone at the cemetery," I say to her as I start to help clean up the paperwork in her office, not planning to leave her side now until she is safe in the compound.

"What did he look like?" I ask her, and I see her hesitate.

"It was from a distance, so I can't really be sure. Tall, dark hair..." she says, getting lost in her thoughts. "It wasn't so much what he looked like, but..."

"But what?" I press, knowing she isn't telling me everything.

"Well, it was more the *way* he looked at me. Like he knew who I was, and..." She swallows, then she looks right at me.

"And what?"

"Like he was expecting me," she finishes, and my brows crease in thought.

Something doesn't feel right.

"What about this morning?" I ask her as I put the lid on the box and turn to stand in front of her.

"It was kind of the same. He kept his distance, but was just... watching me." A small shiver goes through her body as her hands cross her chest and rest on her elbows, her body caving into itself. I don't like it. She is normally so confident and fiery, two qualities of hers that both piss me off and make me hard, but now she is retreating and it makes me mad that she feels this way.

I lean over and pluck the pen out of her hair that has

been buried there since I walked in, brushing the loose strands away from her pretty face.

"Let's go to your place, fetch a few things, and then you will stay at the compound with me," I say with finality.

"No. I don't need to be locked up in your compound," she tosses back, her lips pursed.

"Yes," I say, moving the boxes getting ready to leave.

"No, Nico. I've already told you, I will be fine." Her hands find her hips again, showing me her curves, her sass coming back now in force.

"Yes, let's go." I get everything set, waiting for her to walk through the door.

"Nico! Stop! I can look after myself. I have looked after myself for the past twenty-five years, and I can do it now." She just about stomps her foot.

"Not anymore. Get your things," I grit out, to which she perches herself on her desk, like she has no intention of leaving.

"Nico, stop being so bossy. I. Will. Be. *Fine!*" She raises her voice, trying to get her point across, and I've officially had enough.

"Damn you, bambolina." Stalking up to her, I pick her up, throwing her over my shoulder.

"Arrghh! Nico! Put me down!" she yells at me, and I slap her ass. Hard.

"Did you just spank me!" she shrieks in shock as she tries to lift her head, pushing against gravity before giving up and hitting my back over and over with her tiny fists.

"Enough! You're coming with me whether you like it or not, so unless you want me to spank your ass again..."

"Fine! Okay! Just put me down!" I slowly lower her to her feet.

"Asshole!" she growls, throwing a light punch into my shoulder in retaliation, and I laugh at her attempt. That does nothing else but prove to me that she needs to be with me, as her fighting skills need some serious work.

"You know, I was mistaken. You are not a gentleman. You are a neanderthal!" she says with a shake of her head, and I smirk.

"Grrrrhhh!" I get ready to see a massive tantrum display, but it doesn't happen. She takes a deep breath, huffing out her displeasure as she straightens her clothes. Her mouth opens to speak, but she obviously sees the look on my face and shuts her mouth, pressing her lips into a thin line.

"Where will I sleep?"

"With me," I state, to see how far I can push her.

"What? No. Not going to happen. Absolutely not," she says, wide-eyed. I smirk.

"Come on. We have work to do. Let's work through the weekend and see what we find."

"Fine," she says, knowing she isn't going to win this argument.

Walking out of her office, I get to the elevator.

"Cindy, go home, have a long weekend. I will call you on Monday to talk. I'm not sure how much I will be in the office next week." I listen as she explains to Cindy, who eyes me up and down before she nods.

"Are you okay, Emi?" I hear her ask as the elevator arrives, and I think this is the first person I have noticed that actually seems to care for Emilia. Clearly, they are close, and I now understand Emilia's need to financially look after Cindy. She is probably the closest person she has.

"I'm fine. Please don't worry about me. Go home to that lovely husband of yours." Emilia smiles wide, and Cindy is already packing up as Emilia walks to me. I take her hand and pull her with me into the elevator, and as I turn around, I notice Cindy looking right where our hands are joined before her eyes flick to me.

"Be safe," she calls out, just as the elevator doors close. I nod to her, because as long as Emilia is with me, she will be safe. I will make sure of it.

I don't let go of her hand for the entire drive to her apartment, and I leave Tony in the car downstairs as I walk her up to grab her things.

"I won't need much. Just a few days, right? Then I can come back here?" she asks me as she walks into her bedroom, and I follow her.

"Sure, whatever you say," I mumble to her as she stalks around her room, opening drawers and grabbing out some clothes. I look over her space, seeing it spotless.

"Can you give me a hand?" she asks from her wardrobe, and I see her on her tiptoes, trying to get a bag from the top shelf.

I watch her for a moment, her body stretched, her curves perfect, the light hitting her just right and show-casing her hair flowing down her back. As I step closer, I see her long black lashes shadowing her cheeks. With laser focus on her voluptuous, hot as sin body, my cock's already throbbing, itching to take off her clothes.

"You want me to help you, bambolina?" I whisper out

as I come up behind her, her back now flush with chest. I run my hands up and down her sides slowly, feeling every dip from her hips up the soft curve of her stomach and down again.

"Nico..." she says my name breathlessly before I cut her off as I lower my mouth to her neck. As I taste her skin, I hear her breath catch and her breasts push out a little as her back arches.

I grip her hips tight and pull her ass flush with my hard cock, grinding her into me. "See what you do to me, bambolina. You drive me crazy," I whisper against her skin as my lips caress her neck, gliding up to her ear. Her head falls back onto my chest as she whimpers, and my hands travel around the front of her torso. Running up her chest, I cup her perfect fucking tits, groaning at the feel of her.

"You are such a tease," she mumbles as she turns around in my arms to face me, her eyes hooded, her breasts pushing up against my chest. I drop my head then, skirting my lips across her jaw, inhaling her aroma, and licking up her throat, wanting to eat her whole.

Then... I snap.

My hand reaches up to grab the back of her neck, and I pull her lips to mine. The kiss is instantly just as passionate as it was in front of Piccolina's the other night, but now, in the privacy of her four walls, I am not going to stop.

"Nico, we can't be doing this. I'm working for you," she moans her denial, her body leaning against mine.

"Is that all you got, Emilia? Because you and I both know that nothing I do plays by the rules." I kiss her again, my tongue demanding and hers meeting mine, fighting for dominance.

"But we have to work together. I don't want it to be awkward," she says in between our kisses, her body telling me the complete opposite of her mouth.

"Fuck work. If you keep whimpering and withering your body against mine, I am not stopping. I can't stop anymore," I growl, and she pushes her body against mine once more. Her body is telling me exactly what she wants. And I'm taking it.

Lowering my hands again, I cup her ass before I grab it hard and hoist her up my body. I hear her sharp intake of breath as her feet leave the floor and wrap around my waist, her dress slipping up her thigh, and I get another glimpse of her flawless legs.

"Fuck," I growl, my hands squeezing her ass as I grind into her hot core, already knowing she wants this just as badly as I do.

Her arms circle around my neck, our lips still devouring each other, our kisses frantic, our need explosive. I have never felt like I do right now. I need her body, need to make her *mine*.

I turn and walk out of her wardrobe and make my way to her bed. "You make my blood boil..." I growl out to her, all the while not allowing my lips to leave her skin even once.

"You are insufferable..." she banters back, her hands moving to my chest, where she begins to undo the buttons on my shirt.

"You are so fucking aggravating..." I throw her onto the bed and rip off my shirt, flinging it across the room, before I hover over the top of her, admiring her body that is still too covered for my liking.

"You are infuriating..." she says, as my hands reach her bare thighs. I brush them up her legs, pushing up her dress until it pools around her waist, giving me a perfect view of some pretty black lace underwear that I know I will be keeping.

"You are fucking perfect..." I tell her, my eyes now trained on hers, my hands itching to pull her underwear off, but I want to see more of her first.

"I need you. I want you so bad..." My eyes flick to hers because it sounded like a beg, and I *really* want her to beg. She looks at me with wanting, and as much as I want to take my time, I can't. I want her too damn much.

I grip her waist, feeling her soft skin under my touch before I continue to run my hands up her torso, taking the jersey dress with me, my thumbs skimming her nipples on the outside of her lacy bra. I hear her intake a breath, and she sits up, lifting her arms above her head as I slip her dress right off her body.

Throwing her dress across the room, I grip onto her throat and pull her lips to mine, as my tongue plunges and fights with hers. Each of us fight for control, but there is no match to the flame that is igniting in my soul right now. Laying her back down underneath me, my eyes canvass her curves that are on full display. Her blonde hair splays out on the mattress, haloed around her head, her skin lightly tanned and flushed from her excitement.

I run my hands across her body before pulling her bra down, watching her perfect tits bounce out for me, and I lower my mouth to her nipple. I lick her, suck her into my mouth before I give her a bite. As I reach around to unclip her bra, I give the other breast the same attention, wanting to taste all of her, every fucking inch.

"Jesus, Nico..." she moans as her body starts to tremble underneath mine. I am trying to control my need, but it is becoming very fucking difficult. I pull the straps of her bra off her shoulders and throw it across the room to meet the rest of our clothes on the floor.

Molding her tits in my palms, I lick my lips, already knowing I want to make her lose control with my tongue. "Not Jesus, Emilia, just Nico." I can't hide my smirk. I am very fucking happy right now.

I quickly move from hovering over her and drop to my knees on the floor near her bed, grabbing her legs and pulling her across the mattress. Her body skims down the bed until I have her right on the edge where I want her.

"What are you doing?" she asks, sitting up on her elbows.

"These are mine," I say as my fingers hook into the side of her underwear and I slowly lower them off her legs. Admiring her soft pink toenails up close, I pocket the underwear and kiss her ankle. Her scent wraps around my neck, choking me, pulling my lips to her skin. My tongue and lips trail up her calf muscle to the inside of her thigh, where I could die a very fucking happy man.

"They are my best pair," she says with a quirked brow, watching me. Pure lust shines in her eyes, and I smile against her skin. She is just as confident naked as she is fully clothed, but the fact she is letting me take charge like this makes me think although she likes to win the power dynamic out of the bedroom, inside she knows it is my domain.

"I will buy you more." I push her legs wider, throwing one, then the other, over my shoulders.

"Look at how wet you are for me," I say as I see her glisten, and I rub my thumb back and forth across her clit slowly as I admire her. She falls back onto the mattress and lets out a little moan that goes straight to my cock. Squirming on the bed, her back arches slightly. I love that she is already undone at the mere touch of my hands. I wonder how long it has been since Emilia let a man near her, remembering her slip at the restaurant where no man has ever made her come before. I think about that as I continue to rub her clit with my thumb. I see her breathing quicken, her chest rising and falling in quick succession, and so I don't hesitate.

Lowering myself, I lick her before finding her clit and sucking it hard. I hear her say my name just as her hands come to my head, pulling at my hair.

"Good girl," I murmur, as I do it again, this time faster. Her hips start to rock against my face, and I squeeze her ass cheeks in my hands. She tastes like fucking everything I want, and as I devour her, I can hear her pants, her moans, and whimpers. Little Miss Perfect Lawyer is coming undone at my touch and I fucking love it. My lips and tongue are demanding, my appetite ravenous, and I lick and suck her sex like I need it more than the air I breathe.

She will be my undoing. There is no doubt.

"Nico... I'm going to..." She gasps, and I suck on her

clit as her body convulses. Her fingers grip into my hair, and she lets out a scream that bounces around her bedroom as her body shakes from her orgasm. Lying back breathless, she comes down from her high. I pepper her skin with kisses, not yet wanting to leave the perfect place between her legs as my hands skim across the skin of her thighs.

"That was…" she says, but I interrupt her.

"Just the beginning," I state, leaving no room for questions.

That was merely an entree.

20

EMILIA

"Just the beginning," he says with fire in his eyes as I watch him stand from between my legs and smirk at me as he undoes his belt and makes quick work of his pants. I am still breathless from what was my first orgasm delivered by someone other than myself. It was amazing and now I want more. Many more. I am naked, which at any other time I would be embarrassed about, since my body isn't even close to being perfectly toned. Yet for some reason, Nico makes me feel more wanted and beautiful than any man before him.

My chest is flushed, and I watch him as his naked body stands next to the bed, admiring mine. I don't even have time to get my bearings, my mind still a whirlwind of *what the hell just happened*. As my eyes wander down from his face, taking in all of his tattoos and every refined muscle to the V at his lower abs, my breath gets stuck in my throat when my eyes settle on his cock.

"Oh my God," I murmur in quiet shock. I am not even sure I know what to do with him. He is massive.

"This is all you, bambolina. See what you do to me," he croaks out as he fists his cock, pumping a few times as he walks to the bed and crawls over me. His eyes remain on mine like he is stalking his prey. In any other circumstance, I would hate this feeling, but right now, I want him to eat me whole. "You drive me absolutely fucking crazy, yet I crave you like no other," he says, smirking, and my eyes widen a little at his honesty.

"Are you all words, Nico? Or are you going to put that to good use?" I say, nodding toward his cock, which is heavy and full in his hand. I'm playing with fire, because frankly, I'm slightly terrified of how he's going to put that to use.

"Now, be a good girl and take me, because I'm not playing anymore, Emilia. I want to fuck the sass right out of you."

He lowers his head and bites my lower lip, pulling it slightly, before his tongue swipes across it.

"I'm always a good girl, Nico..." I whisper, because it's true. I rarely color outside the lines, and in this moment, I want to do everything he tells me to.

"Tell me, Emilia," he says, nudging my cheek with his nose, as his lips travel down my jaw. I feel the tip of his cock at my entrance as he positions himself between my legs. "Do you want my cock inside of you?" he taunts, his hands skirting down my body and back up again. He feels like he is everywhere, all over me, his touch soft yet demanding. His woodsy cologne infiltrates my mind, and I can still taste his coffee on my mouth. He rubs the tip of his cock through my center, each stroke hitting my clit over and over, my hips bucking a little, already wanting more.

I don't hesitate. "Yes," I whisper, because I don't think I have ever wanted a man this much before in my life. I know he is all kinds of wrong, but this just all feels so right. He grabs my wrists and lifts them above my head, his face now right in front of mine.

"Then take all of me..." he grits out, just as he pushes inside me, and the air gets caught in my chest. I feel the burn before I start to feel the pleasure.

"Breathe, bambolina. I'll fit inside you perfectly," he says, pausing a little to watch me breathe again.

"Move, please, move..." I plead, needing the friction, needing to feel him over and over.

"You are so fucking tight," he grits out as he begins to do as I asked, thrusting in and out, his forehead resting on mine as he looks me in the eye. He is watching me, his gaze burning into my soul. His ab muscles contract and move in sync with his thrusts, his body truly a work of art. Wrapping his hands tightly around my wrists above my head, his hips pin mine underneath him. I am secured to the bed, a move I would usually hate because I am contained, yet with Nico, I don't mind one bit. He moves his legs, opening mine wider, as my clit tingles with every thrust. I can feel myself already aroused and ready to come again.

"Oh my God... Yes, that feels so good," I say as I close my eyes, lost in the pleasure.

"Look at me, Emilia. I want to watch you come on my

cock." I see a sheen of sweat over his shoulders, his need for me evident.

My heart is racing. I have never felt this wanted in my entire life. Not once. Sure, my few boyfriends were nice enough, but they never looked at me like Nico does. Not like this. Not all-encompassing. Nico looks into my eyes like he will die without having me, and I feel it too.

He continues to drive into me, the sensation like nothing I have ever experienced. It is not slow and steady, seductive or sweet. It is carnal, desperate; we are fucking like animals, chasing our release like it is going to leave us at any moment.

"Nico... Nico... Nico..." I pant, feeling out of control as my toes curl and my muscles tense. I arch my back even more, my nipples brushing against his chest, our torsos pressed together, nothing between us but the air we're breathing of each other's.

"Fuck, I like it when you say my name like that," he growls. "Come for me again, Emilia." And for the first time since I met him, I do as he asks.

My orgasm washes through me like a tsunami, my hips buckling, my limbs locking. His hands let go of my wrists and clasp mine, our fingers intertwining as I hear him growl.

"Fuck, bambolina. Fuck, fuck, fuck," he grits out as he explodes, and together we run off the cliff, into the deep unknown. Albeit very, very satisfied.

His head rests in the crook of my neck, as we both come down from the high. I smile a little because that was the best sex I have ever had in my entire life. I never knew it could be like that. But my smile is short-lived as his hands run down my arms, and he begins to pull away. It is then I realize, we didn't use protection, and I am not on birth control. How has this man embedded himself so far into me already that I lose sight of one of the most important things?

I am a strong, independent woman. I don't make mistakes, not like this.

21

NICO

Fuck. I didn't use a condom. I always wrap myself, yet another thing I lose sight of around this woman.

"Shit. Nico!" she says, her eyes wide as I start to move off her.

"I'm clean. I've never not used a condom before," I say quickly, searching her eyes. Fuck, I am such a fucking idiot.

"I'm clean too, but, Nico, I'm not on birth control." I look at her for a moment, both of us totally out of our element. I see the fear in her eyes, and just want to ease it.

"Don't worry. It's one time. I'm sure we will be fine, bambolina. We will just be more careful from now on." After what we just did, there most certainly will be a next time.

"Seriously! This is a big deal, Nico," she questions, sitting straight up in bed.

"It will be all right." My words only fire her up more.

"We are so stupid! How could I have been so stupid?"

"Take a breath. Or do you need me to calm you down again, bambolina?" I smirk at her, and I see her nostrils flare in response, her anger turning me on again already.

"You need to take this seriously, Nico. This could have consequences. I have never been so thoughtless in my entire life. I don't make stupid mistakes like that. Unless I am around you, of course! " Her hand flies in the air for added effect as she eyes me like she wants to gut me, and all it makes me want to do is push my dick into her pouty mouth.

I'm screwed.

"Come here," I growl, and her eyes thin at me in response. The look she has on her face now making me crack my neck from side to side, because I want to devour her again.

"No. Every time you touch me, my brain fails to work properly," she states, almost whining, and again I smirk. Glad she finally realizes that I can soothe her soul from my mere touch. I brush her hair over her shoulder and cup her face. She is so beautiful. Her cheeks flushed, her lips swollen, eyes sparkling, a look of contentedness taking over her expression.

"You need to get your hands off me," she says, barely above a whisper, not meaning a word of it. Her eyes hold mine, and I groan as she fully relaxes into me. She turns to putty in my hands, exactly how I want her.

"Hands or lips... your choice," I murmur, but I can't wait. My lips find her neck, and I nibble at her skin.

"You are incorrigible," she moans, and I know I've got her.

"Let's have a shower, and then we need to go." I grab

her and pull her up into my arms, cradling her like my bride.

"Nico! Put me down!" she shrieks, making me laugh.

"Nope. You're mine now, bambolina." It's a gentle warning, because she is, whether she likes it or not, now mine.

Walking into her bathroom, I place her feet down gently in front of the shower and kiss her. Slow and purposeful, still feeling guilty about not wrapping it up before I fucked her.

She leans in and turns on the water, steam enveloping the small bathroom quickly. As she pulls me into the shower, I watch the water cascade over her naked body, and I take my time looking at her womanly curves that I can't get enough of.

"You look good naked." I grab onto her hips, holding her closer, wanting to appreciate every inch of her body. I kiss her before she can make any smartass retort, preferring to also show her my feelings with my tongue as my hands move up and down her spine.

Her hands run over my chest, her fingers exploring, and I tense my muscles, letting her feel every ridge before she moves lower and wraps her hand around my cock.

"So do you," she says, her eyes igniting.

"You would look even better on your knees," I grit out, feeling myself getting hard in her hand as she pumps me slowly, teasing me with her touch.

She hates being told what to do, and I wait a beat to see if she will slap me instead. Watching me with darkening eyes, she begins to lower herself to the floor of the shower. The water runs over her breasts, and I am jealous of the way it caresses her pink nipples. I want to lap it up with my tongue, grab her and fuck her against the wall, but I wait to see what she'll do next..

My heart feels like it is going to jump out of my chest as I watch this strong, smart, sassy woman get on her knees for me. I was right. She looks phenomenal on her knees. Her blue eyes are bright as she looks up at me before grabbing my already throbbing cock and licking it from my balls to the tip in one long stroke.

"Open wide, bambolina." I'm itching to fill her mouth, already knowing the sight will be one to behold. "I want to fuck your mouth like I have wanted to since I met you. I want those pouty lips around my cock, and I want to feel the back of your throat when I come."

A small moan leaves her as she does exactly that. I lean my hands against the top of the shower frame, and let her lead. She moves slowly at first, sucking me like a fucking lollipop. I'm already about to bust.

"Fuck, you look so fucking pretty on your knees. So pretty with my cock in your mouth." My hips start to move involuntarily, my knees weakening.

She moves with more confidence then, at seeing me unravel, getting some rhythm. I feel myself sliding deeper down her throat, as her hands grab my ass and she pulls me closer.

"You want more, baby?" I groan, my hips now moving in time with her mouth.

She whimpers around my cock, and the vibrations spark up my spine. I grab her long hair in my fist and help her control the movement, watching as her hand moves around her body, down to her center.

"Touch yourself, Emilia. Fuck your pussy with your fingers and feel how wet you are for me." Her increasing moans have my whole body tingling. I'm barely hanging on.

"That's it. Fuck, that feels so good. Your mouth was made just for me, bambolina. Fucking *perfect*." My breathing is labored, and I feel my balls begin to tighten at the sight of her on her knees in front of me, touching herself, while my cock fills her mouth.

"Fuck," I grit out, as both my hands tangle in her hair and I move my hips more. I hear her panting, and see her hips rocking before her orgasm comes, her scream around my cock causing me to let go too.

"Fuck, I'm coming, fuck, fuck." I thrust into her mouth hard, touching the back of her throat, and pulling her hair tight I explode, my orgasm coating her throat and she swallows it all.

That was better than my dreams.

She laps me up, before sitting back on her heels and taking deep breaths, a smile on her face. I rub my eyes, trying to ensure I don't black out from lightheadedness. That was the best blow job I have ever been given. Certainly the prettiest girl to ever watch, that is for sure. I lean over and pull her up, smashing my lips onto hers, and grab her bare ass cheeks to pull her naked body closer to mine.

"You are full of fucking surprises," I murmur against her lips, again not able to keep mine off her.

"I am an overachiever," she says simply, and I fucking smile.

"Fucking A-plus for blow job skills." I give her ass a

light smack, then squeeze. She moans into our kiss, biting my lip in return. I could stay like this for hours, but I know we can't.

Pulling back, I cup her face in my hands, reveling in her flushed cheeks and swollen lips. "We need to get your things and go to the compound. But make no mistake, the night is still young, and I am not finished with you yet."

22

EMILIA

As I sit on the floor surrounded by paperwork, once again, I look over and watch Nico for a beat, who is deep in concentration. His large fingers flick through a file, his tattoos pure artwork running up his hands and wrists. They make him appear dark and dangerous, yet after what I experienced with him at my apartment this afternoon, I also know they are protective and reverent. I try to reconcile the two, still not believing I am so close to a member of the mob. Have I just made a terrible mistake? Not to mention, he's my boss and looking for my own criminal of a father. I pat my forehead with my palm... I think I have absolutely lost my mind.

Together we made our way back to the compound and Nico hasn't left my side for a minute. He held my hand for the entire drive over here, his thumb continually caressing my hand as he looked out the car window. He's been quiet ever since, seemingly in deep thought.

Once we arrived, he made us fresh pasta, and we ate it

in comfortable silence, both of us starving and shoveling it in like it was our last meal. Our hunger obviously due to all the cardio in my bedroom. His gentle nature of hand holding, coffee making, and pasta producing is in complete contrast to the smirking, arrogant jerk he also likes to be. I sigh to myself as I try to get out of my head and concentrate back on the work I am here to do.

As I comb through my fifth box for the day, I am beginning to feel tired, the events of the week finally creeping up on me. I stifle a yawn as I grab yet another real estate title, wondering how the hell my father could afford all these properties we are finding. Florida, New York, L.A., and Montana. Then the vacation properties in Belize, one in Greece, and a small condo in Sydney.

"I knew he was rich, Nico, but this is starting to become really obscene," I say to Nico, as my eyes run over the paperwork for the title of his Florida property.

"You know what is obscene, bambolina..." he says as he stands and walks over to where I am sitting. "It is obscene how much I want to put my hands on your body." Grabbing me under the arms, he pulls me up off the floor, placing me on my feet. He leans down, covering me in his presence, putting his hands on my waist again.

"Shouldn't we be working, boss?" I tease him with a breathy tone as heat flames my insides. My earlier doubts instantly vanish the minute his hands touch my body.

"Oh, I am your boss, all right, and right now, I want to lay you out on my desk and lap your juices until you are begging me to let you come," he grits out, and I need to swallow my shock. His face is serious, but no man has ever said anything like that to me before. I like it way too much. His lips start to trail down my neck, my skin prickling from the sensation. My heart pounds and my pussy clenches. This man is so overpowering in the best way.

I am about to wrap my arms around his neck, but we are startled by a clearing throat behind us. Nico jumps, pulling me automatically behind him. I look around his shoulder and see Sebastian Romano standing there, staring at us both, his eyebrows creased with concern, looking displeased, yet somewhat inquisitive as well. Nico's stance immediately changes. He stands taller, his shoulders stiffen slightly, and although I know they are friends, he appears to want to please Sebastian and remain professional around him. I suddenly feel like we are about to get into trouble, and that I am the cause of it.

My heart starts pounding for an entirely different reason, because as much as I have seen his face in the news or gossip pages, to see Sebastian in real life is an entirely different experience. He is taller and broader than I expected, his eyes similar in color to Nico's and deadly as they pin us in place. Nico reaches around and grabs my hand as his stance relaxes a little. Sebastian shakes his head with a smile, and I hear Nico chuckle as he gives my hand a comforting squeeze. Sebastian doesn't seem to mind, but now that I am in the same room as the head of the mob, the reality of my situation hits me again.

What the hell am I doing in this compound with a mob soldier? This is so far out of my comfort zone and professional boundaries, I feel like I have lost control. The thread which my career is hanging on by is about to get clipped, because there is no way I can continue practicing law for the good guys now that I am standing in the same room as these men. The lines have blurred for the past week or so, but this afternoon, they were definitely crossed. I am not sure there is any way back for me now. In fact, I'm not sure I want there to be. It feels amazing to be with him, despite it being the total opposite of how I thought my life would go.

"Sebastian," Nico says, addressing him with a nod and a smile. He pulls me up to stand beside him, no longer shielding me from the man I am still not sure I want to actually meet.

He doesn't say anything for a while. Instead, he looks at the boxes, like he is assessing how much work we have done, and although there are still many more to go through, we are setting a good pace.

"We need to move faster," he comments, his eyes landing on mine. I throw up a little in my mouth.

"We will move through some more this weekend. Emilia had a tail, so I moved her in here with me," he tells Sebastian, and although Nico is now standing casually, my grip on his hand remains tight. He brushes his thumb over my wrist, obviously trying to calm me, but it is not having the desired effect.

Sebastian's eyes take in where our hands are joined, then his eyes flick to Nico's, and I see him nod just a little. "It is a pleasure to have you with us, Emilia. Welcome." He walks forward, putting his hand out. I look at it, stunned for a moment. *He wants to shake my hand?* I give him my best professional handshake, and he smirks. What is it about these men and their smirks?

"Thank you," I say, because I know not to piss him off

with my sass. I am in his home. His compound. Whether I like it or not, at least I am safe here.

"Your reputation as one of the top lawyers in the country is impressive, or at least it was before your father's escapades..." he says, watching me, and I school my features, not yet sure what to share.

"Tell me what have you found so far?" he asks, and I take a breath, feeling like I am in the headmaster's office and wanting to escape his scrutiny.

"Nothing too significant, but as I said to Nico, I feel like my father may have some type of support from international borders. I had no idea he owned so many properties. His wealth is astounding and—"

"Obscene?" Sebastian cuts me off, clearly having heard Nico's and my conversation from moments ago.

"Yes," I say with a nod. He looks at me almost like he is waiting for me to give him more, but the only other things I have learned have been about my mother, and that is too personal.

He watches me and then just nods. The hairs on the back of my neck stand as I feel out of my element.

"Well, I will leave you to it. Nice to finally meet you, Emilia." He starts to walk out of the room, then stops. "Nico." Not looking back, he leaves, and Nico leans in, giving me a quick kiss on the temple.

"I'll be back." He follows Sebastian out the door and I stand there in shock, astounded at how quickly my life has changed.

My father lit the spark, and now it is turning into an inferno. Problem is, why do I feel like I am the one who will get burnt while he walks off scot-free?

23

NICO

After chatting briefly to Sebastian last night, telling him I had everything under control, I made good on my promise and licked my beautiful bambolina on the desk until she was crying out for more. I had her two more times last night, and after seeing her naked and wrapped up in the bedsheets this morning, it was a struggle to leave her, but I quietly set a coffee on the bedside table before I left. Freshly brewed with cream, just how I know she likes it. As someone who appreciates coffee, I never understood the need to add cream, preferring straight black myself.

Now, as I look at her deadbeat father, I am trying to figure out how someone so rotten produced a woman like her.

"Did you get my daughter?" he asks, looking at me, eagerly waiting for the cool bottle of water and sandwich I brought with me. It's his usual lunchtime meal. Despite the fact I could easily let him starve to death down here, I know I need him alert. He still needs his memories, because if Emilia can't find what we are looking for, then I am back to square one.

"Maybe," I say, staring down my nose at him, trying not to breathe in the stench coming off him in waves, which is hard, considering he hasn't showered in many weeks now.

"Good, now let me go. She is a good lawyer, can serve you well," he says in a very businessman-like fashion, like he has the right to barter with me.

I laugh then, a low cackle. The arrogance of this man is astounding. Even now, even though he hasn't told us shit, and after all he has done and been responsible for, he still thinks he can worm his way out of it. Not give us all the information, all his money, all his connections.

"Not until you tell me who is funding your activities," I say to him.

"I have already told you. I acted alone," he huffs out.

"We both know that the type of money you were throwing around to get your son a senator seat is not the kind of money you have. So I will ask again. Where did you get the money?" I'm getting sick and fucking tired of this asshole.

While there is no question his attempted push into politics was for the betterment of himself, I am not a fool. I have looked at his finances. His businesses were doing okay, but they weren't as successful as we first thought; obscure transactions, mostly into offshore accounts. They are intriguing, but despite our best efforts, we cannot locate the person paying him. Whomever he or she may be. There is no doubt he is being financially supported in some way, but who would be financing his foray into getting ahold of the streets of New York to compete with us?

"I think whatever you're looking for is in international borders," Emilia's voice repeats over and over in my mind. She came to this conclusion after less than a day of investigation. And I know she is right.

"I had the money. It was all my money." His raised pitch tells me he is lying.

"Was it someone in Europe?" I ask, and I see his eye twitch a little.

"Are you deaf as well as dumb. I already told you, I acted alone," he spits out.

"Oh, I am many things, Mr. Cole. But I tell you what I am not." I watch him carefully.

"I am not merciful. I am not forgiving, and I certainly am not going to miss the opportunity to peel the skin from your body and put you in a bath of leeches," I growl, my anger simmering right on the surface.

"I demand you let me go!" he yells, drawing my attention to his angry eyes. His face is red, and slimmer than it was a few months ago when we threw him in here not long after his son's funeral. The rich prick has remained tight-lipped ever since, appearing to be the gatekeeper to many secrets, making me think he is more fearful of the person funding his activities than he is of us.

"You don't get to demand a fucking thing." I open the water and take a gulp, seeing him swallow at the action, craving it for himself.

"You have my daughter. You can do whatever you want with her. Like I said, she is a lawyer, but tie her up and fuck her all you want. I don't care. A deal is a deal, so let me go!" he shouts again, and I see red. Blood red.

I throw the water bottle across the room, then march up to him, smacking my knuckles across his cheek so hard I hear a crack. I do it again with my left hand, on the opposite side of his face, and hear another crunch.

"You fucking never speak her name again, asshole," I seethe, glaring down at his pathetic, panting face.

"You are a fucking despicable father, a shit businessman, and a poor fucking excuse for a human being!" I scream, my rage not dissipating. His eyes find me, and although he can't smile, I see the glint in his eyes. I am about to hit him again and end him once and for all—

"Enough!" Sebastian barks behind me, and I look at him sharply, my nostrils flaring. I don't say a word, and I give him a sharp nod before pushing past him, walking straight out the door. I need to get away from this asshole, and I need to get my shit together. Because the lines of personal and business are blurring, and that is a dangerous place for a man like me to be.

"Nico," Sebastian says from behind me, but I keep walking, blood pumping heavily through my body. I need to hit something or someone.

"NICO!" Sebastian shouts, and I stop, standing still until he comes up beside me.

"What the fuck is going on?" Sebastian questions, looking at me with a mix of concern and intrigue like a big brother should.

"He is not talking. We have nothing to go on, and I want to fucking kill him already. He is a fucking disgrace," I spit out.

"Yes. Yes, he is. But we knew that from the start," Sebastian says, running his hand through his hair. "While I don't care that you hit him, because the asshole deserves everything he gets, you can't kill him. Not yet. If I hadn't come down, I know you would have ended him. You need to wait." Sebastian searches my face, but I already know he knows.

"Maybe you should just fuck her? Get her out of your system?" I look at him sharply.

"That has made it worse," I reply, scrubbing my face with my hand.

"Fuck," he murmurs, my look obviously confirming Emilia is more than a quick fuck at this point. "Fine. Don't go down there again without me. In the meantime, double time on those boxes and get it done."

"We are moving fast. There is just a lot to get through. Can't we start taking his fingers?" While we have roughed the guy up a bit, we could push him much farther.

"By the look of his nose just now, I would say that you have crushed his bones to the point where he won't be able to breathe normally ever again."

"It is not enough." I clench my fists, pushing the pain in my knuckles to the back of my mind.

"Nothing ever will be. Now get that girl of yours back to work. Less fucking, more working, please!" he groans the last word before stalking off.

I take a deep breath, then follow him, already knowing I need her again. She is becoming my addiction, and even though I only left her a few hours ago, I'm ready for my next hit.

24

EMILIA

I am mid-way through a box when I hear the door slam and look up in time to see Nico walk into the room with purpose.

"Hey, I haven't really found—" I start to explain, but he struts toward me without stopping, then picks me up off the floor in one swoop, linking his hands underneath my arms. I am airborne before I even know what is going on, and he lifts me to his body and slams his lips into mine. My feet dangle and my hands immediately wrap around his neck, and it is all I can do to hang on for dear life as his hands encase my waist and he pulls me close.

"What happened?" I ask breathlessly in question, my stomach leaping at my sudden movement.

"I need you now," he says, sounding distressed. "Right fucking now." His impatience makes my heart thump, loving how his need for me seems greater than anything else. He moves us over to the table in the room and sits me on the edge, his lips not leaving my skin for a moment as he runs them along my neck.

"You are all I can think about. You are in my fucking brain 24/7. What are you doing to me, bambolina?" he grits out, as his lips and tongue trail my skin.

His hands move swiftly, as his lips smash back onto mine, his demanding nature when it comes to getting us naked, startling and addictive. He is already undoing his belt buckle and lowering his zipper before I can even think of responding. My hands shoot out as I take over, lowering his zipper and pushing his pants down, just as eager to get to him.

"You're so demanding," I tease, even though I'm pulling at his shirt, desperately wanting to see him naked.

"Don't push me right now," he growls, as his hand cups my breast, where he squeezes and molds his hand, tweaking my nipple and making me shudder.

"Nico. Condom," I say in a rush. My mouth is barely able to leave his, but we don't need a repeat. We need to be smart and have been ever since our slip up the first time.

"Fuck." He dives into his pants pocket and fishes one out of his wallet, and I lean back on my hands as I watch him slide it on. I wonder what has prompted his insane desire for me, yet not I don't want to question it. I actually enjoy seeing him undone with need for me.

"Come here, this is going to be hard and fast, bambolina," he says in warning as he quickly lifts my dress. It bunches around my waist, exposing my lacy underwear, which he admires for a moment before pulling them to the side.

"You like it when I need you, don't you, Emilia?" he

asks me, running his cock up and down my lips a little, making my pleasure build with the lightest of touches.

"Yes," I say on a breath, because I do. Who wouldn't? One of the most dangerous men in the city, someone who I should have nothing in common with, and no desire to be next to, desires me like no other man ever has before.

"But if you don't hurry up..." My words leave me with a gasp as he enters me quickly, and I lose my breath for a moment. I feel so full. I wrap my hands around his neck as he pulls me toward him, his hands now cupping my ass as he continues his assault, thrusting into me like a man possessed.

"I fucking need you like I need the fucking air." His lips find mine once again and my body melts. I whimper at his words and his insane appetite for me, for us.

"I want you too. I need you too," I pant, my fingers gripping into his shoulders, my breast pushing up against his chest, the two of us trying to get as close to each other as possible. I'm starting to sweat since I am still fully clothed. As I cling onto him, my body feels as if it's no longer my own, and I let him take me exactly how he wants to. He is in total control as he pulls me on and off his cock, putting me where he needs me, turning me on more and more.

"Fuck," he groans, before he lifts me off the desk, putting me on my feet and spinning me around, my back now facing his body. His hands reach up and rip off my panties.

"They are my favorite pair!" I whine, because that is the second pair in a matter of days he has taken from me.

"Head down, bambolina," he grits out, and my pulse

races, loving his demanding tone. I lean on the desk, and he kicks my legs wider, manhandling me in a way I wouldn't like from anyone else but him. I try to hold on with my sweaty hands before he enters me again.

"Fuck, this view is perfect. Your ass, your curves, you look so fucking pretty with my cock inside of you, bambolina," he says breathlessly, and my hands wrap around the edge of the desk, needing to stabilize myself as his thrusting gets faster.

"Faster, Nico... Oh... Harder," I moan, as his hand sweeps under my hip and finds my clit.

"You want to come, bambolina?" he says in torment.

"Yes, Nico... please." I am about to explode.

"You will come when I say you can. Your pussy is mine. Your fucking body is mine. *You* are mine." I feel his strong body over mine, gripping into my flesh, pounding into me relentlessly. Turning my face to his, his eyes look deep into mine, and despite the heat of the moment, I see nothing but truth in them. He says what he means and means what he says. My belly flips, my pulse quickens, his obvious feelings for me thrumming through my veins, and my need for him increases. His other hand reaches for my hair, pulling my hair back, my body now arched back, and I feel him get deeper as he places kisses on my neck.

"That feels so good..." I moan as he hits my G-spot. I have never felt anything this good before.

"Who do you belong to, Emilia?" Nico growls, and I am lost in my arousal. I can only moan in response.

"Tell me. Tell me you belong to me." The two of us are hanging on by a thread.

"You, Nico. I belong to you. Only you," I pant out, the words falling from my lips without any doubt. Nico is branding me as his, and I am letting him. There is no longer any doubt; he owns me. I can't hold anything back. I'm not able to think of anything else.

"Come for me. Now," he orders just as he pinches my clit, and I lose it. Like a wild animal, I let go, my body shaking, silently screaming my release as Nico roars behind me. I hope this room has sound-proofing because I have never heard him this loud before.

I lay against the desk, panting, my skin coated in a light sheen, and I close my eyes as I feel Nico pulling out. "Fucking perfect," he murmurs into my neck as his hand caresses my bare ass, and then he fixes my dress to cover me, making quick work of readjusting himself as well.

"I'll take these too," he says, sweeping down to pick up my panties off the floor as I sit up and look at him.

"What happened?" I ask him. As much as I like to feel wanted, I know something must have upset him to make him walk in like he did.

"Bad day." Walking up to me, he pushes a stray hair out of my face and cups my jaw. "You seem to make it all better, though. Just like I knew you would," he finishes, thumbing my bottom lip and looking at me intensely. I roll my eyes.

He tilts his head. "Did you just roll your eyes at me, bambolina?" A sly grin comes to his face at catching me out.

"No, why would I do that?" I scoff, throwing my hand up in the air with indifference as I start to walk back to the box I was working on, pretending to be busy to not answer him. But I only make it exactly two steps before he grabs my hand and pulls me back to him, and I slam into his chest.

"Good, because I would hate to have to put you over my knee..." His hand squeezes my ass cheek in warning, and I bite my bottom lip. If anyone else dared say that to me, I would run for the nearest exit, but Nico, he makes me want it. I need to press my thighs together just to settle myself from his light threat, knowing I am in way over my head, and hoping he will never let me drown.

"You wouldn't dare," I challenge him.

"You would like that, wouldn't you? You would like me to roll up my sleeves and turn your pretty skin pink?" I swallow roughly, because he is right; I think I would like that very much.

"You need to focus on work, not me," I say, trying to get out this conversation before he does, in fact, drape me across his knee. Then, we'll be hot and sweaty and moaning all over again.

"Hmmm, boxes first, then. Just wait until tonight, Emilia," he murmurs, before smacking my ass with his hand and leaving me wanting, with a wall full of boxes.

25

NICO

It has been two weeks since I brought her here, and she hasn't left this apartment once. Her head has been buried in boxes from morning to night. I have been here to help her too when I can, but her work ethic is strong, and she was one hundred percent focused on the task. For the most part.

In between sorting through the paperwork, I have had her in my bed, on the sofa, on the desk, on the floor, in the shower, even in the kitchen when I've cooked for her. We have had sex in the morning curled up in the sheets, at noon when I saw the midday sun hitting her hair just the way I like it, and at night, when our eyes are exhausted from looking at the various documents and contracts, yet our bodies ache for the touch of each other. And while my sexual appetite is sated, we have found nothing much else to get us any closer to finding out who is helping her father.

Everything we have found, although excessive, seems to be above board. There are no contracts, notes, his phone logs are clean, no mysterious messages, nothing to indicate if or who he is working with. But I know he is. There *has* to be someone.

We need to access his laptop, something we left to the side, thinking we might find clues to his passwords in the boxes. But we are going to have to brainstorm more for that.

"Arghh! There are still so many boxes left!" she says as she lies back on the floor, sounding exasperated, and I feel guilty. I gave her three orgasms last night and then woke her up with a fourth this morning, so I know her body is craving rest. Although the way she is looking, all relaxed and sultry on the carpet, it makes me want to give her another one.

I say nothing as I walk over to her and pick her up, her soft body automatically tucking into mine.

"They can wait until tomorrow. You need to sleep," I say, noticing she doesn't argue with me, and given it is only early evening and her eyes are already half closed, I figure she will be asleep as soon as her head hits the pillow.

We have been sleeping here in the spare apartment, given the boxes are here, but as soon as the last box is done, I will be taking her to my place. I want her in my space, with me. No longer wanting to keep her purely work-related. We crossed that line a while ago.

As I get to the bedroom, I look at her, about to ask her if she wants a shower, but she is already asleep, in my arms, her body heavy, her breathing consistent. So I put her in the bed, cover her up, and turn off the light.

My phone vibrates in my pocket, and grabbing it, I see

Sofia's name on the screen. She has been calling me nonstop all week, and I haven't spoken with her because I have been so preoccupied with Emilia and the boxes.

"Hey, Sorella," I say quietly as I exit the bedroom and walk back to the main room.

"Finally! Where have you been?" my sister exclaims, like it has been months.

"Busy." I sit on the sofa, looking over the huge amount of work Emilia has done.

"Who is bambolina?" she asks immediately, and I knew it was coming. She heard me speak to Emilia the other week and has been calling me numerous times a day since. It is the first time in my life I have ignored her calls. My mind now only focused on one woman.

"No one you know," I say, leaning back on the sofa, wondering if I should go and join Emilia, yet knowing I probably need to go see Sebastian. He and the boys still trying to work out who our intruder was, but we have no leads, no other indications of who he was and why he was here.

"Have you found a girlfriend, Fratello?" Sofia asks, intrigued and almost in awe.

"Ahh... don't get ahead of yourself, Sofia. It's just someone I know." I try to get her off the topic, resting my head on the back of the sofa and resisting the urge to close my eyes.

"Is she Italian?" Sofia asks hopefully, and I sigh.

"Tell me, how is your writing going?" She loves to write. Poetry, fiction, blogging. You name it, she writes it. Sometimes she publishes, sometimes she doesn't. I think it was because she spent so long in hospital and in treatment that she had a lot of time to daydream, so now she is full of story ideas. It never gets dull seeing her books in the bookstores back home.

She tells me about her latest story, and I listen as best as I can as my body grows weary. Then I'm jolted awake by a hand slapping me on the back of the head.

"Fuck!" I jump up and see Sebastian, Dante, and Carter all standing behind me.

"Sofia, I need to go," I say and hang up quickly as I scowl at all three of them.

"Assholes." I rub my head with my hand. "This is the last thing I need right now. I'm fucking exhausted."

"Or exhausted from fucking?" Carter muses, which pushes him and Dante into fits of laughter as they fall onto the sofa and relax. I swear to God, he has been such a pain in the ass since he met Doc.

"Enough," Sebastian barks out, and we all calm down.

"So, we think he might be from Europe," Sebastian says, sitting in the armchair. Looking at the paperwork surrounding us, the dwindling boxes, he nods in approval at the progress.

"Still nothing from your end?" he asks me, and I shake my head.

"Nothing concrete," I say.

"Shit," Sebastian grits out.

"What makes you think he is from Europe?" Dante asks, pulling us back to Sebastian's discovery about the man who was in our basement weeks ago.

"The guy we caught snooping around our compound didn't speak, so we don't know if he had an accent," I say because that would have been a dead giveaway, and now I think about it, it was probably why he didn't talk at all. Never answered questions, never cried out in pain.

"I have been through everyone who has something of worth who resides in this country, and not one is sticking. If old man Cole is getting money, it has to be from Europe. No one from the Middle East would touch him," Sebastian says, and we nod. It makes sense.

"So where to from here?" Carter asks, looking at Sebastian.

"We wait. There will be more. Be alert," Sebastian says, looking at each of us.

"We are allies with all the families in Europe. It can't be any of them?" I ask Sebastian, the two of us talking with various families all the time. Our bond is strong.

"Never say never, Nico." I feel like he knows more than he is letting on.

"Carter?" I get his attention. "When are Doc and Ivy coming to New York next?"

"Why?" he asks, immediately on guard. His protectiveness over his girls is overwhelming sometimes.

"I thought it might be nice for Emilia to see Doc. Maybe bringing them together may spark some memories that may help bring out new information?" I say, which is true. But I think after seeing everything in the boxes, Emilia would also like to see her niece. They are blood-related, and with no one else as family for her, it might be good for her to spend time with them.

"Fuck me," Carter says, rubbing his temples.

"What?" I bark at him.

"You get your dick wet, and already you are in love," he says, smiling.

"Fuck off," I say, yet don't deny my feelings.

"Fine. I will chat to Doc, and I'll let you know." I smile before I look at Sebastian, and then my smile fades.

"She is our fucking lawyer, so be very fucking careful," he says in warning.

"She is good at her job." I crack my knuckles, not liking the focus on what Emilia and I are because I am not putting a label on us yet.

"I know. She may be here for this project, but if she is as good as I think she is, then we might want to keep her. Don't fuck it up." I nod, letting him know I understand the ramifications.

Because I do. Our mob business is everything, but Emilia is becoming a very close second.

26

NICO

S ebastian and I walk into Esquire, one of our strip clubs. It is one of our less legitimate businesses and a fantastic place for a private meeting. We nod to the security boys at the front door and make our way straight through the main bar.

It is busy tonight. The noise of glasses and ice behind the bar mixes in with the loud music, the atmosphere energetic. Unusually so for mid-week. I look at the line at the bar, then walk past the scantily clad women on the poles, who are doing a roaring trade if the dollar bills at their feet are anything to go by.

I watch them for a beat, their bodies twisting and turning. They are good at their job. Fit, strong, and talented. Obviously easy on the eye, because every man in here is looking right at them. But my eyes glaze over, my mind only on one woman. Who is snoring at home. She has been in my bed for over a month now, and I have no plan on her being anywhere else.

The music turns into a dull thud as we walk out the

back, into the offices to meet our man. Rory is a guy in his mid-forties. Married, with a couple of kids, he has been in the NYPD for decades. He has worked his way up the ranks over the years after being recruited straight out of school, and now is one of their senior detectives. He followed his father's footsteps into the police force, just as his father followed his father. His historical commitment to serve and protect is comical since he has been our main informer and insider for nearly ten years now.

"Rory," Sebastian says, shaking his hand as we see him already in the office, sitting in the soft leather armchair.

"Boys." He stands, taking Sebastian's hand, then mine in a confident shake.

"How's Elaine and the kids?" Sebastian asks.

"Good, Sebastian. Little Tommy got onto the baseball team, so he is excited," Rory says with a grin, clearly a doting dad any other time when not dealing with the mob.

"We will make a donation to the team for the season, Rory. Make sure they have enough money for equipment and things," I tell him, offering our support.

"Thanks, Nico. I appreciate it." He nods as his lips thin. No man likes asking for help, but we know his kids go to a shitty school, so they probably do need more than he's able to provide.

"So what's happening?" Rory asks, as we all take a seat.

"The usual. Tell me, where are you boys looking for Brian Cole?" Rory doesn't know we have him, but probably assumes we do.

"Well, every lead we have has run dry. We are scaling back our investigation. The assumption is he has fled the country. Which was always a strong possibility," Rory says, looking at Sebastian and I, neither of us giving him any indication we know anything different.

"What country?" I push him, wanting to know everything they are doing.

"We think China, but Russia is not out of the question. Of course, we don't want him bad enough to go pushing diplomatic lines. The tension we have with both those countries is not worth enhancing with our need to capture a white-collar criminal such as Cole."

"I need you to keep us informed of anything you find," Sebastian says.

"Of course, Sebastian," Rory says, nodding as I pour us all a glass of whiskey and slide one across the desk to him.

"The Police Chief is closing the cases for Old Doctor Wakeford and Daniel Cole this week too. Everything has officially wrapped up, and it is confirmed as a burglary gone wrong," Rory confirms what we already hoped.

"Good," Sebastian says, nodding.

"I need you to look into something else for me," I say, and Sebastian's head whips to meet mine from where he is sitting at his desk.

Looking at him, he raises his eyebrow in question. This is not something I have discussed with him yet.

"Sure, what do you need?" Rory asks as he sits back in the leather armchair, looking comfortable and relaxed.

"Brian Cole's wife. Her name was Jacqueline. She

died in an apparent car accident about twenty years ago."
I state the facts as I know them.

"Yes. I saw her file when I was going through Brian's case," Rory says, thinking it over.

"I don't think it was a car accident, and I want to know the details." I can see Sebastian eyeing me suspiciously from my peripheral.

"Fine. I will look into it. I will get you the file. Odd..." Rory says, then pauses.

"What?" Sebastian asks him, the two of us now watching his expression shift.

"Well, I looked into that car accident for Doctor Wakeford's wife for you too. They would have happened around the same time, I think..." It's clear his mind is now turning.

"Yes. We know." It isn't a coincidence. I am sure both men colluded at the time. Stupid cops had no idea back then.

"Fine. Anything else?" Rory asks, throwing back the remaining whiskey.

"Not today. Thanks, Rory," Sebastian says, shaking his hand again. I do the same, slipping some cash into his at the same time, making sure he is well paid for his time. Rory now has enough money from us to fund college for both of his children when that time comes. No doubt he will have a very nice Christmas this year as well, because we are generous. A fact I know he appreciates. Our boys walk him out the back of the club to his car. Ensuring he is not seen and is well protected until he is far away from here. He is a good informant, but even now, ten years later, we can't be too careful. Every meeting needs to be timed properly, moving locations regularly and often at the last minute. The logistics of being in the mob are exhausting at times.

As soon as our office door closes, we sit back and Sebastian's eyes are on me.

"Her mother?" he asks.

"Yeah. I think Brian killed her," I state, leaving no room for questions. Wishing I could just torture the man for this information because it would be much easier. But we can't kill him, and he knows it.

"Nico. She is not our priority. Brian Cole is our priority and finding out who is funding him," Sebastian warns me.

"I know. Fuck, I know." I jump up and start to pace the room.

Sebastian leans back in his chair and watches me.

"You need to be careful, Nico. Women make you do stupid things." I stop pacing and look at him.

"I'm fine," I grit out. And I am, but Emilia is like a drug, one I need desperately. All the time. She is consuming me, and I want to let her. I wonder if what I am feeling is normal.

"Looks like it," Sebastian says with a smirk, taking another sip of his whiskey.

"Is she happy playing house in our compound? Are the two of you together, or are you just fucking her? Because, like I've mentioned, I think we should keep her on after this debacle with her father is dealt with. She has some serious skills, skills we could use in the business, so whatever you are doing, you should stop if it's not serious. We don't need complications," Sebastian says, and he is right. She is an asset. A very fucking beautiful asset.

"I am fucking her and not planning on stopping. She is ingrained in me, Sebastian." My heart pulsates in my chest just at the thought of her. Sebastian is the closest I have to a brother, so I look to him for guidance often. Now is one of those times. He watches me, looking for a sign that I am joking, but I am not. I am seriously fucked for this woman.

"How did you handle it all when you first met Goldie?" I ask him. I wasn't around him in the early days. I came into the family just after they met.

"I nearly fucking killed her father. Set her mother up in a financially safe and secure home, redesigned the entire mega club, so I didn't encroach into her gallery, which cost me millions, and purchased a picture of her for over fifty grand... all before I even slept with her." He scoffs, and I smile. Sebastian's foray into his relationship makes me feel normal again.

"Like I said, women make you do stupid things," he repeats, swirling his drink.

"She is finding out a lot of personal information going through the boxes. I just wanted to close one of those loops for her. Make it easier for her," I say before taking a seat again.

"Admirable, but she might have a different opinion of you once she knows her father has been living in our cell right underneath her this past month. No matter how bad he has been to her, he is still her father. Her only living relative. She might hate him, but she might hate you more for lying to her."

Sebastian is right again, of course. Not telling Emilia her father is in our cell is hanging over my head like a dark cloud. But that is mob business. Not any business of hers.

"She only has a few boxes left. We should be finished by tomorrow. I still can't believe we haven't found a fucking thing. Her head has been in those boxes since she arrived at the compound almost two months ago, and nothing." I crack my knuckles in annoyance.

"We are close, Nico. I can feel it. We will know who we are dealing with very soon," Sebastian says, a faraway look on his face.

"And then?" I prod him.

"And then, we end them all."

27

EMILIA

I sit up in bed, the morning sun gleaming on my face, and look next to me. No Nico. The bed linens don't look slept in, and as I reach out and touch the pillow, it is cold. He didn't sleep here last night. My heart skips a beat as I think about where he might be.

We have been together every night since I came here, and while I know this isn't his apartment, I didn't think he would just leave me here on my own. I rub my face as I try to let go of the disappointment. We haven't talked about what this is. If it's casual and purely for fun or something else. I usually don't get attached, no matter how close I get to people. I keep a bit of myself reserved, just for me, my way of staying secure and safe from any potential hurt that may come.

With all my previous boyfriends, it is what broke our connections, because I would never give them my full self. But I broke that rule with Nico, and I didn't even know I was doing it until this moment.

Now I realize he isn't here, and I have no idea where

he is, and my heart feels heavy. I feel sick in my stomach as my mind wanders with made-up scenarios. He could be with someone else. Perhaps he has many women, and I am merely a notch on his bedpost. We have known each other for such a short time, and why I feel this deep connection to him, I have no idea, but that is not to say he feels the same. The sex is great, the hottest I have ever had, but maybe it isn't the same for him.

Whatever we are doing, it is unbalanced. He is in total control, bringing me here, locking me up in the compound for my safety, yet not giving me any way of moving around or leaving of my own accord. I don't like it. I have been independent my entire life. I don't need looking after; I have been doing fine on my own.

I slide out of the bed, my feet hitting the floor, and decide to take a quick shower to wake up properly. Hopefully that'll pull me out of this mental mind battle and bring back the strong, confident woman I know I am. I was out cold last night, slept solidly, and now feel almost back to normal, although I am still sore in places I haven't been for a while.

After a quick shower and fresh clothes, I walk downstairs into the living space and look at the few boxes we have remaining. I stand listening; it is quiet, the quietest it has been in the entire time I have been here. You could hear a pin drop.

I stare at my accomplishment, not believing I have worked through all these boxes. It has been nearly two months since Nico walked into my office, and even though I feel a sense of pride at my work ethic, I feel disappointed we haven't found anything. The case of my father is still unresolved. With nothing else left to do, I grab the first box and pull it to the middle of the room, taking my usual spot on the carpet and opening it up.

This box is really full, and as soon as I pull out a few papers, I already know there is a treasure trove of personal items in here. I steel my nerves, ready for what I might find. I feel fragile today for some reason.

I pull out a stack of photos. Many of my brother Daniel from when he was young to some of him and Catherine when they graduated from med school, both looking so innocent and starry-eyed. I wonder briefly if I should reach out to her, maybe get to know her and my niece Ivy better. We spent a little time together years ago, but without knowing exactly what happened between her and my brother, I am not sure she would want to see me.

That thought makes me nauseous. I chose to move away for college and then drown myself in my career, so much so, I buried my head in the sand, not wanting to know all the things my family did.

But I should have done more. Maybe I should have fought harder to find out where my mother was and what happened to her. I never asked for police reports about the accident or anything. Am I a bad human being for running away from it and not helping? What did my brother do to Catherine and his daughter Ivy? Given he learned from my father, and knowing how my father treated me, I can only assume Ivy was a mere annoyance to him too. That is a hard thing to shake, even after all of these years. I still feel like no one will want me. Up until I met Nico, at least.

There is another photo of my father and his cat, then a few more of what look like business events of some kind from decades ago. All of them flamboyant, opulent, and over the top. It is funny because growing up with him, in the same house, I knew he had money, but I was never privy to it. I had a good education, but I was never spoiled. I stayed out of his way.

I put the photos to one side, my head fuzzy, needing coffee. I hope Nico returns soon because I have no idea how to work the snazzy coffee machine he has.

I pick up a stack of papers next, invoices from a company called Dragonfly Industries based in France. This is interesting. Money, large sums of it on invoices for everything from wine, to foie gras, to parfum. I have no idea what my father would have done with any of this type of stock. He probably likes foie gras, and from what I remember, drank wine, but by the looks of these invoices, he would have to consume a shipping container of it every month. It is excessive.

Grabbing my cell, I search Dragonfly Industries, and images come up showing the insect. I am about to ignore them to keep looking, but one image catches my eye. It is small, red, the wings lines like veins. It would be pretty if it wasn't so... morbid looking.

I stare at it, scorching it into my brain before it hits me. It is the same as the tattoo on the man I saw who was following me. I quickly grab the invoices again, and I begin to wonder if France is the international spot my father has got his millions from. Perhaps he sold this product, put a hefty markup on it, and gouged the market, making millions in the process. It sounds too easy and simple, but it is a possibility.

I click back to my search and scour the internet for the same image, seeing if I can find anything, but nothing comes up. Staring at the ceiling, I will my brain to work faster, wondering how they are all connected, because they have to be.

But why is Dragonfly man following me? What do I have to do with it all?

I need to go to my office. I need time to think. Being stuck here in a space that is not my own is not helping.

"Good morning, how did you sleep?" Nico asks, standing in the door, and I jump a little, having had no idea he was there.

"Hi," I say with a small smile, glad to see him, before I school it and mentally scold myself for being too eager. "I slept fine, you?"

"Fine. I slept in my apartment last night," he says, watching me. I feel my brow furrowing in question, before I shake it off. "What's going on? You're jumpy, fidgety. Did something happen?" I need to learn to hide my feelings better. It is 101 at law school, and my training is all out of the window in front of this man.

I let out the breath I am holding, feeling delicate. *It is just sex, Emi*, I say to myself over and over. Great sex. Lots of sex, but it's no need to go developing any serious feelings. The pull I have been feeling is obviously hormonal. No one can fall for a guy so soon, can they?

"Nothing. Just tired," I say, trying to relax my face and seem genuine.

"I'll go make us some coffee," he says before turning

and walking to the kitchen. I sigh. I need girlfriends, I need to vent.

I start to pack up the contents of the box, knowing I should quickly look through the last one before I see if I can leave. Again, my head is buried, and I am packing up the final box when Nico returns.

"Here." He gives me a coffee, and after a small sip, I can feel my world balancing out just a little bit more.

"I want to go home," I say to him, a little harsher than I wanted, but word vomit is my specialty.

"Why?" he asks, and my eyebrows raise.

"I need time. I need time to process what we have and haven't found, and I need to be in my space to do it," I state, keeping it professional. God, I was so stupid to actually get so deeply involved with him.

"Bambolina," he says as he takes a step toward me, and my heart melts a little at the pet name.

"It's fine." I take a step back, putting my hand up, and he stills. His head tilts, like he is trying to figure me out.

"What happened? Something has happened?" His tone is a little more forceful, and my stomach feels like it is going to come out of my throat.

"I'm just tired, and I really need to be in my own space. I have been here for over a month. I need fresh air, my own things, my own environment." His eyes crease as he looks at me.

"Okay," he says, nodding, yet I know he doesn't believe me.

"Okay?" I ask in reply, wanting to make sure I heard him correctly and he doesn't place any caveats on me.

"Yes, bambolina. It's been a big project. You work too

hard, and I have been keeping you awake too much. I understand. But we are not finished here. I want to know your thoughts on the boxes and then we need to tackle his laptop." I am surprised at his genuine concern, my chest warming before I tamp it down.

"I also want to take you to my own apartment. Now the boxes are done, we don't need to stay here in this one. I want you with me," he adds, and my heart almost stops. I want that too. I want to be with him, but my mind is such a mix of emotions, I can't get a grip on things.

I am speechless for a moment. I have spent all morning thinking he just wanted me for sex and now he is saying he wants me in his space, in his apartment. He wants me.

"Make no mistake, bambolina," he says, coming closer to me slowly, like he knows what I am thinking. "You are mine. You work for me, but your body is mine as well, as is your brain, and your smart pouty mouth. Maybe your heart too. I will organize Tony to drive you. You go and get your things sorted and have a break today, because tonight I want you all to myself." Grabbing his cell from his pocket, he walks back out the door.

I don't like her not being with me, but I can tell she needs to think. She was off this morning, and I don't know why. Sitting with her in the back of the car as we drive to her office, I crack my knuckles, not liking that she is hiding something from me. She remains quiet, her body rigid, and I hope the day away from each other helps her with whatever is going on in that head of hers.

I don't want to argue with her or upset her. But I can't stop myself from asking again before she's out of my reach.

"Is there something wrong, bambolina?" I ask, stroking her hand with my thumb as she grips mine tightly. I clench my jaw, wanting to demand answers, but knowing that won't help the situation right now.

"No, nothing," she says with a huff like I am annoying her, which does little to make me feel better.

"I'm just sad to see Cindy go off to the other side of the world. It's a big trip!" There may be some truth to that, but I know that isn't everything. I nod in understanding and let her be.

Tony pulls up outside her office. The city is busy as usual, and I look up and down the sidewalk before I step out. It is a habit us boys have. Always to be aware of our surroundings. I stand and lean into the car, offering my hand to Emilia. She takes it, and I squeeze her hand in mine, before pulling her inside and taking the elevator up to her floor.

"You don't have to come all the way up," she says, and I scowl. *Why is she giving me the brush off?*

"What is going on? Did you find something in the boxes?" I ask, coming to the conclusion she must have spotted something. What else could have caused this change in demeanor?

"No, I mean... maybe. I don't know." Her face scrunches up in frustration.

"What did you find?" I press, now intrigued.

"I just saw some paperwork that made me think of something. But I can't connect the dots yet." Her answer is cryptic, and I don't like it.

"Tell me what you saw." It's not a question.

She sighs, the weight of the world on her shoulders. "Invoices. They didn't look right, but I can't reconcile them until I go through the paperwork again to see if they match up with any other inventory." While the words make sense in theory, I know there is much more to it. Before I can push her further, the elevator stops and the doors open to her floor. Cindy's excited greeting halts my questioning for now.

"Hi, guys!" Cindy says happily, and given she will be

on a plane tomorrow, I am sure she is excited to take her big trip.

"Hi!" Emilia says, just as upbeat. "I am popping in for a bit because I wanted to see you before you go!" The two of them chirp on for a moment, and I wonder how long it will take her to notice the tall, dark, menacing soldier at her office door. I have no problem with her needing to have space to think and work from her office or apartment, but there is no way she is doing it without protection.

I stand back, my hands in my pockets, watching her and Cindy chat, their eyes wide, their excitement palpable. I side-eye the soldier who is standing firm.

"What the hell?" I hear Emilia screech. It took less than ten seconds. "Nico!" she groans, whipping around to look at me. I frustrate her even more by remaining casual in my stance.

"I don't need a bodyguard!" She's now facing me, her hands on her hips, and I feel relief because she is at least now back to normal.

"Yes, you do."

"I do not!" she retorts.

"Yes. You. Do," I say with more grit, aware Cindy is watching this whole interaction.

"Urghh." She spins on her heel and stomps past Romero, our young soldier, and into her office.

Cindy looks at me, wide-eyed.

"Is she only this frustrating to me?" I ask Cindy, whose face softens into a smile, and then she nods.

"Good to know," I reply before I strut into Emilia's office after her, closing the door behind me.

"Nico, I do not need a man standing right outside my office door," she huffs, trying to remain calm when I know all she wants to do is explode.

"Need I remind you that you work for the mob now. You need protection, and I can't be with you all of the time."

"I seriously don't need a babysitter. It's ridiculous." Oh well. I am not budging.

I walk toward her, pushing her body with mine until she backs up to her desk. Looking down at her, she is breathing heavily, her perfect breasts lifting up and down, begging to be in my mouth. She still doesn't seem to understand, and I am about to make it very fucking clear to her. I watch her swallow before I put my hand up and cup her around the back of the neck, forcing her eyes on me.

"Bambolina, you need to start doing what you are told," I grit out.

"Or what?" she replies, and my nostrils flare. She is really pushing my buttons today.

"Do you need something to calm you down?" I ask as my other hand begins to trail up her thigh.

"I don't need looking after. You won't be my boss for much longer anyway." Her words are firm, but I feel her body start to cave for me.

"You are mine, bambolina, and whether you like it or not, I am going to have a soldier on you to protect you when I am not with you." I lean over and brush my lips across hers.

"You're serious?" she asks, seemingly shocked that I want to look after her.

"Yes. I thought I made that very clear to you already." If she has doubts, I am happy to erase them. She looks at me for a beat, like she is trying to understand the declaration I've already made.

"Nico, if you don't mean the words, please don't say them." Now it is my turn to be surprised.

"I mean every damn word I say to you. And I know you know that. No other man has looked after you or cared for you, but when I tell you that you are mine, I fucking mean it. Now get to work, and sort out what's in that head of yours, so I can have you in my bed tonight." I press a kiss to her head, then her lips.

"You are a pain in my ass," she says as her body softens into mine, and I smile, glad that she understands exactly what I want.

"That can be arranged..." I say, making her blush, before I step back and walk toward the door.

"Take him with you, wherever you go, and he will bring you back to me later. Call me with anything." She just nods, still holding the desk white knuckled with both hands, and I leave feeling no more settled than I did before, but happy her mood is lighter.

29

EMILIA

Watching Nico close my office door, I finally take a breath. I was a bitch to him this morning, no doubt, but my feelings and emotions are all over the place. I put it down to not enough sleep and the daily dredging of my father's life. The snippets of my history that are starting to become exposed aren't the easiest to digest.

Sighing, I walk over to the window, feeling the stress of the past few weeks slowly lift from my shoulders, now I have peace and quiet and I am in my own space. There is so much for me to think through and unpack. But the urgency I have is not with my father's financial circumstances, but with my mother.

"Emi." Cindy knocks on my door before entering. "I just need to go to drugstore. Do you need anything?" she asks me, and I am about to decline when a new thought enters my head.

"You know what, I will come with you. I need to go for

a walk and get some fresh air," I say, grabbing my handbag.

"Great, I will just put the phone on the voicemail," she says and I go out to tackle my babysitter.

"Hi. I need to go out," I say to the man standing near my door. "I need to run some errands."

"Fine. We have a car downstairs." I shake my head.

"No, Cindy and I are walking. You can stay here. We are just going around the corner to the drugstore." I fully expect him to do as I ask as I head to grab the elevator.

"What's your name?" I ask him to fill in the void as I wait for Cindy.

"Romero," he says, pulling out his phone.

"Are you reporting my movements to Nico?" I ask, my eyebrow rising in challenge.

"Yes. It is my job. It is at his request to know where you are at all times."

"Fine. Tell him I'm with Cindy running errands," I say without any further commentary, knowing I need to pick my battles and this is one I am not going to win.

The three of us get into the lift comically, Cindy giving me a side-eye and Romero ignoring us completely. I am sure when he joined the mob, babysitting someone like me was not on his list of priorities, but Nico obviously has other plans.

"Tell me again what countries you are visiting," I ask Cindy, keen to get some of her excitement into my weary bones.

"Well, we fly to London and are staying for a week. I want to visit Buckingham Palace and see Big Ben, then we will take the train to Paris!" I smile at the look on her face.

"Tell me about France. What are your plans there?" I ask, my ears now clearly attuned to every word coming from her mouth.

"A few nights in Paris, to see the Louvre, Eiffel Tower and go to the Moulin Rouge, and then we are heading South on the train to the Mediterranean. There is this large chateau right on the water called Dragonfly, which apparently has views of the water that are amazing. It's the best place to watch the sunset, but it gets booked months in advance, so we don't have access yet. We are hoping to go for lunch when we are there." My heart skips.

"Dragonfly? I haven't heard of them before. Tell me about them?" We step out of the building and into the hustle and bustle of the city pedestrians. My eyes are looking everywhere, my ears firmly hanging on every word Cindy says.

"Oh, well, I am not really into wine myself, but George loves red and supposedly, they have one of the best. We just wanted to check them out. We didn't realize how beautiful their chateau was because they never advertise and don't have a website. But we saw a photo of it that one of our friends took last year on their travels and they highly recommended it. It has a casino and everything!" I feel like I am going to faint.

This is obviously the winery my father did business with. Why are all these places now suddenly being pushed at me, when over a month ago, I had heard of none of them.

"Sounds lovely," I say to Cindy with a smile.

"Are you all right, Emi?" Cindy asks me, looking concerned. "You look a little pale." She grabs me by the elbow and pulls me with her into the drugstore.

"Fine, just tired." I wave my hand around nonchalantly as we go inside.

Romero stays outside the store, not willing to look over the makeup and female products we are here to pursue. Remembering I need to grab some tampons, I leave Cindy to look over her sunscreen options and make my way to the feminine hygiene section. As I stand there, I do a rough calculation in my head of when my period is due, and my fingernails dig into my palm when I realize it was weeks ago. With everything that has been happening, I hadn't even thought about it. My daily interactions with the mob and Nico have had me so preoccupied, my monthly is not something I've given any attention to.

I have never been late, and while I can attribute it to the hectic pace my life has undertaken this month, a deep brick of realization is sitting in my stomach as I hear Nico's words in my head.

We will be more careful next time. It was only one time... we will be okay.

My eyes flick to the pregnancy tests and, along with a box of tampons, I grab the early test kit. The one that can test for ultra-early results, and I swallow the bile that is rising in my throat.

I can't be. It would be literally a one in a million chance. The one time in my entire life that I have had sex without some form of protection. I am now cursing myself for going off the pill six months ago, something I chose to do at the time because I wasn't sexually active and I wanted to give my body a break.

Nico coming into my life was unexpected and my desire for him even more so.

Yet here I stand, at the cashier, with both a box of tampons and a pregnancy test, silently praying she puts them in a brown paper bag and quickly before Cindy or Romero notice anything.

"Did you get everything you need?" Cindy asks, just as I grab the paper bag from the cashier.

"Yes. You?" I ask, giving her my best fake smile, even though I am dying inside.

"Did you know that they have this amazing spray on sunscreen now? I can't wait to lie on the beach in Greece and fall asleep in the afternoon sun under those big beach umbrellas!" she gushes as we walk back to the office.

"Cindy, why don't you pack up now and leave work early. We don't have anything on and I am sure you have a million things to do before your flight leaves tomorrow," I say to her as we approach the front of our building.

"Are you sure?" she asks, but the smile on her face tells me she is really keen to start her holiday now.

"Go. Have a wonderful time away, please stay safe, and I can't wait to hear all about your trip when you get back!" I wrap my arms around her shoulders and give her a hug goodbye. I am glad she gets to take this trip of a lifetime, but I'm sad I won't see her for six weeks.

"I will bring you back a souvenir from Paris!" she exclaims happily, and my breath hitches. Paris. If the universe is trying to tell me something, it is starting to become very clear.

I wave as she continues walking to the subway, then I turn to Romero.

"Can you take me back to the compound now? I need to get back to work."

He nods, and within moments, I am in the backseat of a blackened car, my only mode of transport these past weeks, wondering not for the first time what the hell I am doing in my life. As I sit in silence and watch the world flash past, I rest my hand on my stomach and think about options and what ifs. Am I pregnant? If I am, what will Nico think? What will we do? Do I even tell him?

Suddenly changing my name and moving to Mexico to make jewelry on the beach doesn't sound like such a silly idea after all.

30

NICO

Leaving her with Romero for the day is making me as comfortable as sitting on a cactus, but she needs space, and I need to show her I can give her that. In our professional relationship, I know she is a good lawyer, and if we want to keep her, then we need to trust her and she needs to trust us. Trust me.

While the boys and I are sitting around, looking through a few of the more important documents Emilia found, I grab my phone.

Romero sent me a text a while ago saying they were running errands with Cindy, and I am keen for an update. Even though that was only thirty minutes ago.

"So, who do we know in Europe who has pockets deep enough to be funding his role into the senate?" I ask as I pocket my phone again, looking at Dante and Sebastian. They would have a better idea than anyone who we might be dealing with.

"There is the Karra family in Greece, but we periodically check in with them, so I know it can't be them," Dante says, glancing at Sebastian for confirmation.

"I wouldn't put anything past the Greeks, so don't count them out just yet," he says, gritting his teeth, clearly knowing something we don't.

"What about the Moreau family in France? What are they up to?" Dante counters, and Sebastian's eyebrows rise.

"They are quiet as of late, but quiet is not always a good thing..." Sebastian says, again giving us nothing to go on.

"What are those Sutherland boys doing in London lately?" I ask. Those boys are always in trouble.

"It isn't them," Dante says quickly. "I spoke with them last week. They are busy trying to land grab from the Irish at the moment." We all nod.

"The only other ones that are capable of this level of business, then, are the Danes," Carter says, and we all nod once more in agreeance.

The Danish are tough, tougher than most, but I can't see them wanting anything to do with an American businessman such as Brian Cole. It isn't really their style.

Sebastian shakes his head. "I'll put in some calls. I can get our boys in Sicily to start asking around," he says, standing, knowing we haven't got any other leads. The frustration of the situation festers in all of us.

My cell vibrates then, and I look down at it. Romero is on his way back, and I am surprised. She was gone less than a few hours, much quicker than I was expecting, but I am happy about it just the same.

"I'm going to the apartment. I want to check on the

last few boxes Emilia did this morning." I have checked every box she has opened. Some better than others, but I trust her to tell me anything she has found, no matter how small or insignificant she thinks it is. After her behavior this morning, though, something definitely is not right. I hope by looking through this morning's boxes, I will find a clue that may help me piece it together.

"Doc and Ivy are on their way here, so I will get them settled and see you later," Carter says, walking out the door.

"I will call you if we need you," Sebastian says to Carter and I. "Dante, come with me to make these calls. Let's see what we can find out." Sebastian dismisses the meeting, and we all walk out and go our separate ways.

In the apartment, I grab the two boxes and start to sort through them. There has to be something here that upset her, something that would explain why she needed space.

I could have made her tell me, but I know how far I can push her, and today wasn't a day for that.

I see invoices, photos, and random paperwork, but nothing significant. Nothing that stands out. It must be the photos, all of her brother. I wonder if he laid a hand on her... the urge to hurt him comes on strong, even though he is already dead.

Sitting on the sofa, I put my head in my hands and think. I know it must be a lot, going through these boxes, but I am sure there is something I am missing. And then it clicks. I didn't stay with her last night. At the time, I thought I was doing the right thing, letting her sleep while I worked half the night and then fell into bed in my own apartment so as not to wake her, but now I am thinking that her waking up without me might be the reason she feels unsettled.

I stay with that thought for a moment, and let it roll over in my mind. I hear Sebastian's words in the back of my mind to ensure business before pleasure, to keep her focused. But I like that she wants to be with me, feels better in my presence, and my desire for her continues to grow every day. My heart tugs for hers. For years, I have dated, met women, fucked them, and none of them even come close to the feelings I have building in my chest for Emilia.

I look at my watch and decide to go to the basement garage to meet her, see how she is, and bring her back here. We have a lot to talk about.

Downstairs, I run into Carter. Doc and Ivy have just arrived, and he is grabbing their bags.

"Need some help?" I ask him, because the girls do not pack light when they come to New York. He shakes his head, and I see Emilia's car pull up behind him. Opening her back door, I give her my hand and help her out.

"Hey," she says quietly, and she looks exhausted. Like she needs to sleep for a hundred years. The guilt at having her work so hard festers inside my gut.

"Hey, bambolina," I say softly, just for her.

"Emilia?" a voice pipes up beside us as we both turn, startled.

"Catherine?" Emilia's eyes go wide at seeing her brother's ex standing right next to her.

"Oh my God!" Doc says and grabs Emilia, pulling her away from me and into her chest, hugging her close. My eyes catch Carter's over the top of their heads, the two of us watching the interaction closely, not certain how it will go, but relieved it's seeming to start well.

"What are you doing here?" Doc asks, bewildered, and Emilia looks at me. When I glance at Carter, Doc whips her head around to him... and if looks could kill.

"I didn't know you were here, otherwise, I would have seen you sooner," Doc states as Ivy comes up to stand near her.

"Hi, Aunt Emi," Ivy says, a little reserved, but certainly with familiarity, which is interesting.

Emilia looks at her for a moment, and I notice her face going a little pale as she stares at the small girl. Her breathing quickens, so I rub my thumb on her hand and give it a little squeeze, but she is not paying attention to me.

"Did you know a butterfly can fly up to twelve miles per hour?" Emilia whispers to her, and the two of them stare at each other in silent awe. My gaze flicks to Carter and Doc, and they look a little shocked too. I look back to Emilia, who is now shaking, her whole demeanor changing instantly as soon as she sees Ivy.

Ivy nods. "Did you know that butterflies use their feet to taste?" Ivy asks in a whispered return.

Emilia lets out a little gasp, then falls to her knees, and Ivy runs to her, slamming into her chest. The two of them hold each other while the rest of us look at one another, wondering what the hell is going on.

31

EMILIA

Ivy has grown up so much since I saw her as a toddler. I feel overwhelmed. The sight of both her and Catherine setting off memories in my mind that were long buried. She holds my hand now, leading me through the corridors of the compound, a place she appears to know well, as Catherine watches us closely, and Nico and Carter take us to their apartment.

No one knows about the connection Ivy and I have, and now seeing her again, even though it has been years, it is as vivid now as it was back then.

"We're here!" Ivy says, and we walk into an amazing apartment, one just as luxurious as where I have been staying. But this one a little more lived in, with trinkets, photos, and colorful drawings on the fridge, no doubt Ivy's work.

"I think we need to talk. Let's go sit in the living room," Catherine says, and I nod as I follow her and Ivy into the living room, which is a large open-plan space, something that looks like it came directly from a Hamptons mansion.

"How have you been?" Catherine asks me, and I feel my stomach drop.

"Cat, I am so sorry..." I start to say. The guilt I feel for not doing anything to stop my father and brother from hurting her for all those years is eating away at me, even more now that I am looking her in the eye.

"It was not your fault. You were young, only a teenager, what could you have done?" Cat implores, grabbing my hand as young Ivy looks on. When I look at her, she gives me a soft smile.

"But I should have." Instead of going straight to help them, I didn't even look in their direction. I kept focused on work and drowned myself in it in the process, trying to remove myself from the misery of my family and keep them at arm's length.

"Emi, no. This is not on you. This is not your burden to carry. What Daniel did, what your father has done, is not on you. You were right to stay away because they would have hurt you too," Cat says, gripping onto my hand with hers, the two of us now with silent tears running down our cheeks. I feel the pain. Deep in my chest. I know my father would have hurt me too, and as long as I was away from him and kept my head down, he forgot about me. Everyone forgot about me. It was safer that way.

"What was with the animal fact earlier?" a man asks, and I assume it is Carter. Nico having mentioned he was who Cat was with now. I look at him for a moment, startled, because he is huge. Like, really big. Someone you would immediately walk in another direction to avoid. His face is not mean, but he seems certainly inquisitive.

"What do you mean?" I say, confused for a moment as Nico comes and sits next to me on the sofa, taking my other hand in his. I feel immediately more comfortable now, even though all eyes are on me.

"In the garage, you saw Ivy and immediately talked about a butterfly," Carter elaborates.

I feel my breathing quicken, my memories going back to a place I often retreated to as a child and teenager to escape the loud voices, the yelling and thumps I would often hear.

I clear my throat and I start to become a little emotional.

"Well, when I was younger, I would try to stay away from my father and brother as much as possible. Out of sight, out of mind kind of thing," I say, looking up at everyone. Nico squeezes my hand, so I take a deep breath and continue.

"One of the things I used to do is bury my head in books. As I got older, I read a lot of nonfiction books in relation to animals. I am not sure why, but I gravitated toward them and often found myself repeating weird animal facts all the time to escape the reality of my everyday life," I say, and both Carter and Cat are a little wide-eyed, so I continue.

"Often there would be people over, men, a lot of men, and I would lock myself away. They got really rowdy after a few drinks. I was scared a lot of the time." I think back to the few nights when men came looking for me. Those were the scariest nights of all. I feel Nico stiffen a little beside me, and I realize I haven't opened up like this to anyone. No one knows my history, and while I am not going to relive all of it, I will tell them what I think is relevant for Ivy.

"I would hide and recite animal facts over and over to myself, so I could tune out my fear and help ignore the yelling. I guess it was my survival mechanism. One day, Cat, you were over at the house with Daniel, and you both were fighting. He was being really mean, and Ivy must have been only three or four. It was one of only a few times I was home from college. I found her hiding in one of the upstairs bedrooms, so I sat on the floor with her and told her whenever I get scared, I read animal books, and I gave her one I used to read as a child. Together, we sat there in the room and looked through the book and memorized all the facts until the yelling calmed down and I brought her back downstairs to you. I think that was the last time I saw either of you." A lone tear runs down my cheek as I finish.

"Ivy, is that what started your weird animal fact obsession? You used it to help you when you got scared?" Carter asks Ivy, and she nods her head.

"Now I just like animals, but yeah, I would lay in bed sometimes, and during storms I would cover my head and repeat them over and over until the storm went away," Ivy says, and it both warms my heart and breaks it that she took a little piece of me with her.

"Cat, I am not sure of all the details of what my brother and father did to you and Ivy, but please know that if I did, I would have helped. I should have helped." My poor excuse for an apology falls from my lips.

"Well, you're here now, and I am sure glad you are okay too," Cat says, pulling me into another hug. Ivy joins in too, and another tear falls as a feeling of warmth overtakes me. This must be what it's like to have a family.

"Carter and I are going to go and do some work. Leave you girls to chat for a while. I will come back and get you later," Nico says, and I look up at the man who, despite my reservations, has done nothing but offer me a glimpse into the life I tried so hard to ignore. Although it is a bitter pill to swallow, I owe him a debt of gratitude for letting me sift through all those boxes and help me heal, even if it is just a little.

"Okay," I whisper to him and he leans over, kissing me briefing on the lips before walking out with Carter following him.

"Okay, so I need coffee. Ivy, do you want to go upstairs and watch a movie? Aunt Emi and I have a lot of catching up to do, and I am really interested to know why she is here and why Uncle Nico was kissing her just now," Cat says to Ivy, but looking at me with glee in her eyes, and I blush. This is all new to me. Sharing my life, my thoughts and feelings. But Cat knows a lot of the dirty secrets of my upbringing and has no judgment. I feel safe to talk to her about it all. Almost as safe as I feel telling my mother.

"Yes!" Ivy fist bumps. "I'm going to watch Frozen," she yells, already halfway down the hall, going to her room. I laugh at her enthusiasm, and it feels good to laugh. I haven't in a long time, and I really want to do it more.

"So," Cat says as she pulls me up off the sofa and into the kitchen to get the coffee. "I want to know everything!"

And as I stand watching her in the kitchen, grabbing

chocolates and getting the coffee, I feel at peace for the first time ever.

"So, you live here?" I ask, changing the subject while we both wipe the tears from our cheeks.

"Sometimes, or at least we stay here with Carter whenever we come to New York." I know she is in love from the smile on her face.

"I have so many questions," I say, feeling over-whelmed.

"We have plenty of time now," Cat says, handing me a coffee.

"All this time, I wondered where Ivy got these weird animal facts from, and it was you!"

"Sorry!" I can't help but cringe, not sure if this is something I should have done.

"Oh my God, stop apologizing! We have so much to catch up on." We both take a seat back on the sofa.

"Perhaps we can start here? What can you tell me about the boys?" I ask, needing all the information, and I see a smile come to her lips.

"Carter saved me. Just like Nico will save you," she says, tone full of confidence, giving me a wink. My breath gets stuck for a moment, before I release it slowly.

"I work for them. My law firm went down the drain once Dad got caught. So even though I kept my distance, I was still in the firing line of his activities and he pretty much ruined any chance I have of ever practicing again," I say solemnly.

"I'm sorry that happened to you. I know how hard you have worked all these years in your career. It's funny, something similar happened to me," Cat says before she tells me a little about changing her path from Emergency Department Head to now working in Carter's gym. "So I still put my medical career to good use; I just do it in a different way, and let me tell you, Emi, I am so happy. I never knew life could feel like this." She sips on her coffee. "Nico has certainly taken a liking to you..."

"We get along well. I just don't know if it is just casual or something more," I say honestly, with a small shrug.

"Well, I haven't known him long, but I have never known Nico to have a girl here at the compound. In fact, I have never seen him with a woman. So the fact that you are here, and he is kissing you in front of everyone, I would say that he is pretty into you," she says, grinning.

"But what does that mean? These men are the mob, Cat! They are dangerous, deadly, caught up in so many illegal things... I don't even want to think about it." I run my hands over my face, my brain constantly misfiring and competing with a range of emotions and information.

"Look, they do what they need to do. We don't get caught in their business. They look after us. Sebastian treats us all like family. Goldie, his wife, is amazing, and Carter, well, Carter would burn the world down for Ivy and me. No man has ever offered me even a slice of something like that before." She is right. I feel the same way about Nico, like he would do anything for me.

"I guess this is a big fork in the road for me. A career change, a new love interest. I had my entire life planned. I was so sure running a law firm; looking after the good guys was exactly where I was supposed to be. I hadn't even thought about a boyfriend or anything else for years. Now I am practically living in the mob compound, sleeping with a mobster." When I say it all out loud, it is a lot.

"Well, I am not going to tell you what to do. It is your life, and how you chose to live it is your decision, but I will say that sometimes you need to push through the pain to get to the pleasure. And let me tell you, Emi, it is so good once you get to the other side," Cat says, her eyes glistening, a smile on her face.

"I'm not sure happiness is something a girl like me is supposed to ever get. I wasn't raised to expect anything like that and, to be honest, I think some people are just destined for a different life. A harder life. And I think I am one of those people," I whisper out my thoughts, not wanting them to be true, but the realist in me knows I am probably right.

"Everyone deserves happiness, Emi. Especially you."

I hope she's right.

32

NICO

I left her with Doc for the rest of the afternoon, and now, as I take her by the hand and lead her through the hallways, she seems to be feeling much better.

"Where are we going?" she asks, obviously now clued in on the fact that we are not going to the usual apartment.

"My place."

"Oh," is all she says, then remains quiet for a beat.

"Why?" she asks tentatively, which is unlike her, and I stop. Turning, I face her.

"Because I want you with me. I want you with me all of the fucking time. I had one night away from you last night because I was working late with Sebastian, but I slept like shit because you weren't next to me and in my arms." I bring my hand to her waist and pull her to me. Her frame leans against mine, her hands coming up and resting on my chest. I hear her hold her breath as her eyes search mine.

"I have no idea what is happening between us, we only just met, but there is no way I want to be without you, and no way I am letting you leave," I say, grinding my teeth together, waiting to see what she does.

"Is that so?" she replies, her mouth turning upward slightly, and I can see that I won. Her hands grip my shirt as she adds, "You are so bossy."

"Come on, before I fuck you up against this wall for the entire compound to see," I say, stepping back, grabbing her hand again and walking toward my apartment, now itching to get there. I step through my door and pull her in, locking the door behind me.

"Wow..." she says in awe as she looks around.

"You like it?" I stand behind her, watching her take a few small steps farther inside.

"This is insane!" she says, her eyes wide.

"It's a little different from the others..." I trail off, because my apartment is very different from what the other boys have. My space is like a large warehouse conversion. Everything is open on the bottom floor; the living room, kitchen, dining, and office are all open spaces with no walls, no doors.

I can roam around, do my work, and see everything from wherever I stand. Stairs at the back take us up to my private area, including the bedrooms, bathrooms, another private office, and library. Where downstairs is open and industrial, upstairs has a more homey feel, with cream linens and rugs, making it feel warm and inviting.

"This is amazing. I have never seen anything like it," she says, as she walks up the stairs, wandering around my place. If it was anyone else, I would have stopped them by now. Even my sister has only seen it all once. But I let Emilia roam. I want her to feel comfortable, to feel at home.

"Nico, did you design this?" she asks, as she peeks into one of the bedrooms, before she continues walking down the hall to the master at the end.

"Yeah, Sebastian lets us all manage our own space. I like the industrial warehouse look. It's very New York, but I also crave the comforts of home, so I decided to mix the two."

"Oh my God," she breathes as she opens the door to the master bedroom and steps inside. It is big, with a retreat at one end, housing a sofa and armchair with a TV. I have an oversized bathroom off to the side and a walk-in wardrobe hidden at the back. The bed is big, too big just for me, but as she walks through, it is the view that has her attention.

One whole wall is a floor-to-ceiling window overlooking the courtyard we have in the middle of the compound. It is like a park, actually, lush and green, with my sitting area right in front of it, so I still have my privacy, but can sit in my armchair and think while looking out at the world.

"This is beautiful." She moves to the wardrobe, and I wonder how long it will take for her to notice.

"Nico?" She stops, still as a bird, and I watch her, waiting for her reaction.

"All my clothes are here, already hanging up?" she says in question, as she looks at me, slightly confused.

"Like I said, I want you with me now." I walk up to her and hold her from behind, and she leans back into me.

"Nico, I don't know…" she says softly. I run my hands up and down her body, searching her face, knowing that this is something she wants, yet she is still trying to be independent because that is all she has ever known.

"Let's just try it out, bambolina," I say as my lips find her neck and kiss her, my tongue tasting her skin, and she lets out a sigh, relaxing into my grip.

"Okay," she whispers to me.

"Okay?" I question her, needing to hear it from her correctly.

"Yes, Nico, I will stay here with you. Permanently." Her acceptance comes without her usual sass, and I spin her in my arms and find her mouth, kissing her until we're both breathless. Gripping her waist, I pull her body flush with mine. I feel her hands curl around my neck, and I walk her back until her shoulders hit the wall.

Pulling away, I look at her. "I want to take my time with you today." Then I drop to my knees in front of her.

"If this is what you are like when I leave you for a few hours, what is it going to be like when I am gone longer?" she whispers, smiling, watching me as I reach up and drag her jeans and underwear down her legs, skimming her skin with my hands as I do.

"I don't plan on ever letting you go." I lean in and kiss her on her hipbone, as my hands run up her thighs, then I grab her knee and lift her leg over my shoulder.

"Now lean back. I want to taste you," I growl, not wanting her to be anywhere other than my apartment, naked, just for me. I brush my lips across her skin, making my way slowly from her hip to her sex, and I flick my tongue across her, feeling her warm and wet.

"You are insatiable," she murmurs, her breath hitching as my tongue glides across her center.

"I fucking love the way you taste," I murmur in response, her skin sweet like rose flavored dessert made just for me.

"You are so good with your mouth." Her breathing is getting faster as her hands come up and run through my hair, her fingers tools of magic as she massages my scalp. Any tension I had disappears as I move my tongue deeper into her.

"Nico…" she whimpers, as my lips kiss and my tongue licks in tandem, and I feel her relax even more. I decide then and there this is where I want to be buried when I die.

"Bambolina, you are so wet for me," I say as I lick her, savoring every drop she's giving me.

"Always for you…" she breathes out, her lips rocking slightly, telling me she wants more, as her hands continue to run over my scalp.

I move my hands down her thighs to her knees, and I open her right up to me, wanting to have all of her.

"You are so beautiful, glistening for me like this," I say, my thumb caressing her clit, just how I know she likes it.

I flatten my tongue and swipe, trailing my fingers down before one enters her warm, wet core.

"More. I want more," she begs, her voice pitching upwards, and so I put in a second one while my tongue continues to lick and suck her clit. I find a rhythm then, a soft, sultry rhythm, as I slowly tease her, her hips rocking against my face, her fingers digging in a little more into my hair, her orgasm slowly building.

"I want you to fuck my face, Emilia," I say, urging her to take what she needs, even though I am so hard it is killing me. She pushes me into her a little more as her hips grind, and her body begins to shudder as her release washes over her.

"Nico, I can't!" she pants out my name, her body jerking, my fingers and tongue continuing their assault. I feel her come on my tongue and I lick her, over and over, not wanting to stop.

Her grip in my hair loosens, and I hear her breathless, so I slowly remove my fingers and inch my way back up her body, pressing kisses all over her, my hands following, needing to touch every inch of her beautiful body.

"That was amazing," she whispers out, her hand splayed across her forehead, a small blush to her face and neck.

"I like making you come," I say, and she grins, but my look remains deadly, because I haven't finished with her yet.

I stand in front of her, letting her catch her breath as I unbutton my shirt. I watch her eyes travel over my bare chest as I sweep the shirt from my shoulders.

"Tell me about your tattoos?" she asks, lifting her hand to my chest, letting her fingers trace the myriad of lines and drawings on my body. It feels good to have her hands on me.

"What's this one?" Her fingers trace the lines jumping up and down on my upper arm.

I lean over and unbutton her shirt. "That one is my sister's heartbeat." Her eyes flick to mine as I push her shirt off her shoulders and throw it on the floor, and take her in, now only in her bra, before I kiss her softly.

"She was sick for a long time. One time she was really bad, and we thought it was the end, so I grabbed her heartbeat from the monitor and put it on my skin so I would always remember."

"What about this one?" she asks, as her fingers trace my forearm as I unbutton my jeans and push them down my legs before doing the same with my underwear, her eyes honing in on my cock, which is already hard and throbbing for her.

"That one is the time of my birth." I am talking about the clock that displays the time I was born as I pull down the straps of her bra and unclip it before putting my mouth around her nipple, licking and sucking her. I hear her breath hitch and her body relaxes back against the wall once more.

We are now both naked, her blue eyes wide, her blonde hair falling down her back, her body curvy and so fucking feminine and beautiful. I can't stop touching her as my hands run up and down her torso, grabbing her breasts and her ass as I try to be slow and steady, wanting to take my time with her, show her how I feel.

"Come here," I say as I lift her up by her ass, forcing her to grip on tight, her legs wrapping around my waist just how I like them.

"I'm trying to be good, but I really want to fuck you up against this wall right now." The truth falls from my lips as I smash them into hers.

She moans as her hands grip my shoulders tight, and

I can barely hold myself back as I grind myself into her, my dick painfully hard.

"Take me, Nico," she says, in between our kisses. "I'm yours." Her hands run through my hair again, pulling it slightly, and I can't wait any longer. I grab a condom from my wallet, making quick work of putting it on before I hold her body tight and I slowly push into her. I hear her breath hitch as her head falls back against the wall, her pussy squeezing around me.

"Fuck, you are beautiful." Her eyes are closed, mouth slightly open, her pulse throbbing in her neck.

"Fuck me, Nico," she breathes out as her eyes open and challenge mine.

So I do.

I have been wanting her all day, and I am hungry. I hold her ass cheeks tight as I pull back and slam into her, over and over again, watching her tits bounce and her breathing speed up, as sweat covers my chest. Pink blooms across her cheeks, her lips swollen.

"Do you like this, bambolina? Do you like me so desperate for you that I need to fuck you against the wall?" I say, knowing she does.

"Yes, Nico. God, yes." We are both no doubt bruising each other with our holds, my shoulders with her claw marks and her ass with my fingerprints.

"Are you mine, Emilia? Tell me you belong to me, only me," I grit out. The urge I have to own her comes on strong.

"Only yours," she says, as she leans her forehead against mine, and I thrust into her like it is my last dying wish.

"Fucking hell, you were made for me. Fucking perfect. Fucking mine."

"Nico, I'm coming," she screams, and I love that she is loud in bed. Hearing my name bounce around the room from her lips is music to my ears.

"Fuck. Bambolina. Fuck me." I feel her come undone, and I soon follow, both of us lost in a tangle of limbs, sheen of sweat, and with nothing but each other's names on our lips.

I WAKE up halfway through the night to feel Emilia slip out from my arms. Remaining still, I just watch her in the moonlight as she finds her footing and goes to the bathroom. I pay little attention except for the fact that she is in there for a long time.

I wait quietly, in the dark of the room, until I hear the door open back up and feel her cold skin as she sinks back into bed. Reaching out, I wrap my hands around her waist and pull her close, wanting to tuck her into me, and feel her naked body against mine.

"Everything okay, bambolina?" I murmur to her, as I nuzzle her neck from behind, my hand running up and down her body.

"Sure, yes, go to sleep," she scolds me, not wanting me to worry about her, yet I do. I pull her closer and then I flatten my palm against her stomach, my fingers softly caressing her skin. I don't know what is happening. I have never been this infatuated with a woman before. I have never found someone so addictive, someone I want to be with all the time. Touch, fuck, kiss, make coffee for.

"Nico?" she whispers quietly, and I feel her body tense in my arms.

"Yes, bambolina?"

"I want to go and see my mother again soon," she says, not asking me, because she sure as hell doesn't need to ask me. She's letting me know her needs, and I appreciate it.

"Of course, no problem." I feel her body relax again into mine, and I continue caressing her skin.

But something isn't right. She can go to the cemetery, but with me or Romero, because I feel those sharks are circling and I fear blood will soon be in the water.

33

EMILIA

I lie in the sheets, trying to pull myself together. Nico is already in the kitchen getting coffee and now that I am alone, my mind races as I picture those lines on the pregnancy test.

Those two lines had me hyperventilating in the bathroom for five minutes last night before I decided to take a second test just to be sure. I am not sure how long I was, but by the time I calmed down and put the tests back into the brown paper bag and into the bin, I thought Nico would be asleep. But, of course, he wasn't.

Now my heart races because I don't know what to do. I bury my head into the pillow. Pregnancy and kids were not something I have thought a lot about. Being so career-minded, my focus has always been on climbing the career ladder, not my biological clock. I'm only in my mid-twenties; I still have plenty of time for babies.

I look at the door, and my palms sweat. I should tell Nico, but I have no idea what he will say or how he will react. I'm sure meeting me and spending every day in bed together was something unexpected for him too. But he is in the goddamn mafia! What is wrong with me?!

My hands shake as I quietly slip from the bed and pad across the carpet to the bathroom. It is huge, just like the rest of his place. When he brought me here yesterday, it was very unexpected and I couldn't believe how beautiful everything is. Downstairs is large, open, masculine, with dark lines and hard edges. Upstairs is the complete opposite, with light colors, soft linens, and lush carpet. It is a mix of two worlds, just like the man himself.

I splash water on my face and wrists and take some deep breaths.

"Are you okay, bambolina?" Nico asks from where he stands, leaning against the bathroom door. He looks concerned, and I stand shocked for a moment, not sure what to do or say.

"Yes!" I say too quickly, with a fake smile. "Just trying to wake up." I grab a towel and pat my face dry to distract from my nerves. His eyes narrow, knowing that I am lying, but I plaster on another smile as I hang the towel, my eyes flicking to the coffee in his hands.

"Here," Nico says roughly, handing the coffee to me before retreating, and I follow him back to the bedroom. The air between us is now a little thicker than it was just moments ago.

"Thank you. What's on for today?" I ask, knowing even though the boxes are complete, my work is far from done.

"We need to start trying to access the laptop. Are you sure there were no clues in all those boxes?" he asks me again, searching my face.

"Maybe, I don't know," I say, taking another sip, letting my mind wander. I push aside the personal information about my mother, about France and all the loose connections, and try to concentrate on my father's business and what I have uncovered.

"Yesterday, you said that you think you found something. What did you mean?" We both take a seat on the sofa in his room. This is my favorite spot in his whole house. This small living space faces a large window, which overlooks the gorgeous greenery of the courtyard below.

"It's just I found so much personally, and it is hard for me to filter what might be helpful and what isn't. I mean, my mother, I never knew her, could never picture her, yet now I've seen her photos. She was beautiful, Nico. She was really, really beautiful." My eyes become watery, and I mentally curse my hormones because I never cry. Not in many years. He puts his hand around my neck and pulls me close. His fingers caress the back of my neck, massaging my muscles, and it feels so good.

"We will go through your pile of files from the boxes this morning. Maybe we can decipher a password and start trying them," he suggests.

"Maybe. I have sorted everything, so I have a few important papers we need to go back through again anyway. Just in case I missed something," I murmur, my face now resting against his chest, and I close my eyes, already tired again, even though I just woke up. My hand unconsciously comes to rest on my stomach. I feel nauseous, and my thoughts are a jumbled mess.

"I can always go back downstairs to your father and —" He stops himself.

"What?" I pull back from him suddenly and look at him, wide-eyed.

He stares at me for a moment, and rubs his jaw, leaning back and looking like the mobster he is.

"What do you mean, when you say 'downstairs to my father?'" I ask, now very awake, blood rushing through my body faster than before.

He doesn't answer me, but he continues to watch my reaction.

"Nico, is he here? Is my father here?" My voice raises, demanding he answer me.

He remains silent, which infuriates me more.

"Nico!" I jump up, my morning coffee forgotten.

"What is my father doing here?" My words are tumbling out now, not even giving him a chance to reply. I can't stop myself.

"Has he been here this entire time? Has he been here while I am here?" I'm panicking.

Nico leans forward, resting his elbows on his knees, clasping his hands together. I can see his jaw clenching.

"Nico! God, he is here, isn't he? What the hell is he doing here!" My heart feels like it's going to explode with how fast it's beating.

"Emilia, calm down," he says firmly.

"I will not calm down! You are a lying asshole!" I scream at him, not backing down.

"Emilia, take a breath. Lower your voice," he says calmly again, and I want to slap him.

"What else are you lying about, Nico? What else are you hiding from me? Is anything real? Is anything you have said to me the truth? I can't believe you. How can I believe anything you say now? How am I meant to trust you. Tell me. Is. He. Here?" I spit out, my body now shaking in fear, anger, nerves. I don't know, maybe all three.

"Yes, he is here!" Nico roars back at me, his hands clenching at his sides.

"He is business, Emilia, and I don't discuss family business outside of the family. And if you are asking me if what we have is real, then I want you to know that this is the most real I have ever been with anyone in my life. I have told you the truth about everything else. This is the only thing I've kept from you," he states, his chest heaving. And looking into his eyes, I know he's being honest. Almost instantly, the two of us start to calm down. But we're not happy, that much is palpable.

"I want to see him." I ignore his words, even though I want nothing more than to crawl back into his arms. My anger is taking charge for now.

"No," Nico says dismissively.

"I want to see him. I want to look him in the eye. I want to..."

"You want to what, bambolina? You want to talk to him? You want to yell at him? What do you want?" Nico sneers at me.

"I want to get some fucking answers," I bite out, the two of us murderous. This showdown was our biggest one yet, and it's leaving us both panting.

"I want to know the truth."

34

NICO

This woman.

This woman is going to be the death of me.

She fucking pushes my buttons, and I would be lying if I said I didn't like it. Fiery Emilia is the best one, aside from when she is withering underneath me and moaning my name. That one is my favorite.

"Fine!" I grit out to her. "I will take you to him. Get dressed. We will go down now." I take a seat and grab my coffee, not sure whether it is right or not, but I will be with her the entire time. He will not touch a hair on her head.

She huffs around my bedroom, throwing clothes on, tying her hair up in the messy topknot I like, and I don't miss the bite marks decorating her neck. I smirk because they will show her old man exactly what side she is on, and no doubt piss him off to no end.

"Ready," she says, standing next to me. She is breathless, almost panicked, so I stand up and take her hand.

"Let's go." As I drag her out of my apartment, her hand stays in my death grip.

"How long has he been here?" she asks as I pull her along the hallways and corridors until we get to the stairs.

"What have you been doing with him?" Her questions continue, my eyes focused straight ahead as I lead her into the depths of the compound—where no other woman has ever been before.

"Goddamnit, Nico!" she yells, and I stop, turn, and look at her.

"Don't ask me questions I am not prepared to answer. He tried to ruin us, he tried to kill Catherine and Ivy, and he is ruining your business as we speak. He is an asshole who deserves everything he is getting and then some. So don't come into my home, asking questions and demanding things you don't need to know," I shout out at her and instead of shrinking away from me, her eyes meet mine with fire.

"Fine. Just don't leave me alone with him," she says, narrowing her eyes.

"He is not going to touch you. I will fucking kill him myself if he tries."

With a huff from her and a sigh from me, we continue along the cement walkway, the compound less luxurious down here. Colder, designed for function, not comfort. As we walk around the darkened corner toward the cells, I see Sebastian up ahead and stop as we get closer.

"Nico," he says in warning. "What are you doing bringing her down here?" None of the girls are allowed in this space, but if she wants to see her shitty father, then I am going to fucking show him to her.

"She wants to see him," I spit out to Sebastian, and his eyes glance from me to Emilia and back again, obviously seeing the fire in both our eyes. He nods and walks behind us, clearly interested to witness the interaction too.

I slam my hand against the keypad and throw open the door, pulling her inside, wanting to get this over with. Her father is still sitting in the chair we've left him in, his hands and feet tied. He looks disheveled and the smell of him is nearly overbearing. But when he looks up, and sees his daughter, he smiles.

"Ahhh, here she is. Hello, my darling." I see her visibly shake at the greeting. My shoulders are heaving, because I am livid that she won't listen to me, but I am more angry now seeing her reaction to him.

"You!" she yells, her eyes tearing up, her breathing ragged, but I notice her opening and closing her fists by her sides. She is upset and overwhelmed, and I shouldn't have brought her here.

"You bastard!" she screams at him, her face contorting in anger, and my nostrils flare. I want to end him for making her upset like this, but I know this is her fight, not mine. So I wait.

"You selfish, dumb bastard!" Her foot stomps on the cement floor, and she would be totally adorable if we were anywhere else.

"You stupid fucking girl. Get me out of here," he demands, not even having flinched at her rampage, and she pauses for a moment before it dawns on her that he thinks she can help him.

"Get you out of here?" she scoffs. "Do you have any

idea where you are?"

"I know exactly where I am, and apparently, it is a whorehouse if your neck is anything to go by. Now, get me the fuck out of here!" he roars, and I take a step toward him, ready to hit him for taking that tone with her, but she puts out her hand in a silent request for me to stop. Which I do.

Her father raises an eyebrow before a shit-eating grin comes to his face.

"You are a slut, just like your mother, then," he spits out at her, and I am about to explode. Emilia obviously sees my reaction, so she steps in again.

"Why do you even care? You never cared about me ever," she says to him much more calmly, as my anger slowly builds even more.

"I don't. I don't give a flying fuck about you. Just get me out of here. I am your fucking father," he sneers. I look over to the door, and Sebastian's watching intently.

"You never even loved me. Scratch that, you never even liked me! You only ever loved your..." Her voice stops, and she stands in shock for a moment before her eyes flick to me.

"Oh my God..." she says in quiet awe before she turns on her heel and runs past me and Sebastian and back out the door.

"Emilia?" I yell to her, chasing her down the hall. Sebastian closes and locks the cell, following us.

"The laptop, Nico. Where is the laptop?" she yells back at me, as she is trying to navigate her way out of the depths of our compound, where I never want her to be ever again.

"This way," I say, taking her hand and pulling her along, the two of us now running, and while I can't see him, I know Sebastian is tailing us.

We get back to the apartment, and I rush to the desk, pulling out the laptop and opening it for her.

"Here." I pull out the chair for her to take a seat, and she opens the screen to her father's personal files.

"Do you know the password?" Sebastian questions, waltzing into the room, watching her closely.

"My father never loved me, my mother, or anyone else. But he did love one thing."

The screen blinks for a moment before she starts to type, and then hits enter.

Then we hear a distinctive ding, and the program opens.

"Holy shit," I say in shock.

"His fucking cat. Kitty. The password was Kitty!" she says before she stands up and pushes the chair out and rushes to the bathroom, me hot on her heels. She only just makes it before she vomits into the toilet, still standing before she drops to her knees.

"Emilia!" I rush to her and hold her hair back as she continues to empty her stomach.

"I'm going to kill him. No one ever talks to you like that. I am going to fucking kill him," I say over and over. Her reaction to him is so intense, I wonder if there is something else I don't know.

If I find out that he has touched a hair on her head, I will be the one that takes his last breath from him.

That is a certainty.

35

EMILIA

Nico ran me a bath and left me to relax until I was a prune, then wrapped me up in a towel, dried me, and put me to bed. If someone had told me I would be bathed and put to bed by any man, I would have thought them crazy, but for Nico, a man of the mob to do such a thing, well, I think I am the one who has lost my mind.

Now as I wake, naked, tousled in his sheets, my hair everywhere and my eyes adjusting to the light, I still feel exhausted. My body's weak, no strength in my limbs, no energy humming around my nervous system. I feel purely exhausted, like I could sleep for a week.

I'm not sure where Nico is, but I see my phone on the bedside table. Grabbing it, I notice the time and internally cringe. I slept for over twelve hours. I don't think I have ever done that before. I rub my hand across my face, wondering if I need to run to the bathroom or if the feeling of nausea will pass if I lie still for a moment. My body jolts slightly, giving me a hint, and within seconds, I fling the sheets back and run like my life depends on it. Any thoughts of breakfast now erased from my mind as I empty my stomach.

Sitting back on my heels, I rub my tummy. How can something so small have such an impact? I need to tell Nico. I need to tell him because I have no idea what I am doing. It has been days and even though I took three tests, the outcome was the same. Deep down, I know they are right.

Two weeks pregnant, the test said. Standing at the sink, I look at my pale complexion and dark circles and wonder when the pregnancy glow is supposed to kick in. I splash some water on my face to help make me feel human and saunter back to bed, where I feel like I want to spend the day.

So unlike me.

The apartment is quiet, so I grab my phone again and look through my emails and social media before I tap to view my photos. Images of the paperwork I sorted from the boxes come up. I captured what I thought was important, and now, as I stare at one image, I am trying to get my mind to work.

"*Think, Emi. Think. Think. Think,*" I mumble to myself as I rub my eyes, willing my brain to work. The image of those scrawled numbers I found in the plane journal is staring back at me, the ones that could mean absolutely nothing, yet play on repeat in my mind.

42 and 5. I run the numbers through my head, over and over. They feel familiar, but I have no idea from where.

Sighing, I try to think of other things, like how I

need to visit my mom again. I got so much clarity after my last visit. Unloading my life story to her was very cathartic, and maybe that is what I need to do to clear my mind.

Thinking of her reminds me of the flowers, the beautiful red roses on her headstone, and I pull up the florist Instagram page again, just to look at the beautiful arrangements. That's when it hits me.

Le Rose Fleurs.

Corner of 5th Avenue and 42nd Street.

I sit up with a start.

5. 42.

It's the florist!

I jump out of bed a little too quickly and need to grip onto the side table so I don't vomit, before I start again and move slower to grab my clothes and get my things together.

"Going somewhere?" Nico asks, as he saunters into the room.

"Hey. I wanted to go visit my mother."

"How are you feeling?" He produces a coffee, and my insides melt a little. I'll never get tired of it. He is rough on the outside, but so attentive to me.

"I'm fine. It was just a big day, and I was exhausted. But I feel much better," I lie through my teeth. I feel bad, the pull in my stomach to sit and tell him about the baby is overwhelming, but I can't. Not yet.

"Did you find anything on the laptop?" I ask, changing the topic, as he sits on the sofa with his coffee like a king on his throne.

"Sebastian and Carter are looking through it. If we

have trouble, I might need you to take a look too," he says, not looking convinced that I am well as he eyes me.

"I shouldn't have taken you there yesterday." I notice his jaw popping. He is tense.

"I wanted to go."

"Don't ask me to do that again because the answer will be no." I look at him and watch him for a beat.

"Fine. I don't particularly need to see him again. He hasn't changed. He is still the same cruel son of a bitch he has always been," I say, sipping on my coffee.

"Did he ever hurt you?" Nico's question surprises me, and my body stills.

"No. I mean, I don't think so. My memories are not strong; it is like I have blocked a lot of my childhood out. It really wasn't until working through those boxes that some of my memories started coming back."

He nods slowly, and it occurs to me that Nico might be feeling guilty for causing me stress yesterday, which is not his pain to carry. Placing my cup down, I walk over to him where he is sitting on the sofa, and grab his face in my hands, making him look at me. I see his nostrils flare a little as his face tilts up to me, now I am standing right in front of him.

"I'm okay. I promise," I whisper as his hands come to the back of my thighs and trail up and down my legs. His head leans against my stomach, and I run my fingers through his hair, holding him close.

"I don't like seeing you upset. I don't like seeing you in pain," he admits, and I smile before he looks back up at me.

"Unless the pain turns into pleasure and is inflicted

by me," he clarifies with a grin before swooping me up and throwing me on the bed.

The visit to my mother will now have to be an afternoon activity as he crawls over me, his hands working fast at taking off the clothes I just put on.

"I want my mouth on you this morning. You're the only breakfast I enjoy," he says, always so eager to please me.

"I think this is my favorite thing about you," I murmur in jest as he slides my jeans and underwear off, my lower half now completely naked.

"And I think this is my favorite thing about you," he replies as his thumb skirts over my center, my need for him obvious as his thumb glistens with my arousal.

"Your hands and mouth are truly works of magic, Nico." I take a breath, leaning my head back into the mattress as he pushes a finger inside of me.

"Fucking everything about you is magic. You cast your spell on me months ago, and now there is no way I can go a day without you," he says honestly. Before I have time to respond, his lips find my skin and his desire becomes demanding, the air leaving my lungs. My back arches, as my hands automatically dive into his hair, and my hips buckle underneath him.

"Oh God, you are so good at that," I moan, as Nico continues to pleasure me.

My heart bounces in my chest and my body heats as his tongue and fingers move in tandem. His other large hand grips my hip, holding me in place as I squirm and wriggle.

He growls then, low and deep, as he increases his

speed, sucking on my clit, and his fingers curve just how he knows I like.

My hips rock as I start to pant. "Nico... Nico..." I moan his name, as he sucks hard, and I let go. The tension from earlier, the darkness of seeing my father, the stress I have been carrying, all floats away as Nico takes me over the edge. The last of my energy leaves my body, taking all the doubts and fears with it, leaving me a panting, sweaty mess on the bed, with a smile on my face.

36

NICO

I love making her come undone with my tongue. The way she pants my name. The way she moans and wriggles underneath me. Fuck, everything about this woman is my undoing.

"Come here," I say as I pull her up off the bed. Her legs wrap around my waist as I walk us to the sofa, where I sit and place her in my lap.

"Ride me. I want to watch you bounce on my cock." I squeeze her ass cheeks and help guide her until I feel the warmth of her pussy wrap around my length.

"Nico, you are too big," she says breathlessly, her chest in front of my face rising and falling, and I don't hesitate to pull one of her nipples into my mouth. My palms grip her flesh, the feel of her full round ass doing nothing but making me harder by the second.

"Slide on, baby. I want to feel you around me. You know you take me so well," I coax her, caressing her back to help her relax.

She starts to slide onto me, her fingers gripping into

my shoulders, my skin now forever tainted with the half-moon marks of her nails as she impales herself nice and deep onto me.

"Fuck, you feel good," I grit out, as I look at her naked body on top of mine. I rest my head on the back of the sofa, my eyes feasting on the beauty on top of me, enjoying every second of watching her body move.

"It has never felt this good for me before..." she whispers out, her eyes connecting with mine, and I see the truth in them.

"You were fucking made for me, bambolina. I have told you before. You are mine." My possessive nature comes out in full force, needing her to understand that this is it for me. She is it.

I slap her ass hard before gripping it in my fingers, and I hear her sharp intake of breath.

"Nico!" she gasps in surprise, but I felt her pussy clench, so I know she liked it.

"Fucking start bouncing," I warn her and give her my trademark smirk, which immediately turns into my teeth clenching in pleasure as she moves her hips in a circular motion, making my balls tighten.

"Oh God, that feels so good," she says as her head falls back, her long blonde hair skimming my fingers as my mouth moves to her breast once more. Her hips start moving faster, her body bouncing and grinding on top of me, as my hands run up her back and grip onto her shoulders from behind, pushing her down onto me as I thrust up into her.

"Your perfect pussy is all mine," I grit out to her, the momentum of our hips clashing against each other, pushing me to the edge. "You're fucking beautiful, so fucking beautiful." I watch her, her mouth open, her eyes closed, moving up and down my cock. My hand grabs her hair, and I pull her head back, arching her back even more, her clit rubbing against me just right before I feel her start to shake.

"Yes, yes. Don't stop, Nico. Please," she begs, her movements becoming erratic.

"Fuck me, Emilia, take all of me." I lean forward and bite her nipple, which sends shock waves through her body, as she jolts, her orgasm taking over her body. Watching her, I let go, and empty myself inside of her, pulling her up and down my cock as I ride the high, not wanting it to end.

"Nico," she breathes, her head coming forward and slumping on my shoulder. "That was amazing." Maybe I can talk her into staying in bed with me all day today, even though I know I have a mountain of work to get through.

I wrap my arms around her, my fingers skimming her bare back, and again realize we didn't use protection, yet this time I am not as concerned about it as I was weeks ago. It appears neither is she.

"Let's get in the shower, then I will call Tony and Romero to take you to the cemetery," I say as I stand, keeping her wrapped around my waist and walking us to the bathroom.

She remains silent, clinging to me, so I keep her in my arms as I turn on the shower and step inside.

"Do you want me to come with you?" I ask her, feeling

like I need to be near her today. I can still sense she is fragile, not herself.

"No, that's okay. I won't be long. I will just get the boys to take me to the florist, then the cemetery, and then I will be back," she says, slowly easing off me, and I place her feet on the floor.

"What florist?"

"Le Rose on the Upper East Side."

I still then. Le Rose is owned by the Moreau family. Why would she go there? It is nowhere near the cemetery. Not even on the way.

"Why Le Rose?" I ask her, trying to sound normal, as I wash her body with soap.

"Oh, their arrangements are so beautiful. They have lovely roses," she says with a smile before she turns, offering me her back, which I soap up and then rinse.

My mind whirls. The French are allies of ours, the florist their only business in New York, with a handful of other properties reserved for their accommodations when they visit.

"Maybe I should come." I turn her back around to face me.

"It's fine. I'm not going to be there long." She grabs the soap from me and runs it over my body. It feels nice to have her hands on me like this.

"All right, but Romero goes everywhere you go. No question." I stare down at her, her naked body ingrained in my dreams, even more so now as I watch the water drip down her chest to her center, a place I never want to leave.

"Nico, it is really not necessary..." she starts until she

sees the look on my face and decides not to continue, instead nodding.

"Fine. Romero comes with me everywhere." Submitting that easily? Yet another thing giving me concerns.

"Good, now come here," I grit out, pulling her flush with my body and kissing her, looking forward to when she comes home later because I am already eager for round two.

37

EMILIA

I sit in the back of the car, my stomach curling into itself, nervous, but in reality, I know it will probably be another dead-end. The traffic whirls past, the activities of a busy New York City scurrying around us, yet I remain silent, lost in my thoughts, trying to piece together all these bits of information.

Tony and Romero are quiet in the front, clearly not happy about escorting me around today.

Looking out the window, I think about my father. Seeing him yesterday probably wasn't a good idea. It has stirred up a whole pot of emotions I was not ready for and was not really equipped to handle.

I was honest with Nico. He never touched me. Which is astounding, considering how much he hated me. His abuse toward me was purely mental, and no doubt he thought he could wield his sword over me again yesterday, but it didn't work. So even though I am exhausted and mentally drained from the event, I still feel some strength inside, knowing he doesn't affect me anymore. At least not as much as he used to.

Perhaps Nico has a hand in that. Having him there, with me, seeing him angry at my father for all he has done, including the way he has treated me. I felt like for the first time in my life I had someone on my side. A new feeling for me.

I think once I get back to the compound, I might also spend the afternoon with Cat and Ivy. I am keen to get to know Ivy better and understand their life now they are with Carter and all that involves.

The car comes to a stop, and I notice the sophisticated white-and-black striped awnings on the stark white stone building. The front features beautiful black-framed windows, with an explosion of color coming from the inside, the roses acting as a centerpiece.

"I won't be long," I say as Romero opens my door, then I walk into the florist. Surprisingly, he waits near the car and doesn't bother coming inside. Nico must've asked him to keep his distance.

I push open the door, which sets off a small chime upon my entrance, and I stand in awe. The whole interior is white, except for the black timber floor. The walls, the ceiling, the counter, all of it is pure, stark white. The wall shelves are clear and floating, making the vibrant bunches of roses stand out as displays.

It is breathtaking and nothing like I have ever seen before.

"May I help you?" a lady asks with a very thick French accent. She is dressed impeccably. Like she belongs in a corporate office, with tailored pants, patent leather shoes, and bright red lipstick, the color matching the roses just behind her.

"It is beautiful here," I say in amazement, as my eyes move away from her and back to the displays.

"Thank you. We import all our roses from France. We specialize in long-stemmed and perfumed," she states as she walks over to me.

"After anything in particular?" she asks me, and my eyes rake over the selection before they land on a stunning red bouquet.

"I think I will take the red ones."

"Ahh… the Jacquelines. They are beautiful." My body goes still as my breath catches in my throat.

"What are they called?" I ask her, watching her intently to ensure I heard her right.

"The Jacqueline Rose. It is a specialty from one of our farms in France," she says, turning and taking the bunch to the counter to wrap. My heart is bouncing out of my chest.

"Where is the farm in France? Is it a popular place?" I ask, trying to connect dots that I am not even sure are dots in the first place.

"It is a closed private family farm, but it is stunning," she tells me with a smile as she rings up the purchase.

They cost a staggering amount, one I know I can't afford, but I put it on my credit card anyway as I thank the lady and walk out. Romero pays no attention as I head back to the car and fall into the backseat, the soft comfort of the leather at least making me feel safe in this crazy life I have at the moment.

The traffic is light, so we reach the cemetery in good time, and I grab the flowers and step out of the car.

"I won't be long. I will be just over there." I point to the vicinity of where my mother is buried, and Romero nods, leaning his back against the car, and pulling out his cell phone, no doubt checking in with Nico.

But I am too wound up to care. I walk with the flowers tight in my hand toward my mother. My eyes are pinned to her gravestone as I bring them to my nose, their scent so elegant and beautiful. As my gaze roams her plot, I see the same fresh bunch of roses sitting at her headstone. They are pristine, like they have just been placed, and I put my matching bouquet down next to them. The color explosion once again vibrant against the gray, aged headstone.

I quickly look back to the car, seeing Romero still standing there. Yards away, his body is nearly a spec. Feeling secure that no one can hear me, I look back at my mother, and I start to talk.

"Hey, Mom," I say quietly. "I'm back again—" But I'm interrupted.

"Are you Emilia Cole?" a man asks gruffly as he steps out from the tree nearby. My heart pounds in shock because it is the same man who was here last time and the same man who followed me to Bobby's Diner. His voice is deep, lacquered with a French accent, and now my senses are heightened.

I quickly look back to Romero, his head still down, looking at his phone.

"Yes," I say, wondering who he is as I begin to stand tentatively.

"You are coming with me." Then he's stalking toward me quickly. I am about to protest and move away, but his hand grips my elbow and his body slinks up beside me, pulling me close.

"What are you doing?" I ask, my voice pitching up an octave, surprised by his manhandling.

"This way, Miss Cole," He murmurs close to my ear.

"What! Excuse me, but—" I stop walking and start raising my voice, but he continues to pull me along the path to a darkened parked car.

"Quiet and walk, unless you want a bullet in your brain, Miss Cole," the man grits out. This time, I feel a push into my side and look down, seeing the shiny silver metal of a handgun pressing into my ribs.

"Oh my God..." My feet automatically follow him. His face is close, his breath skimming my ear as shivers run down my spine. My throat feels like it is closing up, my heart beats out of my chest, and my palms begin to sweat.

My eyes are wide as I glance around, trying to look back at Romero, but my kidnapper is firm in his grip. Bruises no doubt will color my skin as he pulls me along at pace.

"Hey!" I hear Romero yell in the distance, and I try to slow down so he can catch up. I have a split second to make a decision. Do I scream and run, or do I follow his command? But I am not just thinking of myself anymore. The gun is pressed right into my side, the little bean forming in my belly not safe in the slightest.

The hold on my elbow gets firmer, my body held closer. My hands start to tremble as I am dragged toward the curb where the unmarked black car sits, with a driver already waiting with the back door open. I have no time to think before the man thrusts me inside, slamming the door on me. It is mere seconds before both men get into the front and the car is moving.

I immediately try to open the door to get out again, but it is locked. I start banging on the window, seeing Romero approaching.

"Romero!" I scream, scared out of my mind, knowing he can't hear me, and with the dark tint on the windows, he probably can't see me either.

My mind whirls as the car speeds off, away from Romero and away from the cemetery. My grip on the handle remains tight as I again try to open the door, pulling it, pushing it, hitting the window with my fist.

Panicking, I go to slide across the black leather seat to the other side of the car to try the opposite door, but stop dead. There is a third man.

"Who are you? Where are you taking me?" I yell, trying to remain strong, but feeling the fear creep into my spine. He sits quietly, admiring me openly, his dark eyes running down the length of my body and back up again. He is in a black coat, with a dark suit underneath, very well dressed.

"What do you want?" I ask him hesitantly, my tone lighter as I scoot away from him and bury myself against the side of the car. He doesn't look friendly. His eyes are piercing, burning into mine, and my hand automatically comes up, resting on my stomach as my eyes pin his in return.

He watches me for a beat before he moves swiftly, putting a cloak over my head.

I scream for all my lungs are worth, my hands flying up to pull the cloak from my face as darkness overtakes me. But his hands are firm before one strikes out at me and hits me across the cheek. My head whips back and hits the doorframe hard, my body slumps against the seat before I'm out cold.

38

NICO

My head hangs low, as I trawl through the finances with Sebastian, new ones that we have found on Emilia's father's laptop. I don't know how we missed this. I flick between transaction after transaction relating to Dragonfly. Owned by the French Mafia, Dragonfly is the face of every business in their portfolio. Any public legal entity, anyway.

"I don't understand. We have an alliance. Why are they trying to overthrow us?" I grumble, pissed off that those who were thought to be our friends are actually trying to sink our ship here in New York.

"You know what they say, Nico. Keep your friends close, but your enemies closer," Sebastian spits out, clearly not impressed either.

"Do you think it's the kid?" I ask, knowing the head position is currently being passed on to Hugo, his father Lucas having led the French mafia for decades, now wanting an easier life. Probably to retire to his rose farm in the outskirts of Provence.

"Most likely. Trying to throw his weight around. He has no concept of respect, earning trust. He just takes without thinking of our alliance or the consequences. But if he wants a fight, then a fight is what he will get." Sebastian's voice is deep, assured, and not inviting any questions.

I stand and begin to pace the room, the anger that has been festering inside of me now swelling. The energy rolling off Sebastian is almost suffocating, as he sits and fumes at the table, cracking his knuckles, deep in thought. His eyes haven't left the paperwork, but I know his mind is ticking over. Just like my own.

I feel my cell phone vibrate in my pocket, and I pull it out, eager to hear where the boys are with Emilia, wanting her back here with me now more than ever.

Looking at the screen, I see it is Tony calling, not Romero.

"Are you on your way back?" I spit out, my anger palatable, my shoulders near my ears and filled with tension.

"She's gone!" Tony says in a rush, and my stomach drops.

"What do you mean, she's gone?" I yell, and Sebastian whips his gaze to me.

"Someone grabbed her. A man grabbed her from the gravesite, threw her in a car, and drove off. We couldn't even see where they went!" Tony explains, his breaths labored, so I know he is running.

"Did you get a license plate?" I question, panic crawling up my spine, anger welling in my gut. I see

Sebastian on the phone already, no doubt getting Dante and Carter.

"No."

"What do you mean, no?"

"There was no plate."

"You mean to tell me, my girlfriend was just kidnapped, because no one was with her, our car wasn't parked nearby, so no one could catch her, and there was no license plate?"

"That's right," he answers grimly.

"What the fuck do you know?!" I scream down the phone before Sebastian grabs it from me and tries to get more details.

Carter and Dante run into the room as I start to pace the floor, my hands gripping my hair, the pain in my chest nearly bringing me to my knees.

"What happened?" Dante barks, looking between Sebastian and I.

"Emilia was kidnapped from the cemetery just now," Sebastian says to them both, their shocked faces looking at me as my nostrils flare, and I continue to seethe.

"Carter!" Sebastian yells. "See if you can hack the cameras and get a visual.

"Dante, get our jet ready and on standby. Lock down the compound. I have a feeling I know who has taken her," Sebastian says.

"Who?" Dante and Carter ask at the same time.

"The French," I grit out, my jaw clenching. I am murderous as I watch everyone running around, pulling out phones and laptops.

"Shit," Carter says as he looks at the computer screen.

"I've got the cameras." The three of us look over his shoulder.

I watch the footage and see Emilia by the gravesite, putting the roses down, a matching bouquet to another one already there. Then her head whips up quickly. She is startled by something or someone. We don't see anyone for a beat, but then a large, tall man appears. I lean in and watch as his hand grips her arm, pushing her to the side of the grave and pulling her away. They move quickly to a black Escalade, with dark windows and no plates.

"We need to call them," I say to Sebastian. I know he is hesitant. He doesn't want them to know we are onto them. That we know anything about what they're doing, working with a man like Brian Cole.

He remains silent.

"Sebastian, I need her. I need her back here." I feel myself falling apart as I wait for his response. If they hurt her...

He sighs, looks to the ceiling, and rubs his eyes. "Fuck! Fine!" he growls, looking at me angrily, and I know why. He told me not to get involved. Not to mix business and pleasure. This is what he was trying to avoid. But she is my weakness, just like Goldie is his.

We stand around the table as Sebastian grabs his cell. My heart rate hasn't lowered, my teeth continue to grind, and I know my pulse is thrumming in my neck. I think about her father downstairs. He knew. He knew this whole time, yet didn't say anything. Because of him, she is now gone, and I am going to make him pay.

"Quiet. Let me handle this," Sebastian says, pinning me with his glare. My jaw clenches, but I nod quickly, and I stand in front of him, listening in to the conversation.

"Sebastian, to what do I owe the pleasure?" Hugo's voice slithers down the phone. I have met him once; he seemed nice enough at the time. Now I want to remove his head from his body.

My lips remain closed, but it is taking all my energy to keep them that way.

"Hugo, you have someone who belongs to us, and I want her back," Sebastian says, not mincing his words.

"Really?" he asked, feigning surprise, giving nothing away. "She is a pretty little thing, but Sebastian, you already have your precious Goldie. You don't need another one." If I hear him right, he is starting to sound a little nervous.

I step forward, ready to unleash, but Sebastian puts up his hand in a silent gesture, so I stop mid-stride.

"She is Nico's girl, Hugo. You need to turn your plane around and bring her back."

Hugo laughs, almost uncontrollably. Sebastian and I share a look, both filled with rage that's barely restrained.

"You seem to forget, Sebastian, I am not someone you can demand things from. Besides, you killed one of my men. You owe me," he sneers.

"Your man shouldn't have been surveilling my compound. His blood is on your hands, not mine. But you have crossed the line now, my friend. You kidnapped a member of my family. That is not something that can be easily forgiven," Sebastian says, trying to keep his anger in check.

I sit next to Sebastian, listening in on the conversation, ready to reach through the phone and end him already.

"I took her because I want her father. The piece of shit stole from me and now is in hiding. Hopefully, taking her will flush him out. She is taking a nice sleep at the moment, Sebastian. By the time she is in France, she won't even miss you."

"She is carrying my niece or nephew, so you can be sure she will be missed dearly." Sebastian drops the words like a bomb, and I stand up, reeling. The chair is pushed from my body and skids across the floor, landing with a thud, and my eyes are wide as I stare at Sebastian, words stuck in my throat.

Niece or nephew. Emilia's pregnant?

Sebastian eyes me, his look at me fierce.

I am about to move, but Carter grabs my shoulders, holding me back while Dante comes close and muffles my screams. Even though he isn't at fault, I want to slide across this table and grab Sebastian by the collar.

"What would your father think of this arrogant display of disrespect?" Sebastian spits out, his eyes not leaving me as I wrestle in Carter's and Dante's arms. Carter drags me back, farther away from the table, my legs failing around me as I try to punch, kick, hurt anyone who comes close to me.

"My father has left the family to me to manage, and this is my decision," Hugo states, a little doubt creeping into his voice.

"We will see you in France, my friend." Sebastian ends the call and stands, rolling his shoulders back. I shrug Carter off me, breathing heavily.

"How did you know?" I spit out at Sebastian as he comes to stand in front of me, angry that I am the last person to know I am having a fucking child.

"The cleaning crew found her positive tests in the rubbish and brought them to my attention this morning," he answers honestly.

"It explains her sickness, her tiredness, her moods..." he adds, and my brain starts to catch up with the events. He is right; everything points to the same conclusion.

How and when run through my mind. But as I think about it, I become acutely aware. My breathing slows. Emilia has been throwing up, more tired than normal, her features shallow, and has even had a loss of appetite. I rub my eyes. This can't be happening.

I want to feel joyous, excited. Emilia is pregnant, and we are having a baby. It is soon, but there is no question we will be a family. But with her not here, and currently in danger on her way to the other side of the world, I feel sick I couldn't protect her.

"The jet is on standby. The car is ready for us downstairs," Dante says. Sebastian looks at him and nods.

"Carter, go get the low life scum from the basement. He is coming with us," Sebastian says, and I raise my eyebrows. Carter walks off, a man now on a mission.

"Dante, get the women and children into lockdown." Sebastian continues giving orders, and Dante runs out the door.

"Nico?" Sebastian says, looking at me.

"Let's go get my family." The need to have her with me now overwhelming.

"Let's go get *our* family," Sebastian corrects me, as his hand comes up and grips my shoulder.

I nod to him, as his other hand grips the back of my neck and he pulls me close. Hugging me, he whispers, "You're going to be a great father."

And it is in this moment, I know if needed, I will hand over my life for hers.

39

EMILIA

My head is pounding, and as I rub my forehead, my cheek throbs with pain. *Did I sleep on the floor again?* Because I can't remember my body aching this much before.

Opening and closing my mouth, my lips are cracked a little, and my throat parched. *Do I have a hangover?* As I come to, the need to vomit begins to swirl in my stomach, the morning sickness still present.

I hear a deep thrumming, and as I yawn, I slowly open my eyes. I see white leather seats. I try to move now, realizing I am not lying in my bed, but I am being held tight. I start to panic as my memories come back to me. Being taken. Put in a car. That is all I remember.

"Sleeping beauty is awake." A man's deep voice penetrates the white noise of the aircraft engine. My head whips around, and I see him sitting across the aisle, watching me.

He took me. I'm on a plane!

My hand touches my cheek where I remember his

slap. It then runs down, and I place it protectively on my stomach.

"I gave you a sedative. It won't hurt the baby," he says, and my eyes widen.

How does he know?

As my body begins to shake in terror, I try to slow my breathing, wanting to keep my stress low. I have no idea what is going on, but I know for the sake of my baby, I need to remain as calm as possible.

"Mr. Moreau, we are making our descent now," a woman dressed as an airline stewardess says to the man, ignoring me completely. He nods at her without saying a word, and she continues farther down the aisle and sits, fastening her seatbelt.

Instinctively, I check my seatbelt is low and tight. The man, however, remains unmoved. He has one leg crossed over his knee. He rests his elbow on the armrest, his chin in his hand, his eyes focused on me only. He looks at me quizzically, like he is trying to figure something out.

"Where are we?" I ask, my voice croaky from lack of use, and I internally kick myself for sounding so weak.

The man continues to look at me, and as my question hangs in the air, my stomach choses that moment to rumble. I have no idea where we are, but it feels like days since I last ate something. Nico's pasta now just a dream, my mouth watering at the thought.

"France," he barks out. My eyes catch an embossed crest on the back of the seat, red on the white leather, the insignia I can't make out. I swallow nervously, knowing the men I am with are probably not going to be very welcoming. How the hell am I going to get myself out of this situation?

Looking out the window, I see nothing but sunshine and the bright blue shimmering seas of the Mediterranean. On any other trip, my eyes would be glued to the azure waters, having never been to Europe before. But I turn back to the man, ignoring the view and fighting the daily nausea creeping into my body.

I feel the plane dip, our descent rapid, and my hands are white knuckled on the armrests. My companion sits unfazed, clearly a seasoned traveler.

"What do you want with me?" I grit out, my voice now much clearer, yet he remains unperturbed.

"It amazes me how someone so beautiful can be the spawn of someone so conniving," he says as the plane continues to get lower and lower.

My father.

Again, my father haunts me, and now I am in the clutches of a man who wants revenge for something my dear old dad has done. My breathing picks up in pace, my heart thumping a million miles a minute. My eyes search the airplane cabin, looking for anyone who may be able to help me out of this situation. I try to catch the eye of the stewardess down the aisle, who is looking everywhere but at me. Fear crawls across my skin, and the small hairs on my arms start to stick up. I am on the other side of the world, where no one will ever find me. My heart breaks a little inside, knowing Nico will be worried sick.

"My father and I are estranged. I have no idea what he has done, but I assure you it has nothing to do with me." I see him smirk a little. It is a similar reaction to that of Nico when we first met in my office.

"He stole from me," the man says, and I raise my eyebrows.

"I'm not surprised. He stole from a lot of people," I retort, and already regret it as I see anger in his face.

"Over one-hundred million dollars," he growls. I throw up a little in my mouth.

"Oh my God," I whisper, because while my father has done some really bad things, that sure is a lot of money to steal from one person.

"Sounds like you need to keep a better eye on your money, then." Why I feel the need to be sassy at a time like this, I'll never understand.

He laughs like I just told him the funniest joke, but I know this is no laughing matter, so I wait and watch.

"You have no idea who you are talking to, do you?" he says to me, his face now serious again.

"No idea," I say, shaking my head, trying to act unaffected, but my insides are curling.

He turns then, looking out the window, and I get a glimpse of his neck under his pristine white shirt collar. A Dragonfly tattoo, just like the man in the cemetery.

"Dragonfly..." I say quietly in awe, knowing the dots are beginning to connect.

At my statement, he turns back around, his eyes wild.

"Your father will pay, if not with money, then with his life, and I will kill everyone close to him, including you and your unborn baby," he threatens, his tone low.

"How did you know I was pregnant?" I am not showing. I haven't said anything to anyone. How the hell does he know?

"Sebastian told me," he says, and I lose my breath.

Sebastian knows. If Sebastian knows, then Nico knows. But how?

"It puts a dent in my plans now, doesn't it." My brow furrows, trying to follow what he is saying.

"I was just going to kill you. Bring you to Provence and kill you on the farm for what your father took from me. But now you are carrying a legacy. Now you are carrying the son or daughter of a brother." I can see the land coming closer and closer out the window near his seat in my peripheral vision.

"It makes my original plan a little less appealing..." he says, obviously not knowing I was involved with Nico or working for the mob. Who would have thought that little detail would be my saving grace.

"So what happens now?" I ask, afraid to question him, but needing to prepare myself for what's to come.

"Now I need to decide if I am ready to start a war with the Italians, because if I kill you, then there will be no doubt it will start a war," he declares, just as the jet hits the tarmac, and my stomach drops. The vomit finally rises, and I throw up all over his polished white leather seats.

40

NICO

I fidget in my seat, sweat building on my forehead. I'm itching to get to Emilia. Sebastian and I are in the car on our way to the Dragonfly compound. A large chateau built into the cliff face along the French coast. Designed that way to prevent access from unwanted visitors. They have a casino, accommodation, winery, and God knows what else in this massive fortress. We were in the jet and in the air within thirty minutes of our call to Hugo, so I know he can't be too far ahead of us.

The four of us boys have been frantic for the past eight hours, each of us on the phone to someone. We have rallied all our associates in Italy, everyone we are friendly with. We have teams of people already in France, positioned both inside the chateau in plain view to create a presence and around the nearby town for a quick getaway. Dante has arranged fueled planes waiting for us. Carter has boats manned and at the docks in case a sea getaway is needed.

We are all on high alert.

I still can't believe an ally of ours would dare take Emilia. They had to have known who she was; they had been waiting for the right time, and I served her up on a platter to them. I am furious with myself for letting her out of my sight. I should have gone with her to the cemetery, but she needed space. And she has never done what I have told her to do since the moment I met her, so there was no way I could have kept her at the compound.

But I should have locked her up. I should have kept her with me.

My cell vibrates, and I see Sofia's name light up the screen. I don't answer. I haven't spoken to my sister in days. She knows something is up. But for the first time in years, she is not front and center in my mind. She has been calling incessantly, but I need to focus. I need to focus on getting Emilia back with me.

"We're here. Are you ready?" Sebastian asks, as we pull up to the valet, men in pristine uniforms surrounding the car.

"I'm ready," I say sternly, my teeth clenched, running off adrenaline like never before.

"Remember the plan, Nico. Don't do anything stupid," Sebastian warns me, because he knows. He knows I will do anything to get her back, including stepping away from our carefully laid out plan.

We are going in and negotiating for Emilia's life. It is something I could never imagine doing. Her deadbeat father is currently in a separate car with Carter and Dante, going to a safe location. I am to trade her life for his. Get her out and all of us to Sicily before nightfall.

We are not stupid. The Moreau family knows we are

here. They run this town, so no one gets in or out without them knowing. Sebastian has tried calling Lucas, the famous Godfather and Hugo's father, but he is not taking our calls. The uneasiness of that plays on my mind. We sent a message via his people, because he needs to know that his son is breaking all alliances and potentially starting a war.

His stunt in his new position as head of the French Mafia could well be the end of them.

I give Sebastian a silent nod before we both step out of the back seat and are immediately patted down. I remain stiff, my nostrils flaring, as I breathe in the air, filling my lungs to capacity.

"Clear," the soldier says before sweeping his arm up. "Let's go." Sebastian and I walk forward, and our car leaves the premises.

As my feet hit the cobblestone footpath, I am calm. I have no fear. If my life ends today, then I do it for my child. For my woman. I thought the heartache and anguish I experienced as a young man seeing my little sister ill was the worst thing to ever happen. But knowing the woman I love, who is carrying our baby, is locked inside this fortress against her will, it has overridden everything that has come to me before this.

At least twenty men surround us. All armed, all moving in synchronization, their team one I would regard with envy at any other time. Right now, I just want to kill them all.

We progress through a double glass door, the faint sounds of voices trailing up from the chateau's main floor, and small musical notes from the overhead speakers a distant jingle. Our feet clip on the polished marble hallway to an elevator. Stepping in, Sebastian and I are significantly outnumbered. It is almost comical, as they clearly see us as a threat. I am beginning to wonder if Hugo is regretting his decision to take a member of our family.

The elevator doors open, and stepping out, I can feel that we are well below ground level. My anger rises as understanding washes over me that they have Emilia down here in their cells.

"You are fucking kidding me," I grit out to Sebastian, and he remains silent, but gives me a look to tell me to stop talking. As we continue on, I notice his jaw clenching. He is furious, and I have never been more grateful to him than I am right now.

We come to a door with two soldiers out the front. They immediately step to the side at seeing our entourage, and the door opens, revealing a large cement room. There are about eight men standing around. Hugo is at the end, looking at us, his body rigid, his arms crossed in front of his chest, like a security guard. Then my eyes land on her.

She is to the side of the room, tied to a chair. *Tied to a fucking chair.* Her mouth is gagged, her cheeks are tear-stained, one of which is purple. Her hair's disheveled, mascara's running, but her beautiful blue eyes widen with relieved surprise as Sebastian and I enter the room. I stare at her for a beat, my eyes flicking to her stomach and back to her face again. Watching a solo tear fall from her eye, my chest hurts. It is then I notice blood on her temple and my attention is brought back to that bruise. How dare they make someone so beautiful bleed.

"You have traveled a long way for a woman, Sebastian. She must be special." Hugo says by way of greeting, and I want to rip his head from his body. He doesn't move to shake Sebastian's hand. The disrespect he is showing is astounding.

Sebastian hasn't looked at Emilia, his eyes remaining focused on Hugo. I see his icy stare drilling into him, and Hugo starts to shuffle, losing some of his confidence with one look from Sebastian. There is no doubt this kid is not ready to lead. He is my age, late twenties. He has years to go before he can lead a family.

"I don't care about the girl or her baby, but how poetic it will be to not only kill her and the baby but you as well," Hugo says in a light threat, and still Sebastian and I remain quiet, standing side by side right in front of him.

I watch their exchange before looking back at Emilia. I can see her trying to move her hands and get out of the restraints, and I shake my head a little to tell her to stop. Not only will she burn her skin, but I will have her out of them soon. She understands and stops moving, but then I can clearly see the shake in them, and her fear pains me.

"Does family mean nothing to you, Hugo? You make a bad decision and give your money to a man who didn't repay you, and you decide to throw a tantrum?" I question, stepping toward him slightly, Sebastian remaining beside me. After severely torturing Brian Cole, we now know he stole millions from Hugo. Brian gave him empty promises, and Hugo was extremely gullible. Now in his haste, Hugo kidnapped Brian's daughter for revenge, not knowing we already had him and had her working for us. Not knowing she is one of us. That she is *mine*.

"Step closer, brother. I am more than happy to take the life of Sebastian Romano's protégé," Hugo threatens again as he lifts a gun that was hidden behind him and points it at my forehead.

My blood boils. Hugo has no idea what he is even saying. He isn't even trying to negotiate. He has no business sense, no sense of family or alliances. If he is not careful, this is going to end up in a bloody mess right here in this room.

"Go ahead. Do it," I push him as I step into the gun, feeling the cold steel press against my forehead, and I hear Emilia whimper as my eyes drill into Hugo.

"Get rid of her," he yells, and his men move toward Emilia and lift her and the chair like she weighs nothing.

I feel Sebastian seething, but his eyes stay locked on Hugo. My heart thumps from my chest as I take a step away from Hugo and toward her, ready to protect her body with my own. I am going to kill every last bastard in this room. I am going to take down this whole fucking French family.

"Stop!!" A big booming voice echoes around the room as an older man, surrounded by four men, walks in. Lucas Moreau, Godfather of the French mafia and Hugo's father. He might be in his mid-sixties, but his eyes are on fire and all the men in the room stop and bow to him, showing a sign of respect.

"Release her immediately," he says in a tone that means business, and the men holding Emilia lower her chair back to the floor and get busy untying her wrists, removing the gag from her mouth. Her eyes are wide, looking at the older man as his eyes drill into her face. His men help her to stand.

"You have my eyes, darling," he says to her softly, and I look between him and her, suddenly completely confused.

"Oh my God..." I hear her whisper, her breathing ragged, gulping for air in between small sobs. She looks at me then, water in her eyes, and I take two long strides and I am by her side. Grabbing her body, I pull her to me. Not caring if anyone tries to stop me.

"Papa!" Hugo shouts to his father, again lacking any respect, but the old man gives him a death stare.

"Put your gun away, you stupid boy," his father spits out as he walks to Sebastian.

"Sebastian," Lucas says, putting out his hand.

"Lucas." Sebastian shakes his hand.

"I apologize for my son. It appears he is making some rash decisions lately."

"It appears so," Sebastian responds flatly, not giving him an inch.

Lucas turns to look at Emilia again and walks up to us, eyeing her closely. My grip on her gets tighter. I don't like him looking at her like this. I don't want her to know this kind of life. I dragged her into this mess; it is not a place for a woman like her to be.

"How long have you known?" Emilia asks the man, and I look at her like she is crazy. Why is she talking to him?

"I didn't, really. Not until I saw you just now. You are

the spitting image of my mother when she was your age," he says with a small, sad smile.

"Emilia?" I question, looking at her for clarity on what the fuck is going on.

"Nico, this is my father, Lucas Moreau. Godfather of the French Mafia, owner of Dragonfly," Emilia states, before her eyes roll to the back of her head, and she drops, my arms catching her just in time.

41

EMILIA

I feel something cold on my face. Taking a subtle swipe at it, my eyes remain closed, feeling sleepy and exhausted.

"Bambolina, you need the ice on your face," I hear Nico's voice whisper to me, and I slowly open my eyes to see his big brown ones.

He is hovering above me, his hand holding a cold compress to my cheek, his other hand brushing the hair from my face.

"Nico?" I croak out.

"Here, have some water." Sebastian's voice punches the air, and the head of the New York Mob walks toward me with a cup, passing it to Nico before he takes a few steps back and admires me from across the room.

"Here, bambolina," Nico says, and I try to sit up, but Nico needs to help me as the room starts to spin a little.

"Take it easy," he grits out, and my hand clenches in his tightly. The cool water quenches my dry throat as my eyes dart around the room. We are in a bedroom. It is large, elegant, with sun streaming in the French doors on the side and I can see the expansive bright blue waters outside.

"More," Nico demands, and my eyes land back on his. I stare at him as I take another sip.

"Better," he says, putting down the cup on the side table.

"You're being bossy already. I just woke up," I sass him, and when his eyes alight in anger, I gulp.

"I'll be outside," Sebastian says, as he turns and walks out the door, giving us some privacy.

"When were you going to tell me?" Nico demands, standing up from the bed and starting to pace the room.

"Tell you what?" I ask, because as I start to get my bearings, I realize he could be talking about the baby or he could be talking about the fact the man I thought was my father is not actually my father.

"Bambolina..." he growls, locking me in place with his eyes.

I sigh. "Nico, I just found out about the baby only a few days ago. I was planning to tell you when I got home from the cemetery... I just wanted to tell my mom first," I say honestly, and he stops pacing and comes back to sit on the bed.

"I shouldn't have let you go to cemetery alone." Deep regret etches onto his face.

"Like you could have stopped me."

"You were nearly killed, Emilia! I didn't protect you like I should have." His anguish at not protecting me hits me like a truck.

"Nico, it wasn't your fault. It wasn't anyone's fault," I say gently, but I can tell my words fall on deaf ears.

"I should kill Hugo for touching you," he grits out.

"I can't believe I have another brother..." I say in a whispered tone, my mind racing at everything I recall from this afternoon.

"When did you realize Brian Cole wasn't your biological father?" Nico asks, looking at me inquisitively.

"I didn't until I saw Lucas. As soon as he walked into the room, I just knew. I can't explain it," I say, trying to pull my thoughts together, but still feeling jumbled.

"Lucas wants to speak with you. I told him you need time." I nod. I do. I need time to process.

"What happens now?" I ask Nico, knowing he and Sebastian already have a plan.

"Sebastian has spoken with Lucas, and although tensions are still high over what Hugo did, Lucas and Sebastian remain allies. As soon as you feel up to it, we have a car downstairs waiting to take us to the airport, and we will fly to our compound in Sicily to gather our thoughts and rest," Nico says, reaching up to run his hands through my hair.

"Okay." I say, absentmindedly rubbing my stomach with my hand.

"Are we really having a baby, bambolina?" he asks, vulnerability taking over his features as his hand covers mine and rests on my stomach.

"Well, I am. With or without you, this baby is happening," I state, because the last thing I want to hear from Nico is our options. There are no options. Only one.

"Like hell you are doing it alone. We made this baby together," Nico growls, and my heart melts a little.

"I've been so sick, so tired, then I had to go and get kidnapped and thrown on a plane." I pause, a terrifying thought hitting me. "Oh my God, Nico, is little bean all right? Do you think it's hurt? I can't feel any pain, but do you think that happens when they are this small?" Maybe I need to be checked by a medical professional to ensure something hasn't happened to the new life growing in my belly.

"Little bean?" he asks as his lips turn up a little at the ends.

"It's the size of a little coffee bean," I say quietly, wondering if he thinks I am stupid for calling our child a bean, even though coffee was what first joined us together months ago.

"A good Italian bean," Nico says with pride.

"Or maybe French..." I say, putting out there that I am, in fact, French by blood. French mafia, no less.

"I can't believe your brother nearly killed you. He is such a fucking idiot." Nico shakes his head, rubbing his temples.

"I can't believe my dad isn't my dad..."

"Brian Cole is now in the hands of Lucas. Apparently, they are well acquainted from decades ago. I'm not sure what happened with your mom, but Lucas wanted Brian and we are handing him over." I nod, taking everything in.

"Are we doing this? Are we going to be together, be parents, raise a human being?" I ask him, needing to know his thoughts, needing to hear them again to be sure. I want to do this with him; I want us to be a family.

His eyes look deeply into mine, giving me butterflies, and I feel like I know what he's about to say before he says it. And that in and of itself has every other thought in my mind taking a back seat. What's important is in this room, sitting before me, and growing inside me.

"I love you, bambolina, and I love our little bean too. The heartache I felt when you were missing is like nothing I have felt before, and I never want to feel that again. So, yes, we are together, and yes, we are having a fucking baby. You will be mine, and I will be yours." Nico's statement has me smiling, tears welling in my eyes, knowing that he means every word that he says.

"I can't believe we are going to be a family. You pushed your way into my life and totally took me by surprise, and I have loved every moment with you since." Nico leans forward and captures my lips in his, and nothing in my life has ever felt this right.

"I love you too..." I whisper, and it's barely audible, but Nico hears, his sexy smirk evident of that fact.

There is a knock at the door, and we pull away, Nico jumping in front of me and moving toward the door.

"Who is it?" he shouts, and I begin to panic.

"Lucas," a deep voice says from behind the door, and Nico moves to open it.

Lucas walks in, Sebastian right behind him, and they close the door.

"How are you feeling, Emilia?" Lucas asks, his accent thick, but I see genuine concern in his face as he stands next to Sebastian, looking over me.

"I'm okay. A little sore and tired, shocked, confused, but otherwise okay," I say, sitting up and straightening myself a little, trying to remain strong. I don't know this man, my father, at all. I catch my reflection in the wall mirror and almost frighten myself, my disheveled look not suitable for public consumption.

"I wanted to personally apologize for your brother. Hugo is an angry young man, who unfortunately hasn't learnt how to use his brain before his brawn yet."

"I have so many questions..." I say to him, and he nods.

"I know you do, and I am happy to answer all of them. But right now, your family is going to take you out of here and let you rest. Hopefully, in a few days, I can fly to Sicily to see you and explain everything." My eyes flick to Nico, who nods at me.

"Okay, that would be good," I reply, and see Sebastian nod as well. Again, my hand rests against my stomach, and I see Lucas flick his eyes down and then back to my face.

"How is the baby?" he asks, a little hesitantly.

"We will see once we get to Sicily. I have our doctor waiting for us there," Sebastian answers for me, and I swallow as my palms sweat a little at the thought that maybe there's a problem with our baby. But I would feel something, wouldn't I? I have no pain, no bleeding. Aside from extreme tiredness and a sore cheek and wrists from the rope, I actually feel pretty normal.

"Good. Well, I won't keep you. Your car is waiting, and I will see you all in a few days," Lucas says, shaking hands with Sebastian, then Nico before walking over to beside the bed.

"Safe travels, *mon ange toujours,*" he says, and my heart nearly thumps out of my chest. Lucas then grabs my hand delicately, and as he does, I see Nico take a step toward him. Lucas ignores him, lifts my hand, and kisses it before placing it back down on the bed.

I give him a small nod, and he steps away, paying no attention to the two mob men in the bedroom with me, then walks out the door, closing it gently behind him.

"Are we ready?" Sebastian asks Nico and I.

Nico looks at me, and I give him a small nod.

"Come on then, Emilia. It is time you meet your Italian family now," Sebastian says, a small but friendly smirk coming to his lips as he moves toward the door.

I smile in return. I have what I've always wanted... a family.

EPILOGUE - EMILIA

Nico and I have been in Sicily for a few weeks now. The amazing cliff-top mansion is nothing like I have ever seen before. It puts postcards to shame. Large green gardens surround the place, with bright pink bougainvillea crawling across the balconies. Inside houses the most amazing art collection I have ever seen. All Goldie's work. She has FaceTimed me daily since we arrived here, and I can't wait to meet her in person when we return to New York.

Little bean is fine, although now the size of a fig, the family doctor tells me. I have had all my prenatal screening tests and everything is going along as it should. Inside my body, anyway. Outside of my body is a whole other situation.

"Seriously, I don't think I can eat anymore, Nico," I whisper to him as his mom walks into the kitchen to get me more bread.

"This is what she does. She cooks all day, and now that you are giving her her first grandbaby, she wants to ensure you are well fed," he says as he shoves another forkful of his mom's spaghetti in his mouth.

"It is beautiful food, but I think you might have to roll me out of here." He huffs a laugh as he looks at me.

"I don't want you to get hangry. What if your stomach starts eating you from the inside, bambolina?" He smirks, and I slap his arm with my napkin.

"I agree. I am so full," Sofia says from across the table, leaning back and stretching out her full belly. Sofia arrived at the mansion about twenty-four hours after we did. Swooping in and taking care of me and giving me the feminine energy I needed after all the men swarming my life recently. She knew something was up with Nico after their phone calls became less frequent, and on her first night here, I heard her yelling at him for keeping me a secret for so long. I now get my girl time every day, and I love it.

Nico's mother and father have been here for a week. They are so lovely and very caring, if not a little overbearing. I am simply not used to all the attention I am receiving in my ready-made family.

"Someone is here!" Sofia says, noticing the soldiers letting in a sedan at the gate, and I already know it is Lucas.

"Are you ready, bambolina?" Nico asks, his eyes searching mine.

I would be lying if I said I wasn't a little nervous. I have seen and spoken to Lucas at length since we arrived in Europe weeks ago. I now know all about how he and my mother met, fell in love, and had an affair while they were both married to other people. Lucas was in an arranged marriage, as the son of the French mafia dom. Not able to step out of line, he had to leave me with my mom to raise me with Brian Cole in New York.

Unfortunately for my mother, when I was born, Brian knew I wasn't his after catching her writing love poems to Lucas. Her letters ceasing to arrive to him was the first red flag for Lucas that something wasn't right, and then he heard about the car accident. Like me, he didn't question it and thought I would be well looked after with Brian. Lucas had no idea how lonely my upbringing was, even though he thought about reaching out multiple times.

Dragonfly was able to recoup some of the funds Brian Cole stole from them. A deal he made with Hugo, clearly taking advantage of his inexperience at the time. Hugo was able to track Brian in New York, saw me at the funeral, and grabbed me as leverage, having no idea I was actually his blood. His father never spoke about his love child, or the true love of his life. He thought it was all in his past. Brian's life was relatively short-lived after he arrived in France. Lucas and his men took him to the farm, which I now know is code *for, they took his last breath and burned him in the fields of roses that he sells for an eye-watering amount from Le Rose Fleur florist in New York city*. Apparently, it is great fertilizer...

Now, as Nico and I stand and walk together out the front door, ready to greet our guests, I feel a sense of calm. Nico's hand slides around my back, offering me comfort, even though I can feel the anger rolling off him in waves.

Sebastian and the boys stayed a few days after the incident, ensuring the business side of things was dealt with, and then they flew home. Nico wanted us to stay a while, to have a break from the New York grind and for me to meet his family. We have been hiding in this magnificent Italian compound every day since. With my morning sickness now all nearly abated, New York is beckoning both of us, so we know we need to get back soon.

Not to mention, Ivy and Cat both calling me daily to beg me to come home now they know a little one is going to be in our lives.

I watch Lucas step out of the car, and the bright sun shines on him, his face lighting up as he sees me, and mine reflects his happiness. We have formed a close bond over the weeks, and it is getting stronger with each visit.

"Who is that?" Sofia whispers in awe from beside me, and I hear Nico growl. Hugo steps out of the other side of the car, and my eyes flick to him. It is the first time I have seen him since he kidnapped me from New York, and his visit is why I am so nervous today. Hugo looks dashing, smartly dressed in a black, well-fitted suit, no longer looking angry and menacing, but like he stepped off the cover of a magazine.

Nico's grip around my waist gets tighter, and I feel his muscles tense. But Hugo isn't looking at me; his eyes rest solely on Sofia. Nico is too uptight to notice, but I whip my head to the side and see Sofia staring right at him. Her brown hair flowing down her shoulders gives me a full view of the longing look she is giving him. The two of them eye each other, and I feel my stomach drop.

I am not sure if we will ever be able to move past what

Hugo did to me, but considering he is my brother, I need to try.

"Nico, good to see you," Lucas says, coming up to us and shaking Nico's hand.

"Likewise," Nico says very diplomatically.

"Darling," Lucas says, his hands cupping my arms and pulling me in for a kiss on either cheek. "Looking more and more radiant each time I see you."

"Thank you, Lucas. This is Sofia, Nico's sister." The two shake hands as my eyes flick to Hugo, who is standing back near the car.

"Hugo!" Lucas barks, and Hugo steps forward.

"Nico," Hugo says, extending his hand to shake as he stands shoulder to shoulder with his father.

Nico watches him for a beat, giving him a look I have never seen before and never want to be on the receiving end of. I nudge Nico with my elbow, reminding him to play nice.

"Hugo," Nico grits out, his teeth clenching so hard I can hear them. He swiftly extends his hand and the two men shake, Nico dominating the exchange.

"Emilia," Hugo says, his face showing a mix of emotions as he looks at me.

"Hi, Hugo, nice to see you in slightly less violent circumstances," I say, acknowledging the elephant in the room.

"Thank you for seeing me. I wanted the chance to talk." I look at my younger brother with interest. As hard as it is for me to meet with him, it must be equally hard for him.

"Yes, well, if you hit me again, I won't be responsible

for what you will receive in return," I sass him, and Nico growls, clearly not liking the reminder. Hugo nods, taking it on the chin, as his eyes flick to Sofia.

"Hugo, this is Sofia, Nico's sister." I introduce the two and watch with interest as they both drink each other in. Hugo extending his hand and Sofia taking it. My eyes widen a little when I see a faint pink stain her cheeks. Lucas and Nico are too busy watching Hugo, so they don't notice.

I clear my throat, and they snap out of their exchange.

"Let's go inside," I offer, and let Sofia lead the two men in as Nico and I hang back.

"You okay, bambolina?" Nico asks, his eyes flicking from me to the backs of the men and then to me again.

"Fine. But I am the least of your worries today, I think," I state, and his brow furrows.

"What's going on?" he asks, looking immediately concerned.

"Hugo and Sofia is what is going on," I tell him, and I see him bristle.

"Over my dead body," he grits out, and I curl my lips to try to stop the smile trying to escape.

"I'm serious. It is not happening," he states again before my lips break the hold I have, and I smile, watching my man start to unravel at the news.

"Well, I guess once we go back to New York, you won't be around to watch her?" I state, knowing that I will talk to Lucas about it anyway.

"She will come with us, and I will lock her up at the compound." Nico leaves no room for questions.

"Now let's go inside before they get too acquainted.

The last thing I need is your brother in my family business," he says, grabbing my hand and leading me inside.

But that is what we need to remember. Hugo is now family and Dragonfly is now one of our business interests. He and Hugo need to get along.

For the sake of both.

GRAB a bonus scene to find out where Nico and Emilia are now

ALSO BY SAMANTHA SKYE

HEIR

Men of Dragonfly Book One, featuring Hugo and Sofia is coming early 2024. To be notified when it is due for release please join my Facebook Group Skye's The Limit Books

OR

Sign up to my newsletter HERE.

ALSO BY SAMANTHA SKYE

Want to read the love story of Beth the clumsy Event Planner and Harrison, Baltimore's most Charming Billionaire?

The Charming Billionaire

The first time I met Billionaire Harrison Rothschild, I was looking up at him after the tray of drinks I knocked over landed on his Italian leather shoes. The second time I met him, the drinks spilt on his shirt instead.

I was born with the clumsy gene, but as DC's most sought after Event Planner, I am professional and the show must go on. I have a sick father to look after and medical insurance only goes so far. But when I get a glimpse of his perfect chiseled torso in the coat room, I do what any red blooded woman would do.

I run out the door.

Rumors are swirling that he is going to be our next Governor, and he fits the persona perfectly. With his charming smile, his broad shoulders that look like they can hold the problems of the world and his sultry eyes, that leave me breathless every time he looks at me.

But we are complete opposites in every way, something his mother has no issue in pointing out.

So when Harrison requests me to work with him on his campaign, I am not sure if I should be flattered or annoyed. Because even though I know it is going to end in disaster, I didn't expect it to be dangerous. And I didn't expect to become the target.

Grab The Charming Billionaire, Book One of the Baltimore Boys today! https://books2read.com/Charming-Samantha-Skye

ALSO BY SAMANTHA SKYE

Boston Billionaires

Coming Home

Finding Home

Leaving Home

Building Home

Men Of New York

My Legacy

My Destiny

My Fight

My Chance

The Baltimore Boys

The Charming Billionaire

ABOUT THE AUTHOR

Samantha Skye

Samantha Skye is a contemporary romance author from Melbourne, Australia. A country kid turned city slicker, Samantha writes characters that are as diverse as they are devilishly handsome.

Her unique brand of suspenseful spice deftly combines the risky and the risqué, setting hearts pounding for more than one reason! When she's not plotting her next novel, Samantha can be found chatting on podcasts, or anywhere there's sunshine.

An avid traveler, Samantha is just as comfortable in gumboots as she is in Christian Louboutins...but she's usually having more fun in the latter.

To join in the conversation join Skye's The Limit Facebook group here; https://www.facebook.com/groups/skyesthelimitbooks

To learn more about Samantha and what comes next in her author journey you can find her on;

Website: samanthaskyeauthor.com

TikTok @samanthaskyeauthor